CONVERGENCE

T.R. DOUGLAS

ISBN: 0615760546
ISBN 13: 9780615760544

For Michelle, Ryan, Nathan, Graham, and Vivienne you are my inspiration and taught me the meaning of life. Thank you.

**"In my mind and in my car,
we can't rewind we've gone too far..."**

Video killed the Radio Star.

—The Buggles

Variety; December 2, 1999 – Los Angeles, CA

Studio Prexy's twins nabbed in FBI computer crimes sting

Connor and Lucas Shaw, the twin nine year old sons of Louis Shaw, CEO and Chairman of MGM, were taken into custody this morning by the FBI Computer Fraud Response Team at their Beverly Hills home. The twins were charged with malicious computer hacking into several government agencies and large financial institutions. The FBI claimed their actions impacted national security and compromised financial data on millions of Americans.

The lawyer representing the boys, Emily Gartrell, issued a statement that the intention of the twins was never to do harm or threaten national security. Rather, the boys were simply imitating their favorite movie, *WarGame*, coincidentally one of the most successful films of 1983 produced and financed by their studio chief father.

Calls to Louis Shaw were not returned, and Margaret Livingston Shaw, the estranged wife of Louis, was traveling abroad and unavailable for comment.

The boys are being held in a secure location awaiting their preliminary hearing.

SECTION ONE

CONCEPTION

Present Day

CHAPTER

1

The end of the world started on a rather ordinary Thursday evening in Hollywood. Adam MacArthur sat at the expansive polished wooden bar facing a large antique mirror, clueless to how he would single handedly herald in the end of all things. The light in the club was low as music flowed from the dance floor behind him. A small group of indistinct figures moved rhythmically with the churning bass that reverberated through the room.

Adam dropped his chin slightly to gaze at his own reflection. In the darkness, his light blue eyes looked steely and his blonde hair looked auburn. The rest of his countenance was shadowed. The only visible brightness was the whites of his eyes and the reflection off a dark metallic earpiece on his right ear. In the reflected light he looked and felt like a different person, a better person.

"Hey Casanova, you look good, stop foggin' the mirror!" said Jenny, one of the early shift bartenders who paused from her bar duties and struck an inviting pose just begging for a witty response.

"Sorry, can you blame me?" Adam shot back with a slight smile and shoulder shrug. She turned away giggling and went back to polishing the bar. *Mission accomplished* thought Adam.

Adam turned back to his favorite view in the mirror and chuckled because he really wasn't kidding. He recalled a recent meme that developed around a new demographic group labeled "Listless Dreamers" who were disaffected, over-stimulated, over-educated children from wealthy families, always getting whatever they wanted from birth. Their entire life was a rolling reel of activity after activity, and, as they matured; they cultivated and fed this need for constant stimulation with ever increasing stimulus and experiences, never completely fulfilled. The "mobile generation" of his youth, gave way to this new label. He took pride in the Listless Dreamer title, and smirking at his reflection, decided that pretty much described him perfectly.

I'm empty but I sure know how to have a good time. He thought as he absentmindedly spun his newest mobile device on the bar as he contemplated his evening stimulation ahead. He was going to go with his old stand-by solution, women. He decided he was looking to find a girl and find her fast. He wasn't going to be picky tonight, in fact, it was going to be a handyman, his affectionate label for a fixer upper where the only thing that mattered was if all the plumbing was in place and worked.

He glanced around the room looking for any potential quarry. Since it was still relatively early, no winning trifecta of desperate, insecure, and drunk was presently visible. There was however, an extremely tall and attractive Asian girl sitting at the end of the bar engrossed in her own mobile device. She wore a low cut sweater showing considerable cleavage and her long dark hair was tied tightly back. She had tremendous potential, but she was momentarily preoccupied, and with no drink in front of her on the bar, would probably take a while. He swiveled back to face the bar, biding his time.

Adam waved Jenny over to order another drink but couldn't keep his eyes from wandering to her bulging cleavage spilling over her bra and out from under her tight shirt. He momentarily considered her as the evening's target but then his mind jumped back to the luscious brunette he had about a month ago. Chuckling, he remembered she actually lasted four nights before he stopped calling her, close to a record for him.   Out of nowhere a flood of images came at him.

The brunette was naked lying on his bed. Her feeling of boredom at the awkward morning after coffee in Hollywood sitting outside at a small cafe. His mind and body lurched as he felt her emotions, felt them deep in the pit of his stomach. She felt ignored and then her feelings turned to anger, vicious, aggressive anger. Words and feelings began to flow through his head. No way, you son of a bitch, how dare you call me, you. Go screw yourself, you dick.   The only one who will think it's a good time is you. JERKOFF! Red colors swarmed in front of his eyes and images appeared in his head. He physically felt the pressure and anger constricting around him like a vice quickly closing.

Adam toppled off the bar stool and landed on his back as the tirade and images finally stopped. He whipped around sharply to figure out what just happened. His mind was racing. What he just experienced was indescribable. He tried to clear his head. He looked up to see Jenny leaning over the bar asking him if he was okay. Her massive breasts were spilling from her tight pink shirt. His eyes involuntarily slipped to her chest again, and the now familiar voice erupted again in his head, his vision was lost and he saw red in his mind's eye blotting everything else out. His mind was again filled with a sharp pain and seething anger. It was the most visceral experience he ever felt. His head felt like it was about to explode as words and images flowed across his consciousness.

The images and voice in his head were switched off as quickly as they started. He started to have his first real panic attack. His breath was coming in labored gasps, his heart was galloping like a horse, and he was sweating profusely. He was definitely hearing voices and hallucinating. He wondered if he was having some drug induced reaction. He forced himself to relax and deal with the facts. He was sitting on a bar floor with some hysterical woman's screaming voice and images rolling through his head. He wasn't drunk yet and there wasn't anyone near enough to him to talk so loudly. For some reason, his first thought was he needed to talk to his mother and get the name of the shrink she'd been having an affair with for the last several years.

His head was filled with images. For a split second, he saw himself as a young boy, sitting on their old porch at their Greenwich house. He saw himself as someone else saw him, an almost impressionistic view of him through the ages. He paused as he thought he looked nothing like the images he was experiencing. He felt a tremendous love, mixed with concern, disappointment and an undercurrent of contempt. Words (Thoughts?) flowed through his head. Hello, Adam heard his mother's voice through his head. Honey are you there?

Suppressing a scream, he raised his hands to his head. It finally dawned on him that he was wearing his new Dakarta phone earpiece and that the voices he was hearing were actually people that he was somehow calling. Exhaling and composing himself, he said outloud, "Sorry, Mom, didn't mean to call you, I will call you this weekend. Bye."

Adam laughed to himself as he pulled off his earpiece. Somehow he must have triggered a series of calls and ended up calling the girl and his mom. He wasn't sure why the images and feelings occurred, though. Maybe Jenny had slipped some new mood drug in his drink.

Noticing something odd, he picked up the device from the bar and looked at the phone screen. No calls were registered.

Adam felt a moment of frustration. The geeky girl at the mobile store had spent considerable time with him to make sure he understood the operation of the phone. She told him repeatedly the earpiece could only make calls through voice recognition to his preconfigured contact list. As he put the ear piece back in his ear, he was greeted with another tsunami of feelings and information.

Feelings of boredom, frustration, and aggravation flowed over Adam. Robotically spoken words followed. Hello. This is TG Mobile Santa Monica. How can we help you? Hello, are you there? Hello?

It then hit him like a slap across the face. Adam made a call just by thinking about it. He didn't use voice recognition or his handset.

He replied "Sorry, dialed the wrong number."

No problem. Thanks for your ca—. Adam disconnected on the perky voice.

He took the earpiece off of his ear and held it out to examine it, as he turned it in his hand, the pieces fell into place and he made the connection. Somehow the device was reading his thoughts. His head began swirling with the implications. He felt compelled to leave the bar to better understand what he just experienced. Ideas were forming quickly as he realized what he just discovered and how he could use it. He placed the mobile device and earpiece into his jacket pocket and headed for the door.

The attractive Asian girl with the long black hair continued staring at Adam as he left. She looked down to her Dakarta mobile device and instantaneously retreated back into her own mind's eye.

An image of a non-descript room appeared as multiple shadowed figures materialized around the Asian girl. Each figure stood at different spots in the room all perfectly still. Her thoughts flowed across the room, visibly tracing a colored and shifting path around each figure, as she opened up her mind. We have our first pawn. He took the bait easily. He was a perfect target. I was able to imprint ideas without any challenge. Each of you will have no issues with your implantations. Rejoice my sisters, it has started.

A deeper, powerful thought stream fell across the room, not emanating from any one figure, but surrounding and engulfing them all and wrapping them in ribbons of colors and pulsating energy. A powerful feeling of warmth and belonging embraced each person. Excellent. I told you all it will happen easily. We need to remember how this will propagate. Faster than anyone can imagine. Overnight our world will experience monumental change and no one will even pause to consider what has happened. Each of you must continue to develop your networks. Our journey is just beginning and our path is clear as our goal is in sight. Many will need our guidance. Many will try to stop us. We must remain strong and focused. Together we will succeed in changing the world forever.

The Asian girl blinked out her mind's eye as she removed her earpiece and quickly left the bar while the eyes and thoughts of every man followed her out.

CHAPTER

2

Connor Shaw couldn't recall the line ever being this long. *Apparently today is the day when everyone decides to start drinking the amazing coffee at Caffe Luxxe.*

"Double espresso" he finally said to the cute and impossibly young barista wearing large black frame glasses. He deftly stepped around the supermodel thin lady in a bright red jogging suit who was fixated on returning her change to her wallet while the line behind her continued to grow.

The woman casually glanced up and stared at the well-dressed, athletically built, tall dark-haired man. Her eyes grew wide with recognition as she blurted out "Oh, my, hi there. Aren't you Connor Shaw?"

"Hi there back to you and yes I am." Connor replied, smiling, expecting the now familiar cadence that was surely about to follow.

"Wow. So nice to meet you. I absolutely love your show. My kids think you are great," she replied as she pointed at Connor, reinforcing the point that she was referring to him. "You know, I've always wanted to tell you this, your episode on Einstein's Unified Theory was utterly amazing. We were all talking about it for days. I've never been much a science person, but the way you explained it, I felt like I really get it. Do you know what I mean?"

Turning on the charm, Connor replied "Thank you so much. I'm really glad you liked the Einstein episode its one of my favorites as well. Keep watching." Connor handed the money to the barista who smiled nervously. The woman walked away smiling, pleased with her celebrity interaction.

Connor, of course, liked the attention and expected that everyone else in the coffee shop was now trying to play the recognition game. It was like the lady pulled the string on the neon sign that was now pointing at him saying "Look at me and try to figure out who I am." He resigned himself that this was the sentence for celebrity.

Connor moved away from the counter and joined another line waiting for his order. He briefly considered shuffling his feet, to reinforce the unshakeable sense he was in some kind of ironic Russian soup-kitchen line for coffee made from the finest hand-picked beans in the world. Fighting this urge, his gaze made a circle of the room as he waited. He vaguely recognized many of the morning regulars, people to whom he had never spoken, didn't know their names, but whom he saw every morning. Everyone moved slowly in an early morning rhythm, nursing their coffee to gain the strength and resolve to face the day. As he continued to survey the room, he realized every single person was using some form of personal technology.

Mobile computing had everyone connected to a greater network. The four-dollar-a-cup of coffee was actually a substandard complement to the sophisticated wireless technology and data that pulsed through the room. Everyone was in their focused private space, posting, replying, sharing, reading or playing. It was utterly amazing. A moment ago, Connor assumed the room as a flurry of human interaction and activity. Now he realized that everyone was tuned into their own network, their bodies inhabiting the physical space of the coffee shop while their minds were elsewhere. He realized he may have just found a topic for an upcoming show.

"The connected but disconnected world" and its implications on human psychology was the idea that popped into his head.

Connor's thoughts were interrupted by a shrill voice, "Double espresso" called by yet another cute, energetic barista, this one luckily sans the Scorsese frames. Connor grabbed his coffee, glanced again at the connected room, and headed out, steeling himself for the long commute to work.

As he merged his black R8 Spyder onto the 405, the thoughts of the coffee shop wireless world were quickly dispelled as the reality of the coming day returned. Like many other reality television celebrities, the combination of who you know and timing got him to his current situation. His break came when he was a last minute substitution on a reality show about recent college grads trying to make it in the world. One of his good friends was the line producer and due to an illness of a cast member, he had to fill a slot on the show, Connor got the call. Connor fit the reality television model perfectly; he was smart, confident, well-spoken and extremely smooth and he looked great on camera. After the first appearance on the show, the web erupted around Connor and his celebrity status was building. After the show completed, his agent and family connections got him his own show which quickly became a ratings juggernaut. He made science personal and used humor and his charisma to explain some of the most complex and mundane scientific principles. The combination of movie star good looks and brilliant intelligence made him who he is today. He checked his look in the rear view mirror and smiled.

Now he was both a television celebrity and the unlikely head of a research and development team for Banner Corp., unknown to the public Connor had an exceptional research pedigree and worked at the center of a vortex of brilliant scientists. He knew that his Banner job was probably due to his celebrity status and the corresponding ability to bring investment and exposure to the company. Many times he felt he had to remind people that he had done post-doctoral work at Cal Poly, and he really did know what he was talking about. A good friend told him to get over it. He tried to heed the advice and go with the flow, but sometimes felt like he needed to prove himself and show what he really was inside.

As he drove, he forced himself to clear his thoughts and focus on his current project at the lab. The team was under constant pressure to speed up the rollout of a new design for a molecular microchip. In addition to unheard-of processing speeds through the use of organic components, it also was designed to enable a basic interface with the human mind through a superconducting quantum interference capability. Put simply, the human mind could connect to the processing power of a computer through thoughts. He felt that familiar rush when he thought that Banner and his team was going to enable the age of human augmented computing.

Shaking him from his daydream, Connor's phone rang, and looking at his car's integrated display he saw the smiling face of Emily. Connor automatically smiled back. Slow and steady Emily. The yin to his yang, the head of his substrate design and technical architecture team and the only person who had been with him from the beginning of his career right out of school.

He recently read a blog about work spouses, people whose relationship at work mimicked a marriage with open communication, shared experiences, and loyalty. If anyone would ever qualify as a work spouse, it was Emily. His only concern was that unlike every other woman he ever met, she never stirred any romantic feelings in him. He once tried to force the consideration and he finally gave up because it just wouldn't process.

"Em, good morning sunshine, how are you this beautiful morning?" Connor answered, actually happy to talk to her with his mood lightening.

"Did you hear about it?" Emily replied in a breathless and rushed voice which echoed through the car.

"Hear about what?" Connor asked, perplexed both by the question and her unusual demeanor.

"Connor, this is unbelievable. I don't know where to start. Hold on, let me organize my thoughts." Emily paused as her breathing filled the car's interior.

"What's wrong Em? What happened?" replied Connor, uncertain he wanted her to continue as his mind turned to a worst case scenario of a terrorist attack or something much, much worse.

"Well, I don't know how to say this other than directly, I guess. Thought sharing is now generally available in the newest TG Dakarta phone. It is absolutely incredible. I'm not really sure how such a monumental discovery could just come out of the blue, but here it is. There were a series of announcements this morning and several press conferences coming online simultaneously. Where are you, by the way?" Emily finished while still sounding somewhat distracted and not entirely confident in what she just said.

Connor couldn't believe what he was hearing. It was literally impossible. "Whoa, whoa, hold on just a moment here, Em, nice prank, but there no way this could be true. You have to be kidding." Connor swerved his car back in his lane as he absentmindedly drifted to the left. An older guy in a black seven series laid on his horn and flipped him off.

"Connor, well, yes it is true and I am as surprised as you are and I'm not kidding. This is accurate. Seriously, I can't believe you hadn't heard about this previously. The reports and press releases claim it translates human thought and allows people to share their thoughts. We will be viewing a press conference in twenty minutes from Tribe on Broadcast One. Hurry up and get your ass in here. It is amazing." Emily clicked off the connection

Connor's mind raced and he felt like he was drowning, as he quickly tried to process the information. It was simply incomprehensible. What the hell had just happened? Who is Tribe? What announcements? How could he not have heard about this previously? There was no way that any of this could be true. Nothing like this happens out of the blue. Nothing.

"This doesn't make sense. Something's not right." Connor said out loud as he dropped the car into fourth and nailed the accelerator. He caught the older asshole's BMW in a matter of seconds and swerved around him, blasting into the HOV lane. He had an ominous feeling that something was very, very wrong.

Experience Pod 887.13.765

California Department of Commerce

Department of Technology Enablement

The Wireless Network Convergence Factors and the

Implications of Governor Mandate 1-04-2005a

Executive Summary:

This brief summarizes the full report attached herewith that was created to study the effects of Governor Mandate 1-04-2005a on the wireless connectivity across the State of California.

On October 18th 2005, Governor Arnold Schwarzenegger signed a state mandate that in summary provided:

"To promote and invest in the wireless connectivity across the state of California, creating standards, objectives, and goals, in an on-going effort to improve wireless network access to support both the private and public sector capabilities."

The mandate was an exhaustive review and recommendation of wireless standards and wireless network capabilities for California. The catalyst for the study and report was to ensure that all Californians has equal access to the benefits of the Internet and the information superhighway.

At its time of initial passage, many business interests held that the mandate prescribed standards that were onerous on wireless carriers and hardware manufacturers. Conversely, there was considerable public support for the mandate, in that it created consistency and standards around public wireless access and usage.

Since going into effect in February 2010, the state has witnessed dramatic development of its wireless access capabilities and is now experiencing unprecedented growth and usage of wireless communication and network usage. The state has created the first public wireless "cloud" that covers the entire state. The primary driver of the State's wireless proliferation is the adoption of the WiMax41c standard for connecting all governmental offices and locations. The standard selection ensured that the WiMax41c standard was the chosen approach for wireless networking development across the state.

As a result of this mandate and state standards, California today has one of the most comprehensive wireless networks in existence. There is no area within the state that does not have access to a high bandwidth wireless network connection. The state joins other leading US states such as New York, Oregon, Washington, Florida, Michigan, Texas, and New Jersey who have also implemented these wireless zones.

Due to this standardization, the state has witnessed steady progress in its business community utilization of the wireless connectivity. Examples include state-of-the-art supply chain, inventory, and warehouse management capabilities that span the entire state. Through the use of the wireless network, distributors and retailers are able to track their product from the time of manufacture until the time of sale. Furthermore, the wireless network allows companies to study and confirm consumption patterns from buyers after the sale. The now ubiquitous "Need Milk?" campaign and service, whereby milk consumption is monitored by wirelessly enabled refrigerators that heralded the return of fresh milk delivery, began in California.

In addition to the business community, the wireless standard has enabled advancements in education. With almost every university, high school, and elementary school now wireless networked, students are able to enjoy real-time connectivity and access to information. This has created unprecedented immersive educational opportunities and collaboration.

California was also the first state to enable wireless voting and government participation. Today, California voters can vote wirelessly through a variety of access points. This has shown considerable promise as the state voting turnout was the highest since it has been measured. In addition, State Senate and departmental hearings are available via a live network feed. The wireless connectivity and availability has made government more accountable and collaborative with every Californian.

Finally, the wireless network has improved the lives of Californians. In the world of medicine today, the wireless standard has enabled physicians and patients to interact like never before. Diagnosis and review can occur regardless of either location. Pharmacy and clinics are able to communicate to share patient history.

In conclusion, the wireless standards that have been defined and realized in California have changed the state for the better. For the first time, the entire state is connected and networked. This connection only promises of greater things to come.   The full report can be cross referenced with ADAKSD-213213.

CHAPTER
3

Alexis woke at her habitual 7:00 am and lay still with her eyes still closed huddled under her duvet. Her dark hair spread out like a large fan across her pillow, as she slowly moved her head side to side to shake off the sleep and start her day. She loathed leaving the comfort of her bed, and like every other morning, she unconsciously swung her leg out to lightly touch Lucas, checking his location. She smiled and opened her eyes. All was right in the world at that precise moment.

The slow comprehension of her schedule finally motivated her to slip out and stand on the apartment's cool wood floor. She stretched, reaching for the wooden beams crossing the ceiling, and slowly walked across the room to her computer. LA mornings had a special light and smell that constantly reminded her why she chose to live on the West Coast.

As she soaked in the stillness and silence, she started her Keurig and logged onto her UCLA network to check her email and any schedule and class updates. For two years she followed the same morning routine before heading to campus. She liked her schedule and the consistent pattern she had formed.

As she logged on the familiar ping of an IM immediately sounded. Dawn, her close friend and another psychology doctorate candidate was already awake and on-line, apparently ready to talk.

Dawn72: Did you see the news?

Alexis paused, hoping that it wasn't another terrorist attack or outbreak of another war.

Alexis87: ???

Dawn 72: It is amazing. The new TG mobile phones allow us to link with the thoughts of our patients. No wires, no fuss. Think of the possibilities for treatment. We can literally read our patient's minds.

Alexis87: I just woke up and need coffee…and I have no idea what you are talking about…

Dawn72: NO YOU DON'T NEED COFFEE. LISTEN TO ME. WAKE UP! This is huge. We can connect to our patient's minds in real time. We can understand their feelings, how they respond and process their thoughts. We can literally get inside our patients' heads.

Alexis87: Is this a dream. Need to process what you are saying. Still not awake…

Dawn72: Let me make it simple. We can now see what people are thinking in our therapy sessions. Think about it! Wake up.

Alexis87: Nice joke. Doesn't seem to make any sense. Need to get moving. You in class today?

Dawn72: I'm not joking. Go check the web. Look for Tribe. We'll talk later for sure.

Dawn72: BTW - how's Lucas??? Lover boy ever make it over????

Alexis87: yeah, he sure did…

Alexis glanced over her shoulder and looked at the sleeping form of Lucas, still ensconced in the warmth of the bed. He didn't get in until 3am last night, claiming he was working on something for his advanced AI seminar. Alexis had her doubts, but couldn't really come to the point of a confrontation. She momentarily wondered if Lucas was seeing someone else and then summarily dismissed it. He had been loyal to her since her first days at UCLA as a coed. She was the one that strayed, never Lucas. Nope, he was old-faithful. She added it to her mental list of to-dos to discuss with him later.

Almost on cue, Lucas sat up in bed and rubbing his eyes returned Alexis's gaze and added a cheerful "Good morning, everything ok?" he smiled as he threw back the covers and stretched his long and muscular torso. He was in very good shape and Alexis's seemingly newly found libido stirred seeing him across the room.

"All good, just checking emails." she replied, deciding not to indulge her momentary desire or bring up the late night arrival. She was amazed at her self-control.

"Ok. We are still good to see my mother this weekend, right?" Lucas said as he headed to the bathroom.

She wasn't ready for that topic however. Alexis had completely forgotten about the visit, and was immediately frustrated that the first subject today was about his mother. She was sure there was some unconscious mental block, based on the difficulty of her relationship with Margaret Livingston Shaw, as every time they were together the woman would make some snide and mean remark about Alexis. Lucas was blind to her behavior and Alexis was tired of pointing it out to him. Fortunately or unfortunately, due to Alexis's training, she quickly diagnosed a potentially bi-polar and conditional woman, who clearly contributed to Lucas's father depressive decline and eventual suicide. Lucas once blamed himself for his father's suicide. Eventually in high school, he used drugs and alcohol in high school to cope with his guilt. He had been clean and sober for several years, but Alexis still felt his mother was an enabler and she held her responsible for Lucas's hardships. Even with all of her training and clinical experience, she just didn't like the woman and her territorial instinct was aroused whenever she had to interact with her. It was at moments like these where it was hard to love someone as much as she loved Lucas.

"Sure, it actually slipped my mind, but I can make it." Alexis replied in the direction of the bathroom her voice not showing any of these feelings.

"Ok. Cool." Lucas replied and shut the bathroom door.

Alexis exhaled with a loud sigh, adding another item to her mental to-do list.

Experience Pod 445.44.3211
St. Margaret's School – Pacific Palisades, CA

The executive director of the prestigious upper school fashioned herself as one of the enlightened and intelligentsia. She was East coast educated and for the last twenty years had been living and working in Southern California, yet she held on to her "other" coast ideals and approach and cultivated her persona of being an innovator and educational trend setter. Recently, she picked up chatter about something called the experience world, a place where people can share their thoughts and experiences with others in a totally immersive and enlightened manner. She knew immediately that she must try it for herself. However, since it was so new, it was hard to figure out what it really was and how to connect. So, relying on her extensive and connected parent network, she went to one of the top entertainment agents to get an education and direction on how to connect. She was referred to an experience pod focused on education - the Children's Learning World. It was described as a collection of current and former educators and adventurers leading the way into the experience world.

As she struggled with the new technology, she had a flash of a memory back to the early days of the internet, where a clumsy interface and noisy modem making a connection to a broader network, defined her initial foray into the world-wide-web. This time, however, as she inserted her earpiece and simply thought about the experience pod location, she felt a tingling sensation travel across her scalp, an electrical charge that cascaded through her mind. As she connected, there was no whirring and chirping, but rather instantaneously her mind's eye was thrown open to images and feelings.

An image of a classroom materialized. She looked down and around and realized that she stood in the doorway entering the room. The space was somewhat familiar and comfortable, she felt like she had been here before and she was safe. Five rows of desks four deep made up the classroom with large windows long the side wall sitting above long grey radiators. She was reminded again of how familiar the room felt. Afternoon sunlight streamed into the space, making it a peaceful and inviting space. She looked down and colors swirled about her feet and pulsated like flowing sand or slow moving water. She realized these were the physical manifestation of her thoughts and they moved with her and changed as her thoughts ebbed and flowed.

She took a tentative step into the classroom and now saw others moving through the space. The others were shadowed and their features were not precise, yet their thought streams were colorful and distinct. She remembered that her contact suggested she connect to this experience pod and attempt to interact with one of the others in the room. She changed her thoughts to move her across the room which she did, floating to another space. She reached out to one of the other forms to touch its thought stream. As her ethereal hand passed through the dark blue thought stream, she felt as if she had grabbed a moving train. The images washed over her in a massive wave and the memories of thousands of schoolchildren flooded her consciousness. She felt as if she saw them all at once. All unique and special, all individuals. She was in someone's thoughts and sharing them as exactly as they were remembered. There was Joseph Addison, who (she?) taught 20 years ago. He was always such a nice boy. The Executive director became disconcerted as she began to lose clarity between her own memories and those of someone else. It was too much and she pulled back her hand and thoughts to retreat.

Sensing the change, the other figure turned slowly and reached out its own ethereal hand, beckoning her to connect. The Executive director began to feel real fear and her thought stream pulsed with red colors and began to move faster. She quickly retreated realizing that she wasn't yet ready for this new technology.

Pulling out her earpiece, and slowly clearing her head, she found herself lying in front of her desk on her expensive Persian rug. Her shoes were off and flung to the corners of the room. Her body was covered in sweat and she had to blink several times before her eyes focused. She slowly sat up and tried to comprehend what she just experienced. A feeling of dread settled in the pit of her stomach as she tried to figure out what just happened.

CHAPTER

4

The assassin sat alone at a small outdoor table sipping coffee. The old Brasserie sat just off the Rue de Malesherbes in Paris. The weather was beautiful. Summertime in the city brought everyone outside, the streets and cafes thronged with people enjoying the day and avoiding work. Li easily blended in to her surroundings, looking like any other Parisian enjoying an especially pleasant afternoon.

From her sidewalk seat, Li was positioned to simultaneously watch the heavy steel doors that led into the Societe Generale building, the location of the target, and connect to the experience pod to review the dossier. In Li's mind eye, a long steel table sat in an olive green room and was set out with a variety of documents arranged to provide background and the directive on the target. Of course, none of this existed. It was a mental construct that Li had been trained to create when on assignment. In the real world, to the casual observer, Li sat behind dark glasses sipping coffee. In the experience world, Li was a blur of movement, preparing for every contingency, poring over and rehearsing every detail of the plan and the target. The juxtaposition of these two existences weren't lost on her, she rather enjoyed the façade of her real world self, hiding the experience world activities.

The target was a French National working for the US government in its advanced weapon research team. He was the leading expert on next generation cerebral weapon control interfaces. He had been under surveillance for several years and last week made an appointment with his Defense of Department contacts to deliver his research on the new TG mobile devices. Following strict

DOD security protocols, he backed up all research from his local computer and was personally delivering the report and the hard drive to his contact this morning. Li had already hacked the network drives and deleted his work. The only copy of the research was the physical copy and the hard drive that he carried on his person.

Shortly after 11am, the scientist emerged from the office building and briskly headed for the Metro station. Li blinked off her mind's eye and disconnected from the experience pod and left the table. The scientist looked older and somewhat rundown from the images in the dossier. In mere seconds, Li took in every aspect of the target, the scuffed black shoes, the battered briefcase and the long black coat that flowed behind him as he hurried down the crowded street. Li matched the scientist's pace on the other side of the road. The target moved with a determined purpose, and just as predicted, clearly on his way to meet his contact.

The target headed down the stairs for the Metro. Li entered the station from the across the road. Joining the crowds, Li quickly caught up to and paced immediately behind him as he headed for the yellow line toward La Defense. Moving into the crowded subway car, Li stood impassively to the his left, looking like just another French commuter leaning against the window, as the doors closed and the train moved from the station.

With an imperceptible move of her wrist, Li palmed an auto injector that contained the life-saving chemical cocktail of atropine and obidoxime. With a practiced move beneath her coat, she plunged the auto injector deep into her own thigh muscle, delivering a massive quantity of chemicals into her bloodstream. She was trained in chemical weapon development and response, and had personally mixed the antidote to ensure it reversed the effects when she released the nerve gas. Her training and tests had worked flawlessly so she knew she had limited personal risk.

She fought the immediate and inevitable nausea and light-headedness. With a memorized and practiced movement produced a small blue egg shaped packet from an inside pocket. Compressing the gelatinous egg in her triple gloved hand, the A-232 nerve gas was released into the train car. She felt a momentary rush as she breathed the gas, but then the antidote overcame the reaction. As the gas spread, Li admired the elegance of the weapon, A-232, is an almost perfect killing tool. It was the most powerful and fast-acting nerve agent coming out of the former Soviet Union in the early 90's, designed and developed to be undetectable to chemical weapon monitors, and meant to bring down large groups of people in confined spaces with a near perfect fatality rate. She knew it created a perfect recipe for the current assignment.

As the gas was dispersed it immediately began to affect the passengers and impact muscle response and bodily functions. Li wanted to immobilize the target prior to his imminent death and confirm the assignment. Passengers began collapsing throughout the car, falling off the seats, many falling from their standing position, hitting the floors and anything else that got in their way on the way down. In a matter of seconds, Li was the only person standing. Moans and the smell of urine filled the car as the passengers began to lose control of their bodily functions. Many shook as the seizures began to overtake their systems. Li didn't register any of the other activity. The focus was on the target as he collapsed to the floor, landing on his side.

Stepping over the bodies and using her foot she shoved away an older woman, knocking her head into a pole, Li knelt next to the scientist, rolled him over and picked up his head to look into his eyes.

He couldn't respond, the nerve gas was moving fast, and he probably didn't even realize what was happening. Li had to make sure there were no loose ends. The man looked desperately into her eyes, and even without the use of words, the message was clear when she smiled. She knew everything and was in complete control. Li ensured that his last moments were filled with a terrible desperation and unfathomable sadness. His death would be horrible and painful and she was relishing the control and ultimate superiority.

He kept looking at Li until his eyes glazed over and his body and nervous system shut down. Watching the last light of life leave his eyes, Li abruptly dropped the target's head which made a loud thud as it hit the floor. She retrieved the target's briefcase, watch, wallet and phone just as the train pulled into the next station.

Li ran from the train as the doors opened, hysterically yelling for help, playing the part beautifully.

There was a momentary pause and then people began to move. Li was lost in the crowd. Alarms were sounded and general panic broke out. The review of surveillance cameras would later show a tall blonde haired woman hysterically running from the train, moving too quickly to get an accurate description, her face covered by her long hair and sunglasses.

As the crowd became frenzied and people pushed for the exits, Li knelt down in a spot not covered by any surveillance cameras, and tossed the overcoat, wig, and sunglasses into the trash. She was wearing a slim blue running jacket and pulled out a baseball hat from her bag and quickly tucked her dark hair up into the hat. She added new sunglasses and in a matter of seconds joined the crowd as she ran up the stairs transformed. Paramedics and emergency response personnel were already responding and came running down the opposite stairs.

"I wouldn't hurry, boys, no one is going anywhere down there." Li mumbled under her breath and smiled as she moved into the light.

CHAPTER
5

Connor Shaw quickly traversed the expansive stone walkway leading to Banner Corp.'s Building One. His black Armani suit was stifling as the sun beat down on him. He was still rattled from Emily's call and obsessively ran through every possibility to reconcile the news. Something nagged at his unconscious, just below the surface, he knew there was something he was missing but he just couldn't connect the dots.

Banner Company headquarters was an ominous two million square foot facility that housed 8,000 employees. Arriving to work each morning, Connor reflected on the size of the building and the scope of the company's operations. The building was designed to represent the enormity and scale of Banner's global operations. The design and materials were not subtle or understated. At the time of the original building development, a small Los Feliz architecture firm created a unique diamond shape, each side exactly the same size. The building was twenty stories high and appeared to have a seamless almost liquid black exterior. Several smaller black buildings surrounded the diamond, creating the expansive Banner campus. The dark diamonds, as it was called in LA, became a common site for travelers flying into LAX. Its sheer size made it both an easy visual landmark for pilots and an intriguing view for passengers.

Banner Corp. was a well-known and often quoted Southern California success story. Almost forty years ago, the company was founded in a small garage in the Pacific Palisades to develop electronic testing equipment for the emerging programmable control industry. The two founders R.B. and James Banner were the perfect complement for each other. R.B, the brilliant scientist, became known for his ability to take existing designs and improve them, leapfrogging the competition with superior technology. James, the older brother, became the consummate sales executive, courting the large defense contractors and government officials, and was instrumental in growing the firm's top and bottom lines. With this complementary approach, the company grew rapidly and branched into multiple scientific pursuits. Today, the company was recognized for its electronics, semiconductor, and research capabilities, and served the telecommunications, aerospace, and defense industries. James still had a seat on the board and was involved in more of the strategic aspects of the business. The unfortunate footnote to the story dealt with R.B. He had disappeared twenty years ago while working late in the office on a highly classified military experiment. He was never heard from again.

Entering the giant thirty foot high doors, Connor shivered as he adjusted to the considerable temperature change. Outside the heat and noise of the one of the world's largest cities surrounded him. Inside, as the massive doors slowly shut behind him, gigantic corporate shields balancing against unseen counterweights, they set a tone for the silence and coolness of the large Banner reception area. With the doors closed, the quiet interior took on an almost spiritual air. The environment reinforced an unwritten code that whatever lay outside these doors no longer mattered. Banner existed and operated separate from the world. Today, like all the days before, Connor experienced a sense of zen-like calm as he entered the building.

The doors were only a small part of Building One's main atrium. The massive black glass doors were dwarfed by the even larger black glass walls that framed the lobby of Banner Corp. headquarters. The walls were infused with wolfram from South America mined especially for the building. The glass walls reacted to the sunlight and darkened and lightened as the outside light changed. This effect gave the reception area constant light and color, no matter what the time of day.

Connor angled towards the right side of the reception desk. He nodded briefly at the guard and showed his badge and then placed his right thumb on the print reader and quickly headed for the elevator.

As he walked into his work area, he caught his reflection in the door. His dark curly hair looked appropriately stylish and his green eyes stared back at him. He scowled back at his image, challenging himself to figure out the puzzle that he walked into this morning. He was greeted with the usual mechanical swoosh of the high pressure door. It was unnaturally silent in the lab. The bullpen wasn't teeming with activity of his team. No one was working in the clean room. He surveyed the room and quickly realized his entire team was in the glass-walled main conference room, participating in a video conference.

He shrugged off his jacket and tossed it over a chair. Connor joined the others and acknowledged Emily with a nod of his head. He looked around the room and mentally ran through the people. He turned his attention to the video feed and watched a handsome guy approach the stage and prepare to start speaking. Before he even started speaking, he exuded confidence and charm. Smiling, he began.

"Good morning and welcome to the dawn of a new world. I'm Adam MacArthur, the CEO of Tribe and I am here today to share with you our revolutionary discovery. I am humbled, truly, in what I am about to discuss. But, before I start, I want to acknowledge the hard work and dedication of everyone at Tribe. Without your contribution and commitment, I would not be standing here today." Adam stretched out his arms with his palms up in a sign of acknowledgement. He paused, reset and began again in a more professional, trained voice. "We have created a revolution, we have achieved a goal that in many ways will change the world. We have broken through a barrier in human existence that was only a dream, a concept, an idea, but today is a reality. We are truly making history here today." The screen behind Adam showed a pastoral scene with trees swaying in the breeze and a small stream running through a grassy field.

Adam turned to another camera and continued "As many of you are aware, the scientific community has been experimenting on integrating microchips and the human mind for several years. Our initial goal was to enable functions for those less fortunate, those who have lost the use of their limbs, whose bodies had failed, yet their minds remained strong. The first experiments, in the early 2000's, allowed us to implant a microchip in the brain and have our test subjects control specific external actions via hard wired connections. These were successful as our patients experienced control of their external environment, they could now interact with the world simply through their thoughts. The scientific research community continued to push the boundaries and was eventually met with the limitation of current communication technology that required the use of physical connection." Adam gestured to the screen behind him which showed several pictures of various patients connected to machines through a mass of wirings. "As a result, every experiment and potential application of this technology was limited by hardware and network capabilities."

Adam paused and looked at the invisible audience beyond the camera. He looked calm and collected. He was a natural. "Even with this limitation our experiments were successful in demonstrating the connection or more specifically the potential for integration between the human mind and machine. We got our first glimpse of what this new world promised and it was awe inspiring. So our success and vision led us down a path to research and develop other mechanisms to harness the brain's electrical impulses to interact with electronics and the external physical world. Within the last several years, we finally overcame the hard wired connection challenges, as the wireless technology and protocols caught up to our requirements. We felt like we were close to cracking this challenge. But then we ran into a brick wall, the limitation for all the research and work came down to a simple and unchangeable fact. The human mind, at its most basic level, operates one hundred thousand times faster than our most advanced computer. We were faced with a paradox of how could we slow down our minds or speed up the computers. We had limited success with some very basic mind control tasks, but they were limited to pre-programmed activities. The research slowed and our constraint based on the binary nature of the microchip and the inability to have an operating system that could control more than a limited amount of pre-defined tasks stopped us in our tracks." The screen behind Adam became a desolate scene, grays and brown colors of a windswept landscape devoid of color.

Moving across the stage, Adam looked down and collected his thoughts, He continued in a thoughtful, hopeful voice.

"In the last several months, we made a breakthrough. We realized that we simply required a translation mechanism. A service, if you will, that understands both sides of the dialogue, and can translate this for the two parties, man and machine. Our Rosetta stone bridged the divide. We created the technology that allows the connection. We have the ability to enable our minds to operate and communicate with machines. Our company Tribe was born and we can now integrate the human mind to the machines through our software and service model. We are most pleased, however, to announce that today Tribe and TG are releasing the next generation mobile device, Dakarta." The screen behind him changed again to the Tribe logo and people interacting with the TG Dakarta phones.

"Dakarta is a revolutionary piece of tech. We have broken through the last barrier in communication with TG and are pleased to announce this is available everywhere today. Out of the box, the phone interacts with the users' minds through an external Quantum Interface Device in the shape of a standard earpiece. This device can detect the smallest changes in the electrical field of the users mind and translate that into commands that can be received and used by wirelessly enabled machines. The tech connects the human mind across a full spectrum of alternatives. A user can control electronic equipment wirelessly, use apps, play games and communicate like never before."

Adam paused for full effect as his words and message took hold "Yet, even with this revolutionary discovery. We realized one more byproduct when we brought the Tribe service and software online. Admittedly, the result was not something we ever anticipated. Simply, we can now share our thoughts. Any two people using the TG device and Tribe can actually and literally share their feelings, experiences, emotions. It all happens in our mind's eye. Let me pause for a moment because you did hear me correctly. People can now share their thoughts." Adam paused and waited for his statements to sink in.

"None of this would be possible without Tribe. Tribe is a very special place. A place where people can become a part of the experience world. It's a place that exists only in our minds, but it's a place that you can now share. In the experience world, people interact within experience pods which allow our users to connect in a unique world. An experience pod is a place, operating in our minds eye, where we can share experiences, our thoughts, feelings, and emotions. It transcends anything you have ever known."

Adam MacArthur turned slightly and faced another camera, paused momentarily, then began more forcefully "Today, Ladies and Gentlemen, we have finally crossed a chasm between both man and machine and our fellow man that has existed since the beginning of time. Think about the potential in terms of advances in human existence. Think about the potential in science, technology, medicine, psychotherapy, business, education and philosophy. We now can now truly communicate and connect with our fellow man. Thank you."

The room erupted with questions and movement as various reporters rushed forward to ask questions.

Emily picked up the remote and clicked off the screen. Speaking to no one in particular said "I'm not sure what to say." The room sat silent, no one responding. Connor stared across the room and couldn't process what he heard. Impossible, completely impossible.

Experience Pod 109.14.215

2600 Foundation Members Only

A diminutive man materialized in front of the group waiting for his appearance. The man was no more than five feet tall and wore a green vest over a khaki shirt and brown pants. His hair was severely parted to the right side and a pencil thin mustache underlined his rather unremarkable face.

The physical appearance of this man, however, did not foretell the power of his mind, for as he began his experience world seminar the thoughts flared like sun spots from him and engulfed all of those in the room. Pulling them into his mind, he began his narrative, Friends, <a wave of warm loving feelings washed over the crowd> I am saddened to announce that yesterday, my friend, Dr. Claude Mautignon was killed. A brilliant scientist from the French Institute of Computer Science and a pioneer in molecular computing died in the horrific terrorist nerve gas attack on the Metro. His death was shocking and unexpected and unfortunately reminiscent of the Tokyo disaster of many months ago where we lost another pioneer in the world of distributed computing, Dr. Kozi Nakamura. <A powerful wave of sadness and despair pulses through the room> my only hope is that the authorities will capture the perpetrators of this horrible crime and pay a swift and decisive retribution. My heartfelt condolences to Claude's family and colleagues in this time of loss.

I want to turn however <emotion changing, becoming positive and hopeful> and continue my briefings on the positive impact of the experience world. We all know that the experience world is influencing and improving our world. I want to share with you an early example of where this discovery has advanced *our world for the better.* *<The entire room transforms to the sidewalk and plaza outside of the UN building in New York City. The man stands with his back to the iconic building as the participants' images surround him. Movement across the plaza draws the views and scores of young students in poor fitting suits file into main building.)* *The Model United Nations or MUN for short, which brings together students from across the globe, was an early adopter of the experience world technology and has been able to show the tremendous promise of this new world order.* *<The scene transforms instantly and the seminar is now sitting in the viewing area of the great hall>The MUN sessions have been conducted entirely in the Experience World and students from countries that have been at war for years have come together like never before. These former adversaries can now share their thoughts and experiences and in the thoughts of one participant <A thought stream from one of the students washes over the seminar> everyone has the same feelings as me, my former enemies are just like me at their core, our differences are simply accidents of birth and location. <Image of Palestinian and Israeli boys standing next to each other, arm-in-arm, and smiling, feelings of belonging and camaraderie>*

The leader continued his thought stream. < The output from the MUN sessions has been tremendous. The participants have drafted multiple resolutions, the highest recorded amount ever, and have moved into problem solving how to get their countries aligned to these new realities. Many of the participants' left realizing and committing to get their politicans and leaders into the Experience world to achieve the same result. <Feelings of pride and the future promise>

But most of all, thank you Adam and Tribe for all you have done and for changing the world for the better. <Final feelings of excitement, small part envy, and acknowledgment of the accomplishment and discovery before the experience pod blinked out>

CHAPTER
6

Connor Shaw ran his fingers through his hair. He couldn't process what he was seeing in front of him. He approached the problem from every theoretical way he knew in an attempt to unravel the impossible announcement from earlier in the day. With each passing hour, he became more convinced that something wasn't right. He now sat in the open area of the bullpen and tried to re-focus his thoughts on the reports that lay open on his desk. It was already late yet he felt that he needed to go through everything one more time. Something was just out of his reach and he needed to figure it out.

He absently realized his lab was unusually empty for a Wednesday night; normally the room was full as his team was wrapping up their days work. Tonight, however the room felt deflated. He was still joined by Emily and Li, who sat at opposite corners of the massive room. Emily characteristically bit her nails as she read, while Li was working on her computer the glow illuminating her distinctive features.

Connor continued to return to the question of how could something this monumental come out of literally nowhere. The soft ping of another email arriving, he glanced down and saw a response to his request from the Banner London lab, which like every other response he received tonight, confirming their knowledge of the discovery and lauding its potential to change the world. He stabbed the keyboard and deleted it immediately. Every single response was the same - it was the greatest discovery in the history of the world. Was he the only one that thought this was impossible?

"Connor," shouted Emily over her shoulder, "Why are you staring at me? Did you figure something out and are just waiting for me to catch up?"

Connor saw his reflection in the glass window in front of Emily's desk and realized she was looking at him as well. "No. I have no idea. It's all a mystery to me. What do you think?"

Emily swiveled in her chair to face Connor "Well, every report reads like a summary, with eerily almost the same content, it gives no sense of the methodology or the process the team went through to make this discovery. Based on these reports, and the summary of their work, it is amazing that Tribe developed this capability. No one on the team is a leader in quantum mechanics, SQUID, or organic molecular chip design and they don't have the lab facilities to manage this type of research. You see, there's this feeling I get, bordering on a nagging certainty, that a lot of the work is ours and that something is missing in this report."

Connor exploded unable to contain his frustration any longer "Really Em? So what I have been saying for the last five hours about this not being possible didn't sink in until now? You have a "nagging certainty" is that what you said? Did I hear you correctly? Just to be clear let me repeat my position very slowly and clearly so everyone can hear it. It is not possible that this happened today. It's not possible that this team came up with this discovery. It's not possible that there weren't previous discoveries that led to the announcement today. It is not possible."

Connor was exasperated by the whole situation. A blind man could see there was something wrong here. He was really starting to worry about his team and their inability to process the obvious.

Li got up from her workstation and leaned against a desk that was between Connor and Emily. Her black pencil skirt rode precipitously up her long tanned legs as she joined the conversation.

"First, Connor you have to relax. We are all dealing with this in our own ways. Second, I agree with both of you, something is seriously wrong. But I think we are missing a critical piece. None of us have actually participated in the experience world. It seems to me that we need to actually connect and see what this is all about. Only then we can truly understand this discovery and the potential implications." she said in her heavily accented and clipped English.

Connor raised his hands in the air to signal stop. "Nope, I don't think this is a good idea. I am unsure of everything here and every instinct is telling me to learn more before jumping into this world."

"Connor you're being a massive jerk, but unfortunately you may be right" Emily said agreeing. Something didn't feel right to her.

Li shrugged her shoulders and stretched like a cat for the ceiling. "I think you are both over reacting. We are scientists. Testing and analysis is what we do. Eventually we will need to experience it first hand to truly understand it. But maybe not tonight, I suggest we wrap it up and get out of here. We can start again in the morning."

Connor turned back to his desk and ignored Li. He went back to the report and absently flipped the pages. He still knew that something was missing and it frustrated him that he couldn't find the clue that would lead him to the culprit. He stopped at the section on the chip membrane development process.

"…during the chip development the current insulation membrane was unable to conduct the electrical impulses required for integration with the human brain at the required frequency range. As a result, the membrane was removed and replaced with a thinner membrane that had a different compositional substrate conductive and receptive ratio, specifically the amount of silicone and selenium, and gadolinium as a percentage of the inactive materials. This substrate change improved the electrical conductivity and increased frequency range receptivity and transmission/receipt of low level electrical impulses, consistent with those found in the human brain."

Connor re-read the paragraph three times. Thinking back to his own team's work, he opened his research drive and accessed the report which held the results of their testing on their membrane material. One of the larger challenges in their research and development of the microchip and the subsequent human implantation was the surrounding membrane. The main problem was the membrane required an extremely conductive, yet stable substance to interact with the relevant electrical impulses.

Connor flipped through hundreds of pages of his team's lab results measuring the different attributes of all materials and their interaction with the human body. This component of his team's testing had taken seven months of development, painstaking testing and measurement. In addition to the laboratory unit testing, the team also had to system test on human subjects for extended periods of time. As a result, the final membrane report, not including the supporting data, was 425 pages.

Connor looked up from his desk and pondered why any researcher would test the chip and membrane together and not separately like his team. The fundamental difference in his team's approach and the Tribe approach was that the report implied Tribe tested both together.

"Hey, Em. Before you leave, I have a question." Realizing he just yelled at her and hoping she cooled down.

"What is it?' Emily said curtly while turning toward Connor, oblivious to Connor's intent.

"Well, it appears that they tested the SQUID together with the membrane. There is nothing in their report indicating that the membrane design and testing was separate from the SQUID design and testing. It appears it was an integrated system test and they didn't first do unit testing." Connor finished.

Emily was always amazed at how fast Connor's mind worked, she sat in deep thought considering this question, knowing he just found the fundamental flaw in the TRIBE report. After several moments Connor continued "Emily, you still with us?"

"Hold on, I'm thinking," she answered "it is an interesting question. I would never consider testing a membrane in a combined state. To me and our approach, the membrane and SQUID are two separate development items. You need to test each individually first and then test them together. Now if they didn't test it separately and only tested it together, it would seem they already knew something about the membrane," Emily said, her last words dragging out into a question.

"My thoughts exactly," Connor replied. "It just doesn't add up. They would need to know that the membrane already worked, and how could they do that if they were developing the membrane?"

Li pushed herself up from the desk and slowly began to close the distance to Connor.

Emily kept talking, running with her thoughts, "To answer my earlier question. There are only two possible explanations. First, if they didn't do any testing on the membrane, it could mean that they didn't design the membrane, that somehow the membrane wasn't a variable, it was a control item."

"Ok, and what's the second explanation?" Connor asked

"They are the luckiest shits in the world." Emily replied quietly.

Connor paused, feeling a presence behind him and looked over his shoulder to see Li was now standing with her arms crossed holding her chin with her right hand.

He gestured toward his computer screen while still addressing Emily. "So I am looking at our 425 page research report that details all of the work you and the team did to design, develop, and test membrane materials. I can't believe that we did all this work and we weren't aware that something was already out there that worked."

"First, trust me, there was nothing in existence that was capable of achieving our requirements. Absolutely nothing. We were pioneering new areas of material composition and chemistry, truly breaking new ground. If there was even a substrate component of the material we would have known about it." Emily replied curtly. "Therefore, I go back to my earlier hypothesis that some element of the membrane was control and was already in place. This allowed the unit testing immediately. My head is starting to hurt thinking of the implications. I need to disconnect and return to the problem in the morning after a warm bath and a good sleep." Discussion over.

Connor sat back in his chair and crossed his hands behind his head. He sighed deeply. Almost on cue, Li came up from behind him and placed her hands on his shoulders. Her hands were surprisingly strong and she began working his shoulders with a practiced touch relaxing him relatively quickly.

Li leaned close. "We'll figure this out, don't worry, you need to clear your head and try again tomorrow" she said while standing directly behind him. She lingered for a moment, gave his shoulder a squeeze and then walked away.

Connor turned his head and watched her leave, wondering what that was all about. He wasn't against office flings, as demonstrated by the many conquests he had made over the years. He filed it away and finally decided it was time to go home.

He had his first clue and wasn't going to let this go. He was going to figure this out. He was on the hunt and felt like he just made a breakthrough in this mystery. Before he consciously realized what he was going to do, he felt like he needed to find his twin brother Lucas and talk it through with him. He was the person Connor most trusted. He would be able to help him figure this out.

Experience World News Clipping Service

Brecksville Gazette Newspaper

Headline: Experience World enables Doctors to cure Danny Cooper

Danny Cooper was seven years old and for most of his life he was in a hospital bed. At birth he had slight facial deformities with higher cheekbones, a narrow jawline and long face. At age 2, Danny began to turn pale, his skin became almost pure white and he was plagued with excessive fatigue and weakness. His condition only worsened as he got older.

Local doctors were at a loss to diagnose and much less treat Danny's ailments and had run out of options. That was until the local doctors found the Experience World, where doctor, patient, and a host of scientists and specialists could come together across three continents to finally diagnose and identify a treatment plan for Danny. Most surprising, was once this group was assembled, a mere twenty minutes was all it took to solve years of pain and suffering.

Danny was diagnosed with a rare medical condition called beta thalassemia, a blood disorder that reduces the production of hemoglobin. The doctors were able to quickly identify the disease by sharing and combining their thoughts and thinking. The best part is that they connected to the CDC and were able to get Danny into an experimental program to provide a fusion protein for treatment.

Danny's parents and doctors are overjoyed at the news and credit the experience world discovery for saving their child.

Danny is now planning for his first day of school which he will be starting next week.

CHAPTER
7

The three women stood equidistant from each other in a large white featureless room. Each remained perfectly still as they carefully surveyed each other, the tension in the room was evident as the thought streams swirled around each of the figures creating an ominous quilt of colors and movement. It was impossible to repress every feeling and thought in the experience world and although each of them physically existed elsewhere, with their image coming from their mind's eye representation, the trio of Assassins regarded each other as if they were actually together in a room.

The first woman, a tall Asian with beautiful waist length jet black hair, wore a black one piece leather jumper that accentuated her near perfect figure. Her outfit was sleeveless showing off toned arms and she wore two cuff silver bracelets on each wrist. She wore black boots and a simple wide belt. Her arms hung loosely at her side as she surveyed the other two women in the room. Her thought streams swirled around her like a snake, black and dark green, moving rhythmically and hypnotically.

The second woman had a more voluptuous figure and wore her blonde hair long and wavy. She wore a white Dolce and Gabbana open back dress and high heel Christian Lauboutin nude heels. She leaned slightly forward on the balls of her feet looking like she was ready to move quickly. Her thought streams pulsed around her like a shield, gold and auburn, flexing in and out as she stood motionless and kept her eyes fixed at a spot in between the two other women.

The final woman wore a silver leather bomber jacket with silver studs and zippered sleeves over a tight white cotton shirt. She wore tight fitted jeans with brown ankle boots. Her auburn hair was cut shoulder length and her green eyes contrasted with her light honey colored skin. The final assassin's thought stream sat curled at her feet, blue and silver, looking like it was a spring ready to release.

There was no movement or expectation as a fourth figure materialized from the shadows and walked to the center of the three. His shape was clearly that of a tall, sturdily built man. His features were purposefully shadowed. Powerful and distinct thought streams began to emanate from him and spill across the participants like waves of thick oily water, visible in words, images, emotions, concepts, and colors.

Welcome, my disciples. Our journey continues to create a new world order. We are today breaking down the walls of oppression that have ruled the world since the beginning of time. Our actions will both destroy our current civilization and save it at the same time. We are the harbingers of the new world. Arising from the ruins, a new humanity will be created, a world where our small group will control and rule everyone in the world making this a better place. We will be the angels that will end conflict, end violence, end poverty end hardship. We will solve the world's problems by controlling it all and dictating the change. Each of you has been chosen, you are my disciples, and through you we will reshape the world.

The thought streams begin to pulse outward from the figure, cycling like solar flares as the energy and power in the room builds.

Our days of hiding in the shadows are no more. You three are the foundation for which we will build our church of the new world. You are the rocks from which our new world will rise.

The years we have labored to create the technology and the infrastructure to achieve our vision is gone in the blink of an eye when people connect to the experience world. Once connected, we have them. Memories are little more than a chemical and electrical reaction in the brain, something that can easily be rewritten, reprogrammed if you will, to a new reality. Today is the day that everyone believes heralded the dawn of a new world, but yet, each of us knows the truth that this is but one moment in a long history of discoveries. Our ability to control the memories and thoughts of all those that have worked on this project is our greatest gift my disciples. They are merely vessels that carry our work and allow us to reset humanity and the history of the world.

The room began to shift as the leader in the center began to glow a dull red and increase in intensity. Each of the participants involuntarily felt their heart rate increase, they felt the aggression, the power, a godlike force of will in the room flow through them, and the energy was building and reaching out from the experience world into their physical beings. Each became more powerful, working together their path was clear.

Continue your journey and we will be triumphant. We are the makers of the new world. We are the disciples. We are gods that will control it all.

Li's mind's eye went dark and she was returned to her physical world. Her heart was still racing as adrenaline coursed through her veins. Her path was clear.

CHAPTER
8

Alexis stood at the entrance of Lucas's apartment at the bluffs on Ocean Avenue and waited impatiently. She decided to make a statement and wait outside the door. At times, she felt like she had been waiting outside for Lucas their entire relationship. Being a clinical psychologist, she knew there was a level of emotional dependence driven by meeting Lucas when she started UCLA so many years ago. Her mother's recent death and her father's physical distance compounded the need for her to reach out and replace these bonds with someone else quickly and Lucas was the answer that fit the bill perfectly. He was a large bundle of damaged goods from his family of origin and was constantly fighting an internal struggle to overcome his perceived shortfalls. His adjustment disorder drove him to exceptional accomplishments while he never felt worthy or satisfied with himself. It was a match made in heaven.

Unfortunately all of her rational analysis couldn't explain away the fact she loved him deeply and cared more for him than anyone. Her heart always skipped a beat when she saw him and she still got butterflies when they kissed. She mentally admonished herself for thinking like a silly teenage girl, but reluctantly she admitted liking the feeling.

She knew that eventually she needed to evaluate their relationship and determine where this was all headed. Connor, Lucas's twin brother, added a whole new challenge to her relationship. She loathed any interactions with Connor, although they were identical twins, she recognized that Lucas was exactly opposite and that was why she was attracted to him.

She returned to the present and waited for Lucas. He texted her as he got out of his last teaching seminar and pleaded with her to meet him at his apartment.

Alexis reluctantly agreed, even though she was still slightly aggravated by him getting in late last night. When he left this morning he had mumbled an incoherent explanation about working on something for his advanced AI seminar and told her he would call her later to explain everything. She suspected that there was something else going on with Lucas and she really didn't need the drama.

"Alexis, hey sexy." Lucas said as trotted over to meet her. He was wearing a white polo and jeans that accentuated his athletic build and dark hair. He still had his college rowing body and carried himself well. He lightly grabbed her elbow as he gave her a welcoming kiss. She pulled away and glared at him setting the ground rules.

'I'm still upset about last night. You don't call and you get back late without any explanation." Alexis said actually surprised how emotional she was becoming.

Lucas pushed out his lower lip and looked at her in a playful manner completely missing her emotional cues. "Hey, relax, I said I was sorry, I didn't mean to be back so late. It's just that I have been working on some amazing stuff."

"You got to remember we are in a relationship," said Alexis, raising her voice realizing now she wasn't really mad about last night, and that something else was bothering her. "I can't continue guessing about the when and how of our relationship. You have to open up with me. Simple things like what time you are planning to be back is a start."

Lucas barreled ahead oblivious to the context of the conversation 'Well, the truth is that I really wanted to show you what I have been working on. Her name is Alex and she is a fully functioning organic android, with all of the right equipment, if you know what I mean. OW!" Lucas yelled as Alexis hit him on the arm.

'Cut it out" she replied "you're not taking this seriously. How old are you anyway? Why did you really want me here? For a brilliant computer scientist and professor, you have the emotional intelligence of a teenage boy" She retreated realizing she didn't have the energy to fight it out today.

Finally catching on, Lucas replied "Ok, sorry, let me start again. I wanted to share something with you based on the announcements that came out today around the experience world. It is really interesting and I wanted you to experience it with me." Stepping deftly around her, Lucas hurried up the last two steps to open the door for Alexis. She exhaled, resigning herself to tabling any solution and handling it later.

As she entered the apartment, she was always reminded of the ironic juxtaposition of the twins. Connor and Lucas had followed a common path, inseparable since birth, but yet completely different. Connor was rarely home and his celebrity status guaranteed he was out at the hottest club or party. Lucas kept to himself and rarely went out. The whole situation immediately made Alexis furious and she checked herself to figure out why she became so emotional when she thought of Connor.

The twins' parents were extremely wealthy and each boy received a sizable trust fund and real estate at their twenty fourth birthdays. The boys had kept their assets separate except for the joint purchase of their Santa Monica condo. As she entered the apartment, her eyes were instantly drawn to the expansive ocean view looking out over the Pacific. It caught her every time. The twins' interior designer had created a masculine yet comfortable and refined living space. The apartment smelled slightly of lemon cleaner as Elba their long time housekeeper had evidently just left.

Lucas unceremoniously pulled off his shoes and tossed them into the corner, "Please follow me to the couch." He said, bowing low and extending his arm toward the couch.

"Sure" Alexis replied curtly, feeling instantly aggravated by his behavior.

Lucas turned on his media center with the remote sitting on the dark wood table.

"So, by now you have heard about the Tribe announcement and the new TG Dakarta phone that can share thoughts and control electronic equipment right?" Lucas asked already knowing the answer.

'Of course" replied Alexis "we discussed the discovery this morning, and you already know that. Get to the point."

"Right," replied Lucas "I want to tell you a very interesting story. So about a month ago I was sitting here playing Halo Resurrection in networked mode, using the wireless keyboard, and battling with some dudes at UCSD." Lucas moved his hands when he talked, getting visibly excited.

"Very impressive. An accomplished professor indulging in boyhood hobbies." said Alexis actually disappointed.

"Ignoring the comment" he continued "I was in the middle of this mission and my phone rings." Lucas picked up his earpiece from the table in front of him and held it out.

"Ok, I know what an earpiece is and did you just call it a mission. Seriously?" said Alexis wondering where this was going.

"Right, ignoring you again, so when my phone rings, I put down my wireless keyboard, put in my earpiece and walk over to the kitchen to get a beer. Well it turns out it's my mom, calling me to ask me to come home for my sister's birthday. So as I am talking to my mom, facing my desk." Lucas points to the wall where a Jackson Pollack hangs "Someone on the other team yells that Boo44, my avatar, is kicking some serious ass."

'Ok" said Alexis, mentally willing him to finish the story, hoping it was going somewhere.

"So, I turn around and look at my Marine and he is running through the tunnels, switching to the electromagnetic pulse gun, and targeting the leader of the UCSD team who is holed up behind an energy field" Lucas moved forward on the couch and can barely contain himself and pointing at the screen.

Alexis couldn't take it anymore, "Lucas, this sounds really fun, and I am ecstatic you beat the UCSD undergrads in a video-game, but if you dragged me up here to talk about some video game strategy, it's falling on deaf ears." She got up and moved toward the kitchen ready to get her own beer.

"Alexis" said Lucas reaching out to lightly grab her arm "Hold on, just a second. You have got to understand what I am telling you. My character was playing without anyone on the keyboard or controller, my thoughts were controlling the character. Most importantly this happened a month ago."

Alexis stared at Lucas for several moments trying to process what he was saying. "What in the hell are you talking about? You were controlling Halo through your thoughts a month ago. Were you using the new Dakarta phone or something?"

"Exactly my point. Yes, I was using an earlier version of the Dakarta earpiece and device. But the announcement today of the release stated it just came out and it would become generally available to the public over the next several weeks." Lucas stood up and grabbed her shoulder looking grim faced and totally serious. 'Don't you get it. This tech is already in the marketplace and it's been experience world capable for at least a month."

She turned back and looked at the screen and then at Lucas "I still don't understand. What do you mean?" unable to process what he was saying.

Lucas stared into her eyes "The thought sharing and machine control functionality has been available for at least a month. This is not some new invention. Somehow last month the tech allowed me to control the game machine. I'm not sure how, but this has been publically available for some time now. Who knows how long!"

Alexis blurted out the next question without thinking. "How could this be possible?"

Connor agreed. "It doesn't make any sense, if that's true then what was the announcement today about. Wouldn't this be something that everyone already knew if the tech was already generally available?"

"Why do I have the feeling that this isn't going to end well?" Alexis replied realizing that the world was changing rapidly and careening down an unknown path.

Experience Pod 113.14.215
Film Farm Productions

It wasn't really that good of a film and Sam knew it.
He knew it in his gut. He had survived long enough in
Hollywood to know you are only as good as your next
picture and this picture wasn't going to get him anywhere.
Sam also knew that even though the film was utter
garbage there was always a way in Hollywood to make a
buck. He just needed to figure out his angle.

It was with this backdrop that Sam literally stumbled
across the experience world and the potential to create
a movie trailer like never before. The film was your
standard supernatural slash fest with some ancient evil
ghost chasing a group of clueless and defenseless students
in an abandoned mine shaft. "Come into the Light" did
have one thing going for it, the film was excessively and
dramatically violent, to the point where some of the
scenes had to be toned down to come in under the rating
requirements. Sam's PA suggested that the production
company make a trailer where the viewers can feel the fear
of the students to the distorted evil of the ghost. Sam gave
it the green light thinking he had nothing to lose and not
really sure what he was going to get.

A week later, Sam arrived at the production office for
the meeting with the trailer design and production team.
They had put together thirty seconds of rough footage in
the experience world to represent what could be achieved.

"Alright, I am ready to be impressed." Sam said while looking at a group of hipster twenty year olds making up the production team.

A tall dark haired woman stepped forward "Please insert your headset and sit down. This is a real bumpy ride." She commented while handing Sam a black earpiece.

Sam inserted his earpiece and sat down in one of the large black leather chairs around the conference table. *His mind's eye was immediately darkened and he saw himself in a dark mine shaft. He felt nervous and scared, actually terrified. His heart rate increased as he began to smell a damp and dusty scent, he turned his head and the dark of the mine opened behind him. He turned back and saw a distant speck of light at the end of the tunnel. He felt an overwhelming need to get out and escape to the light. He forgot he was experiencing a movie trailer and felt his life depended on it.*

As he started moving forward, he heard a metallic scrape against stone, turning quickly he saw sparks coming from further back in the tunnel as someone was walking toward him with something metal being dragged across the wall. He was focused on the sparks and he didn't see the girl coming out of the darkness until she was almost on top of him. She fell into his arms and he immediately felt something wet and sticky on his hands. She gurgled unable to get any words out and then her head fell back at her neck. Her throat was slit and the blood splattered all over Sam. He screamed dropped the girl and turned and ran. He was terrified and needed to escape. He heard someone behind him and stealing a glance behind for a moment he lost his footing and fell to the floor of the mine shaft. He turned and saw the face of the ghost, the most hideous and otherworldly vision he ever experienced. The ghost raised the long scythe above his head and brought it down on Sam.

Sam shot out of his chair and ripped off his earpiece. He was momentarily disconcerted and bent over and vomited. Sam slowly stood up, his shirt covered with vomit and sweat. He looked around the room as the production team stood motionless not sure of his reaction.

Sam slowly raised his hands to the ceiling and screamed in the small conference room "That was amazing, Holy Crap. I have never experienced anything like that. We are going to make so much money on this film. Brilliant, absolutely brilliant"

"Come into the Light" went on to become the highest grossing independent film of the year and spawned a new industry in experience world film trailers and film making. Sam went on to become the most prolific producer of experience world content.

CHAPTER
9

James McLaughlin couldn't believe his luck. He glanced down at dark hair that spilled across his lap as he leaned back in his seat. He watched the near perfect hands move delicately across his thighs. He had to keep reminding himself this wasn't a dream.

The coincidence that got him to this spot was unbelievable. Only two hours ago after stopping for a few beers, he literally bumped into her in the parking lot of The Reel Inn. She wasn't watching where she was walking and collided with James, spilling the contents of her purse, just as he was about to get into his car.

As she gathered her things, she looked up and a flash of recognition crossed her face. She asked if they had met before. He exhaled slowly, as he already knew who she was, since he was the head of internal security at Banner. He personally cleared her security and access clearances only a few weeks ago and remembered her specifically because she didn't look like any of the other scientists and employees. She could have been a supermodel.

She was extremely relaxed and they continued talking while standing in the parking lot. She eventually asked if he wanted to go for a nightcap. They returned to the bar and after several drinks she suggested they go back to his car.

James was full on drunk and readily agreed. He stumbled after her and when she suggested, rather coquettishly, he should move the car to the rear of the parking lot in the darkened last row, he thought he had hit the jackpot. As he parked she moved closer to him and he quickly became aroused. He thought this was easily working out to be one of the best nights of his life.

"What did you think when you first saw me and provided my security clearance?" Li purred in his ear as her hand rubbed his chest.

"What do you mean?" James replied

"Were there any issues? Or concerns?" Li replied while moving against his thigh.

"None, of course. Everything was perfect. I guess the only issue was I couldn't understand how a scientist could be so hot." James said smiling crookedly as his eyes fought to focus.

"Did you ever contact Banner's Asian Operations?" asked Li as her fingers moved down his chest towards his lap.

Even in his near completely inebriated state, an alarm bell went off. His Army training told him to trust his instincts and he got an immediate hint of "What the hell?" from this line of questioning. James clumsily shifted his weight to the door, trying to get his thoughts in order.

"Did you hear me?" Li asked moving closer as her hand moved into his pants.

"Yes, sorry. Um, I followed procedure and contacted Banner's Asian Operations to cross-reference your file. Why do you ask?" James replied, unsure of the turn in the conversation and trying to get focused as the alcohol made everything cloudy.

Li moved her hand and in a matter of seconds she had found him again and he began to relax, letting the concerns of moment drift away.

When he was near full arousal, Li changed her position to straddle his torso. He skirt was pulled up and her blouse was open as she settled down on him. She felt strong and taut as she sat above him. James admired her near perfect body.

"Does anyone else do the background checks?" Li whispered in his ear as she moved slowly up and down.

The little voice from his military training was lost as he began to go to a different place. "No, just me. Keep doing that, it feels good." he replied as he closed his eyes and let his head go back on the headrest.

Li looked down at the pale, doughy security guard while a look of disgust came across her face. She spread her hands as she caressed his head with her fingers. The garrote she was holding was stretched behind his head, and with a practiced move she wrapped it around his neck and with an incredibly strong pull crossed it in front. The force of the garrote was so strong that it immediately crushed his trachea.

James reacted immediately and reached for this throat, and fought to get out from under her. He tried to sit up but she pushed her legs against the dash and held him tight. He reached for the door at which point Li put even more pressure on the wire. Blood began to flow in a perfect line as the wire cut into his skin. His skin began to turn from red to blue. Li held her position for three full minutes as he lost consciousness and then stopped breathing. She sat for another five minutes, applying constant pressure to guarantee she had eliminated the potential risk.

Confident he was dead, she slid off the body, rearranged her clothes and got out of the car. She didn't see anyone on her way to her car and pulled out of the parking lot without turning on her lights until she got to the road.

She had one more task to do this evening. She got on the 10 freeway heading downtown. She was heading to the warehouse where she hid the body of the Chinese research scientist who she eliminated five weeks ago when she arrived in Los Angeles. Posing as her driver, she had killed her while driving downtown and now had several cutting instruments to finalize her disappearance. She sighed realizing that she would be driving all night dropping pieces all over the city. She really wanted to get home to a warm bath and get to sleep because it had been a long day.

She briefly considered that someone else in China had also done a similar drive when they eliminated the research scientist's family and relatives. At least she didn't have to drive around Beijing with six people's remains. Besides it was a beautiful night in LA, so she rolled down her window to drink in the night air.

She smiled broadly. She loved it when a plan came together.

CHAPTER
10

It was only a few days since the discovery was announced, not more than 72 hours thought Connor, and yet it seemed like everyone is now using the experience equipped phones and connected to the experience world. He pondered these thoughts as he sat outside the small café and watched the people walking down Montana Avenue. He stopped counting how many people had the new phone when he reached a hundred in a matter of minutes. It seemed every person was using the new tech. He began to look for people who didn't have the new phones. He didn't spot anyone.

As the weight of his observations compounded, he felt something deep in the pit of his stomach that clawed at his subconscious. Something was very wrong, none of this made sense. It is impossible that this tech could be in the hands of so many people so quickly. There was no company or supply chain in the world that could move so much product this fast. He ran through every conceivable scenario in attempt to reconcile what he was seeing, and nothing came up as possible.

Emily pulled a chair and sat down across from Connor, pulling him from his thoughts.

"Hi, you look tired. Everything alright?" asked Emily with genuine concern.

"Yes, I guess or maybe I'm not sure. I can't break the feeling that something is really wrong with these phones and the experience world. Look around, every single person has these experience phones and is connected to the experience world." Connor replied truly exasperated. "It is not possible that this many phones can be in the hands of this many people in only a few days."

Emily was tired from spending the entire evening in the experience world so she paused and collected her thoughts before she responded to Connor, her mind was moving slowly as she chose her words wisely. "Connor, I think you are confused and I'm not sure you have your timeline straight. The experience phones have been out for at least half a year, maybe more, people have been buying them for some time, they are at every store and there are multiple versions of the phone. The initial rush to get the phones died down months ago, we haven't seen any runs on the stores for a while. All of the interaction in the experience world over the past six months has moved beyond the novelty of the discovery and we are now really thinking about how to make this valuable to industry and the general public. Do you understand that? I'm not sure how you are so confused. I am really becoming concerned about you."

Connor checked himself because Emily's voice had perceptibly changed, sounding flat and without emotion. He was reminded of a computer voice program ever so slightly. His instinct kicked in and although he couldn't believe what he was hearing, he knew that this announcement was only a few days ago. He looked down at the small notepad that he carried with him and flipped it open. He found the entry he made after the press conference four days ago. He remembered everything clearly, he knew exactly what he wrote down and when. There was something very wrong here. Somehow he was on a different temporal line than everyone else around him. He knew the physics and the potential for this, but while theoretically possible, it wasn't anywhere near practical.

He felt Emily staring at him and realized, for no specific reason, that he needed to admit that he was confused. Some basic survival instinct was pushing him to lie and admit he was confused. He followed his instinct.

"Wow, I'm not sure what I am saying, Em. This is clear to me that I need more sleep. Not sure what all that was about and where I got these crazy ideas." Connor laughed while closing the book and putting it back into his jacket pocket.

"Like I said, maybe you should see someone. Get a check-up with a doctor, make sure that there isn't some tumor rattling around inside your skull?" Emily replied

"Well, that's a positive thought. All kidding aside, I will check with Dr. Becker" Connor replied.

"Good, you had me worried there for a moment. Now, do you want some coffee?" Emily asked her voice and cadence returning to normal.

"Sure" Connor stood up to follow her.

He looked around again at everyone with the new tech and had a shiver of pure terror. He needed to get to Lucas and figure this out.

CHAPTER
11

Lucas entered his apartment and set his computer bag on the antique mission table by the front door. He stretched for the ceiling as he walked, trying to remove the ever present tightness in his neck. He sat down on the couch and with a flick of his finger turned on the media console. The different components came to life as the screen descended from the hidden spot in the ceiling. As the projector warmed up, the twelve foot screen began to faintly display the game menu for Red Badge of Courage.

As Lucas waited for the screen to get to full contrast, Connor walked in the door. Lucas didn't turn around but simply said "Hey" facing forward knowing instinctively it was his brother.

Connor didn't respond and sat next to his brother on the couch with an audible sigh. Lucas glanced at his brother and immediately realized he looked tired, run-down and anxious. As a twin, Lucas actually felt Connor's current condition, as only a twin could appreciate.

"What's wrong?" asked Lucas cutting to the chase.

"Don't ask." Connor replied while absentmindedly waving his hand in the air and after several moments he continued with tension and emotion in his voice "Lucas, for the first time in my life I feel like I am going to really lose it. I'm feeling unbalanced and confused. I'm not thinking clearly and while I realize it, I can't get myself off this downward spiral. I have this constant trepidation in the pit of my stomach. I am filled with irrational and obsessive thoughts. All of it centered on the experience world. I know there is something inherently messed up with this entire situation and yet I can't figure it out. I really think I may be having a psychotic episode of some sort. The stress and anxiety are becoming too much."

Lucas sat back and turned so he could face Connor, the twin now internalizing even more of his stress and anxiety. "Connor, first, you need to relax and remember that whatever the problem we can work through it together. Understand? A confused and irrational mind will do nothing to help you to understand the root cause and define how to deal with it. So, first, please calm down."

Connor leaned back on the couch and looked up at the ceiling visibly calming his breathing.

Lucas continued "Now, let's break this down? What is the specific issue that you are dealing with regarding the experience world?"

Connor paused and collected his thoughts before responding. He was already feeling better talking to his brother "Well, the core issue is that I cannot reconcile the rapid adoption and proliferation of the experience world and phones to my own timeline. No one seems to really know when these devices were actually released and how quickly they have become an integrated part of society? For instance, I spoke to Emily yesterday and we had a completely different recollection of the timeline. I am almost completely certain that the press release for the devices was only four days ago. Also, the Tribe launch of the experience world coincided with the device launch as well. Now, four days later, millions of people have the experience phones and are connected. There is no way this timeline makes sense. It just doesn't add up for me."

Lucas replied "First, you're not going crazy. I can confirm for you that the discovery was announced only four days ago. I also agree that there is something fundamentally wrong with the public perception and timing of the phone proliferation. I just told Alexis yesterday that the TG phones could control electronic equipment months ago, when I showed her how I was able to control a video game with my wireless headset. So, I think we first need to consider a more relevant question of why and how could there be a difference in the first place. What is the reason that we have a different recollection of the timeline than others? How could so many people have a completely different fact base and perception? That's the real issue here. The technology has been available for some time, that's a given. We figure out why is there a difference and we can begin to unravel what's going on here."

Connor felt immediately calmed and relieved by Lucas' admission, yet he became even more disturbed by the disconnects around the timing of the invention. "Thank God I'm not going crazy. It was really scary to think that my reality was different than everyone else. I have to admit that I have been focused on solving the issue around the difference, trying to prove that I'm correct. I haven't spent any time contemplating the potential of why there could be a difference. I have to give it to you it's a fundamental formative question and admittedly allows us to look at it from a different perspective."

Connor sat still for several moments. Lucas could feel his tension release as his mind began to contemplate the larger and potentially more complicated question. Lucas knew exactly where Connor was mentally and it helped that they understood each other as only twins can.

"So what is your theory?" Connor asked, breaking the silence, while he was still trying to work through the question.

"I'm not sure, but the simplest answer is usually the right answer" Lucas said. "The simplest answer, which we have already confirmed, is that the tech has been out in the public for more time than originally assumed. We are dealing with two factors, the physical reality and the mental perceptions. The physical reality is that the devices have followed a normal manufacturing and distribution process, going through the standard supply chains to get to consumers. No mystery there. The perception, however, is where we diverge. I'm not sure how the two perspectives can be so different."

Connor sat calmly as he contemplated what Lucas just theorized. "How is that possible? How can so many people be confused on the timelines? Do you realize how terrifying this could be if it is true."

Connor had the sinking feeling return to the pit of his stomach. The connections started falling together. Connor felt numb.

"Connor, it has to do with people's interaction with the phones and the experience world. It's the only viable reason for the differences. Listen, when I'm connected to the experience world, my thoughts sometimes get fuzzy, almost like I'm drunk. I feel that something is making my mental processing slow down. Again, it's not a constant feeling, it's more like a gentle wave that comes and then passes quickly." Lucas finished looking down at his folded hands while leaning on his knees. Looking up directly at Connor he continued "If I followed my advice of identifying the simplest answer as the reason, I would guess that something is affecting my thoughts when I'm connected, but for some reason it hasn't changed my perception as much as I can tell."

"How do you know it hasn't changed your perception or recollection?" asked Connor. "What if we are talking about a situation where the experience world begins to distort reality and truth? Do you have any idea how dangerous and powerful that could become?"

Connor's eyes traveled to the two black earpieces sitting on the coffee table in front of him. He looked up at his brother "We need to go in together. Our twin connection can keep us strong and clear headed."

Lucas laughed loudly "Connor, come on, we both know that our bond is unique as identical twins, but you're sounding like we have some superpowers. Cut it out."

Connor stared at Lucas "I'm serious. We need to go in together. We are used to sharing our thoughts, we can now do it in the experience world and see what's really going on here."

Lucas actually shivered when he realized what Connor was proposing. Deep down he knew there was a risk and was frightened to consider the real possibility.

"Lucas, come with me and enter the experience world. It will help us understand and answer these questions. We have to do it and you know it." Connor said.

Connor took an earpiece automatically placing it in his ear. As he linked in, he felt a warm tingling across his scalp. It felt like a thousand small bugs were crawling over his head. It was a feeling similar to how circulation returning to an arm or hand feels after it has fallen asleep. He also sensed an almost imperceptible electrical hum in his head that accompanied the connection. He felt slightly disconcerted as he lowered his eyes while his mind's eye was thrown opened. He was overwhelmed with images, feelings, colors, and sensations that were not his own. He felt queasy. His mind seemed to pause as it was catching up with the other thought flow. He felt like he was stepping onto a moving walkway, with a slight tug as his mind adjusted to the new speed.

As he gained his mental equilibrium, the jumble of images and feelings coalesced and he saw himself standing in an old barn, hay filled the corners and old rusting equipment sat strewn across the floor. It reminded him of his grandparent's farm in upstate Michigan where he and Lucas used to go in the summer. Sunlight streamed in from the gaps in the walls. He smelled the distinctive scent of lilacs. Lucas stood across from him, dressed in a Civil War soldier's uniform, looking decidedly buff and hardened. His brother and his thought streams circled both of them and merged and separated in a constant blue grey color. Connor realized that their thought streams were identical and looked like one, inseparable. Maybe he was right, they were different.

Are you ok. Feelings of fear/uncertainty. Connor realized that he and Lucas were sharing the same experience and thoughts. It felt very comfortable and natural being together in the experience world.

Lucas pushed his thoughts toward his brother. *Let's figure this out together. We need to release ourselves and explore.*

Connor mentally forced himself to flip into his mind's eye and the scene focused him back into the barn. *What is this place? Are you controlling this Lucas?*

Yes. This is my starting point in the experience world. I'm not really sure where I came up with this, but it reminds me of Grandpa's farm where I always felt safe. Outside of these doors is the experience world. I don't think there is any risk in here <Lucas gestured around the barn>

Connor became physically queasy as he became more absorbed into the scene. He also felt the ever slightest pressure building on his thoughts, something was pushing at the edge of his consciousness. He felt like a small worm was trying to burrow through his memories. He felt it moving and with it re-ordering his thoughts. He instantly regretted his decision to enter the experience world. He reacted quickly and pulled the earpiece from his ear and returned to their apartment, breaking the link to the experience world. He struggled to comprehend what just happened on multiple levels, but he was certain that something was trying to get into his head when he was in the experience world. Connor removed himself from the experience world and looked at his brother.

"What happened?" he asked.

Lucas replied. "I think I know what's happening and why people have different recollections and memories. The experience world is trying to change them."

Experience Pod 111.33.4444
Stephen Hawking Daily Fireside Chat

A tall dark haired man walked confidently across the front
of a massive auditorium toward the front of the hall, in one
quick leap, he covered the stairs to quickly reach the stage.
He grabbed the sides of the podium and looked around the
auditorium. The man looked the picture of health and vitality,
strong, tall, and lean. He wore wire rim glasses that gave him
an air of intelligence. His confidence and intelligence were
evident as his dark blue thought stream, solid and substantial
flowed and flexed with power and fluidity, moving quickly and
confidently.

The man raised his hands and all movement and noise
were silenced. He looked out to an audience that went back and
up as far as the eye could see. He knew that millions of people
were already coming to his Experience pod and this energized
him even further as he realized that he was sharing his thoughts
and feelings in ways never imagined. For a moment, he paused
and remembered his broken down body that existed in the real
world, his physical vessel had been slowly sinking for years, while
his mind, alive and strong and powerful, was begging for the
experience world to set him free. He collected his thoughts before
beginning.

<As he started a wave of the faintest light blue light washed
across the crowd and filled the space> Ladies and Gentlemen,
welcome to my Experience Pod. My name is Stephen Hawking
and I am a theoretical physicist, mathematician and thinker.

Thank you for the opportunity to share with you today <A ripple
of energy flowed back across the audience, like the ripples in a
pond. Each successive wave built the energy and excitement in
the room.

So let us start <Another wave of energy pulses as the
power of this man's mind is breathtaking> we today are
experiencing something that I never thought possible. The
ability to connect with each of you across our thoughts and
the powers of our minds. Had someone asked me last year
if I ever imagined such a capability and experience, I would
have laughed them off as a crackpot. Yet, today, here we
are all joined together around a common interest, a common
connection. Today I would like to share with you some of
my thoughts. <As the man began to move across the stage,
the thought streams began pulsating across the participants,
causing a wave of energy flowing across the millions of figures
facing the stage>

I want to share with you, in this experience world, my
thoughts on black holes. Now it is important to note, that in
the past, my speeches have been, well, speeches for lack of a
better term <feelings of humor flow across the audience> These
simple words did not fully express or explain my perspective
or thinking on black holes, and it took me, actually it takes
all of us, too many words to get our point across. So today,
I'm going to take another approach, I'm not going to give a
speech, rather each of you are going to share my thoughts and
experience and participate in how I see and understand black
holes. <Immediately the scene changes and the entire hall

becomes a large black hole. The darkness was near complete as the participants looked into a bottomless hole in space and time. Hawking's thoughts and mind enveloped the crowd > So let us begin...

CHAPTER
12

Lucas sat comfortably in front of his monitor and looked at the data flowing across the screen. After his shared experience with his brother, he knew that Connor was right and that there was something happening on a much deeper level in the experience world. He needed to figure out the mystery of the perception changes and memory modification for the experience world users.

The good news was that Lucas was now in his element as he floated among the data in cyberspace. He used a virtual reality data viewing tool that allowed him to access multiple data sources using an Oculus Rift headset. By simply moving his head around, he was able to view and manipulate multiple data sources. He wasn't yet sure what he was looking for, but he knew there was always a trail in data that would lead him to the answer.

His first object was to learn more about the timeline changes and recollections of the general public. He started with comparing as many media and information sources as possible. It took him over an hour to find his first clue, a news article that had been orphaned on a server that was taken off-line to install a new OS and hadn't yet been reopened to the web. The article was postdated six days ago and talked about the Tribe announcement and the amazing surprise this had been to the general public. No other news sources that Lucas searched had the correct date. Each of them referenced back six to eight months ago as the timeline for the discovery. When he dug deeper into the log files for many of the major news servers he found a pattern that each of the articles were edited, all by different authors, around the same time on the day following the Tribe announcement. The pattern was eerie as it showed up across millions of different sites and locations.

Satisfied that there was a massive inconsistency and pattern, Lucas acted on his instinct and started looking at the people that surrounded Connor. He always chuckled about how easy it was to reassemble a person's interests, activities, and personality by just paying attention to the digital tracks they made across cyberspace and even more compelling across the experience world. Most of Connor's team led boring and mundane average lives, one person apparently was interested in narcolepsy, but on the whole nothing was interesting or out of the ordinary.

That was until Lucas got to Li, the new employee from China. Her connections and activity were off the charts, both in the normal cyberspace and in the experience world. She had extensive ip jumps across the globe and she was moving tremendous amounts of data through a variety of servers across the world. She also deployed a fairly advanced mask program to avoid detection of her location. Lucas blew through the protection program and began assembling his dossier on the mysterious Li. She was in the experience world all the time. Her usage was constant and he wondered if she existed in both worlds simultaneously.

A few minutes later, Lucas hacked into her mobile device and began building a dataset of her calls, texts, web requests and emails. He ran his mirror program from her device to his computer so he could avoid any potential detection. Once he assembled the information, he began to rebuild the pattern behind her activities. It was fascinating.

Later that afternoon, Connor leaned against the kitchen counter as Lucas relayed his early findings. "First, to confirm again we are not crazy. There is a massive inconsistency in data on a global scale that I never thought was possible about the actual release date of this discovery. It is probably the most terrifying concept I have ever considered that someone or some group can change facts and perception on such a global basis. It's also important to note that it's not just the specific structured data, but also unstructured data and people's opinions. I couldn't find any records of anyone contradicting the timelines. It's like everyone's memory has been replaced and we are the only ones who know the truth."

Connor stood dumbfounded "Lucas do you realize what you are saying? There is a global conspiracy that is rewriting facts about a discovery that fundamentally changes the world. The scale and power necessary to do this is incomprehensible and terrifying."

"I know, I know" Lucas repeated shaking his head acknowledging the almost impossible conclusion "but we have to deal with the ways things are. We have to deal with the real situation. Something is manipulating the thoughts and memories of the experience world users. They have figured out mind control on a global level."

Connor just stared at Lucas trying to process the implications. After several moments Lucas continued "One other item, your colleague Li at Banner, is all over the place," Lucas described "she has connections in India, China, Russia, and pretty much all over the world. I suspect she has traveled extensively and she uses advanced protection and encryption programs to mask her identity and her actions. She is also constantly in the experience world. I suspect that she never disconnects. Not sure how a person can exist simultaneously in both worlds, but somehow she has figured out how to do it."

"So what do you think it means?" asked Connor

"Right now, I really don't know, but my instinct is that somehow she's involved. I expect that as I continue to dig into this I will find some really, really interesting connections across the timeline and her activities" replied Lucas "If I were you, I would make sure that you let someone else know what's going on here. Aren't you friends with someone on the board of Banner? I would reach out to someone like that to make sure you are covering your ass. My feeling is that this could get real ugly, real fast."

"Yes, we need to bring others into this, I just hope they will believe us." Connor replied feeling the weight of the implications sitting on his shoulders. " I will reach out to Dan Roberts, he knew Dad from a prior life and always told me to call him if I needed anything." Connor replied and nodded in the direction of Lucas "and keep digging. We need to figure this out and what we are going to do."

"Oh, don't you worry, I will definitely keep digging, this is starting to get fun." Lucas replied with a massive grin spreading across his face. A hacker with a mission. A dangerous combination.

CHAPTER
13

Adam sat looking out the window of his top floor Tribe office and stared at the Santa Monica Pier. It was a crystal clear day and the ocean was calm and a deep blue. The pier was quiet at this time of day as a few people could be seen walking the boardwalk. He glanced to his right at the foothills of Pacific Palisades. The morning sky was clear and two sailboats moved gracefully across the water. Adam felt a momentary peace as he gazed at the idyllic scene.

He came back to the present as Rina stood up in front of him. She adjusted her skirt and tucked in her blouse and walked over to the hidden mirror to check her make-up. Adam smiled as she walked away, amazed by the chemistry between them.

The intercom buzzed, breaking his momentary serenity, as he swiveled in his black leather chair to face his dark walnut desk. He reached out and roughly punched the page button, and brusquely said "Yes"

Tess, his current secretary, said, "Sorry to interrupt, Mr. MacArthur your 10:00 am is here."

"Ok, give us two minutes and then escort them in." Adam hung up and bolted out of his chair.

Adam headed to the recessed closet door that blended into the dark panel walls. He pulled out a black sport coat and quickly pulled it on. He stopped to look at his reflection in the small mirror on the back of the closet door. Not bad for a soon-to-be newly minted multi-billionaire, he thought.

He closed the closet door and strode back to his desk. As he walked he heard his executive coach's voice in his head – make sure you are sitting and working on his computer when guests arrive in the office. To cultivate a specific image of a hard working charismatic intellectual you must reinforce it with every interaction.

He sat at his computer and opened his email and began looking at his daily correspondence when a courtesy knock announced his guest's arrival.

Rina had already taken up a position on the arm of a chair her skirt climbing up her long legs, waiting for the guests' arrival.

Tess led three men into the room. All of considerable significance and power, they carried the demeanor and confidence of success. Adam stood and moved around his desk to greet his visitors. He mentally checked himself trying to remember if he should have given away his position so early. Did he lessen his executive aura if he came to them, or should they come to him? He made a mental note to ask his coach during the next session.

Tess stepped aside, as the three men moved forward to shake hands with Adam and Rina. Dan Roberts extended his hand first. Tall and lean, he still held his swimmer's body from college, and had a perpetual Southern California tan cultivated from many afternoon walks on the golf course. Dan's grip was warm and firm and he looked deeply into Adam's eyes while saying a simple "Adam."

Adam returned the nod and turned to Sam Ford, who carried his extra twenty pounds like a badge of his success. He wore a black polo and light khakis. His dark curly hair was gelled back from his forehead. His grip was softer and cold. He shook Adam's hand with "Nice to see you, Adam," while he looked over his shoulder at the Pacific.

The final member of the group was the legendary Tarun Patel. He was one of the world's most successful venture capitalists. His business started with several computer hardware companies, moved into early Internet and enterprise software and recently led the largest social media IPO in history. He sat on the boards of some of the largest and most powerful companies in the world and was notoriously tough in negotiations and excessively rewarded his employees and board of directors' success. He was also a frequent target in the gossip magazines, as a notorious womanizer and billionaire playboy. He was Adam's idol.

He stood back and let Adam come to him. Adam spoke first. "Tarun, it's an honor to meet you and thank you for coming today."

Tarun replied in his distinctive accented English, "My pleasure. We have many plans for you and I am excited about your role and involvement. You are somewhat of a wunderkind, aren't you?"

Adam swelled with pride. "No, not at all. Really just fortunate to have a good team and support."

Tarun smirked a knowingly look and moved toward the four leather chairs that sat to the left of Adam's desk. Rina moved to a footstool that had been pulled into the circle of chairs. Tarun's eyes drifted toward Rina and looked her over; it was obvious to everyone in the room, especially Rina. She didn't flinch and returned his stare with a slight nod of her head.

As the group sat, Tess returned with four bottles of water and a bowl of frozen grapes. She shut the door quietly and left the group to their business.

Dan grabbed his bottle of water and twisted off the cap. "Adam, it was good to see you last week at Geletas. My wife commented that you and Rina make an excellent couple. Is there something we should know about between the two of you?" He raised his eyebrows as he finished, clearly amused by the implication.

Adam shook his head and smiled. "Nope, we are business partners who fancy ourselves as foodies when we aren't working."

Rina supported Adam's statement with a coquettish smile and nod.

Adam glanced down for a moment and looking up he spoke. "So gentlemen, what can we discuss with you today?" Adam's coach advised him that men of power are very specific and to the point. Powerful men have very little need for small talk.

Tarun glanced at Dan and Sam, then started. 'Well, Adam, we are interested in getting an update about Tribe and get a sense of your perspective on the continued growth. The early discussions were very interesting to our team and we would like to get a sense of where the business is today as well as your current growth trajectory."

Adam smiled his executive smile, practiced many times in the mirror, and replied, "Gentlemen, it would be my pleasure."

Adam briefly recollected the last several months that led to the meeting today. Returning to the present, Adam started his review. "As you both know, spring boarding off our research, Tribe was very fortunate to develop the ENS, Experience Name Service early in the company's existence. This patented technology allows us to provide the primary mechanism to connect people in the experience world. The establishment of the ENS was rapidly followed by the development of the application and network infrastructure to support our concept of experience pods. We modeled the technology after the communication styles of whales, essentially allowing communication to a group of people who shared a common interest, desire, or question. We now call these groups LMIs for like-minded individuals."

"Our users create their experience worlds that are aligned around common interests. We have some really interesting experience pods that I can provide a tour of later if you are interested," Adam said with a chuckle.

"So with these two pieces of technology we essentially own the only way that people using the experience phones connect in large massive groups. Our revenue model is simple. We make money by the connection to the pods and usage of our technology. We pass all of our billing through the phone and network providers, therefore obviating any need for our own billing systems. The network usage also makes the phone and network providers some of our best marketers. Our usage drives their usage and so on." Adam paused and briefly glanced out the window to reset his thoughts.

Turning back to the Venture Capitalists, Adam shifted in his chair and began, "So that brings us to our financial performance. The last quarter yielded a 500% Quarter over Quarter growth. While we thought that was good, we actually now know that it was only the beginning. In the last two months, we have seen unparalleled growth. We have a rate of 100,000 new users per hour, with new pods being established at a rate of five thousand per hour. Our user revenue continues to grow and we have started to see initial usage in overseas markets."

He paused for effect, in a few moments he started again "at this rate we will have around one billion users by the end of this year, with approximately forty million experience pods. Our first full year revenue should be approximately 900 million dollars with a continuing annuity stream from the ENS usage, experience pod usage and pod maintenance. It goes without saying that the network effect of the experience pods drives the demand and rapid growth. Once a person enters the experience world they are hooked. I call it the MacArthur principle."

The bankers sat back in their chairs and silently considered the statistics. Dan was the first to speak. "Adam, I have to admit, that's unbelievable and unheard of for a year old company. If those projections hold, we are way ahead of our plans."

Sam continued, "With all due respect, I think these projections are powerful, and I want to discuss accelerating the discussions of taking the company public. Both Goldman and Credit Suisse are ready to go, and quite honestly, Adam, I can't really see a reason why I would disagree at this point. Tarun and Dan, we need to move quickly."

They both turned to Tarun. Tarun paused and then simply nodded validating Sam's recommendation.

Adam's stomach dropped. He knew exactly what this meant. They were moving forward with the equity event. His dreams of being one of the wealthiest young men in North America were almost complete. Although he could hardly contain himself he kept his smile perfect, not letting on any of his internal feelings show.

The bankers stood up and shook Adam and Rina's hand. They exchanged pleasantries and agreed to schedule a golf outing later in the week.

Tarun and Rina lagged behind, talking in quiet voices. Adam glanced backward observing the dynamic between the two and wondered what they were discussing. He was momentarily jealous and wondered if Tarun targeted Rina as his most recent conquest. He realized he needed to think through the implications of that happening later.

Dan and Sam reached the door first, Dan stopped abruptly, clearly remembering something they had to say. "Oh, sorry Adam, I almost forgot, someone named Emily from Tribe keeps calling my office wanting to get an introduction to you to discuss Tribe. She has something important to talk about and she said he has requested several meetings with you and asked me to forward her request since I sit on both boards. Do you know anything about this?"

Adam replied, "No, I haven't heard from her, although I am of course familiar with Banner. I will check with Tess and see if she called in. I will schedule something with her if she calls again." Adam escorted his guests to the elevator promising to see them soon.

He turned from the elevator and asked Rina to come back in for a discussion. Bowing slightly and motioning her to go first, he stared at her rear and wondered if his morning could get any better.

Experience Pod 213.78.781

Inspector Wu still couldn't get his mind around the idea
of a stakeout in the Experience world and he cursed
his chief as he connected yet once again. The Hong
Kong police department made it a key element of the
department strategy to be ahead of criminals through
the use of technology. The chief had discovered the
experience world and almost immediately had all of his
detectives begin to connect and pursue criminals and
conduct experience world stakeouts.

*Inspector Wu moved through the dark underbelly of the
Experience world. He found himself in his minds' eye walking
through something called an experience world marketplace, but
instead of brightly colored stalls with various products and wares,
it was dimly lit, still, and unnervingly silent.*

*In the stalls, various shadowed figures sat motionless waiting
for someone to approach at which point a negotiation would
occur and the transaction would occur. Inspector Wu shivered
considering what these experiences could yield. He felt mentally
compromised each time he pursued a suspect in the Experience
world. He pushed down these feelings and focused on the task at
hand.*

*They had been watching the woman for two weeks and
suspected she was conducting some form of human trafficking or
exploitation. Each day she would arrive at her small stall and
sit on the stool waiting for her first customers. She was unique
in the experience world as she always had a small baby with her.
This was unusual as normally only adult figures were found in*

the experience world. Wu suspected this had something to do with her criminal activity but had been thus far unable to specifically determine the connection. Inspector Wu wandered slowly down the row of stalls, pausing at random points, yet always keeping his minds' eye on the woman. Each day, almost on cue, a group of shadowed men would arrive outside of the stall and wait patiently. The woman would move slowly and deliberately and joined her thin yellow thought stream with each man, who after a short connection would disappear behind a curtain at the rear of the stall. Inspector Wu understood that none of this existed and the imagery of the curtain and the stall only represented a mental construct, yet he knew he had to get behind that curtain to understand what was happening.

Inspector Wu decided to move in, he moved quickly toward her and reached out to join her thought stream, almost instantly, he knew everything, he saw what she was doing in selling the connection to the young child. She also immediately understood she had been discovered and quickly physically disconnected from the Experience pod.

Inspector Wu planned for this and disconnected as well. Blinking his eyes several times to return his focus in the real world, he saw the woman running from the doorway where she had been sitting. She roughly pushed her way through the crowded Hong Kong streets, bumping against people and receiving stern shouts as she fought against the crowds. She continued to steal brief glances over her shoulder, looking for Wu while clutching her two year old daughter close to her chest.

A gap opened and she saw her chance for escape in a small alley lined with shopping stalls eerily similar to the Experience world. In the real world however, the people were thick on the small alley and she was sure she could lose her pursuers in the chaos. She paused before she entered the alley and looked behind her. She saw Wu closing the gap and saw the recognition on his face when he caught her eyes. Her fear energized her and she ran like she was struck by a bolt of lightning. She sprinted down the alley realizing she didn't have much time to escape. The alley was on a steep hill and she was running wildly at this point. Her legs were tired and she didn't see the old man step out from the fabric shop until she was on him. The woman tried to dodge the feeble old man, but instead managed to catch her leg on his hip. She went sprawling and her baby was thrown from her arms. As she fell, the woman watched in horror as her baby landed on the hard concrete bouncing slightly and then rolling forward. The wails pierced the street as people rushed to the women and infant's aid. She struggled to her feet ready to continue her escape when a pair of strong hands grabbed her arm and pulled her up. Wu looked into her eyes and held her tight.

"You will need to come with me" he said in Mandarin to the woman, as others arrived on the scene to retrieve the baby. Wu glanced around at the crowd realizing he needed to move away quickly to avoid a confrontation.

She spat at him and fought to remove his grip. She started gesticulating wildly and screaming, "Help me, help me, this man is trying to kidnap us. He is a slave trader and wants to take me away." She pleaded with the group around her "You all just saw him chasing me. He caused me to trip and fall and hurt my baby. Give me my baby back."

The crowd edged closer as they heard the pleas of the women. Several taller men began to angle towards Wu. He stopped and reached into his coat and pulled out a badge. "I am Inspector William Wu from the Hong Kong Police Department. I work in the Vice and Human Trafficking division and this woman is suspected of taking advantage of her child. I am taking her into the police station and I need to protect her baby. I kindly ask everyone to step back" he looked around at the crowd to determine if they understood.

Raising his voice, Inspector Wu continued to ensure that he was heard by the crowd heard, turned and addressed the woman directly "You are under arrest for violating Hong Kong Penal Code Article 146." As he finished, he noticed that his sunglasses reflected the woman's disheveled hair and dirty face. He was disgusted. The crowd had a look of complete disbelief and began to turn its anger toward the woman.

One of his partners came up and provided an update, "We apprehended one of her customers, and Sir, we have a problem. There is no way to determine what they actually were doing in the experience world" Inspector Wu stopped and looked at his partner.

"What do you mean? When I apprehended her in the experience world I connected to her thought stream and saw everything." Wu looked perplexed.

"Inspector, I'm sure that what you say is accurate, however we don't have any physical evidence. There is no way to track the thoughts in the experience world once they are gone. We can't go back and find a thought. Once a user disconnects they disappear."

Inspector Wu turned and looked down to the woman, switching back to Chinese, he asked "We both know what you were doing. I'm going to make you talk." he tensed his grip on her arm, and pulled her slightly higher, his frustration starting to build.

The woman smiled a knowing smile, her rotting teeth showing and replied "I was doing nothing. You are harassing me. Let me go"

The Inspector knew this woman was taking advantage of her daughter, but felt that unfamiliar feeling when a case begins to slip away. "You are coming to the police station and we are going to talk about this until you remember something." The Inspector pulled the woman and led her into a waiting police car clearly dreading the Chief's rage when he found out the evidence was limited. The woman looked longingly back over her shoulder at the baby. She began to cry. Inspector Wu wasn't sure if she was crying because she was losing her baby or because she had been caught and lost her source of income.

The baby continued to cry, as the paramedics tended to her injuries. The baby looked around for its mother unaware of the terrible mistreatment endured at her mother's hand.

CHAPTER
14

After his experience world scare, Connor focused his time on researching and learning everything he could about the experience world. He reached out to an old friend at the NSA and requested any information they had assembled on the experience world. Connor now sat staring at the NSA report he had just read for the third time, the report confirmed that the thought sharing and machine controlling capability was present and available now to the general public. It wasn't clear on when the technology was introduced but it reported that there were now several manufacturers who were shipping the new phones and that business had rapidly developed around the capability. He closed the report and decided he would visit his source, Hamlin.

Hamlin and Connor were unlikely friends and confidants. Hamlin was Alexis' uncle. She had heard that Connor was heading to the same symposium and suggested that the two do a meet and greet. Neither had any interest in meeting the other, but because they were both presenting they struck up a conversation while waiting and immediately hit it off. They were unlikely friends as they were as opposite as two people could ever be. Connor the science celebrity and seasoned Hamlin the government researcher, both living in two different worlds, but still connected and close. Their friendship had grown from mutual admiration as well as Connor's need for someone to validate his show and some of his thinking. He hated to think that Hamlin filled in some paternal need, but if he were honest, it would probably be the correct conclusion.

Connor wasn't fond of visiting Hamlin's lab deep in the bowels of the Federal Building in LA. Besides the seemingly never-ending walk, in which he passed numerous anonymous offices and labs, he always became slightly claustrophobic as he thought of the millions of tons of concrete and steel that sat above his head just waiting for a massive earthquake. The pressure exerted on these walls had to be enormous.

Finally arriving at the non-descript lab, he pushed through the heavy steel door into a large open laboratory. Connor saw Hamlin almost immediately. He wasn't hard to miss. Hamlin's tall thin frame stood at least a foot above everything else in the room and his head was bent slightly as he was talking with someone much shorter. Hamlin's back was to the door as he engaged in an animated conversation with a young attractive research scientist.

The young research scientist, noticing Connor entering the lab, motioned to the door, to indicate that Hamlin's guest had arrived. Hamlin turned and nodded to Connor. He briefly turned back to the research scientist said a few final words and then turned quickly to intercept Connor at the door.

"Connor" Hamlin extended his hand visibly happy to see his friend.

Hamlin's slim, long fingers wrapped themselves around his friend's proffered hand "Ham, we need to talk." Connor replied simply.

"Right this way." Hamlin led Connor toward the rear of the lab toward a large glass walled conference room. The conference room looked different then the outside lab and was diffused with dim lighting. The walls were paneled with a dark blue sound suppressing material and the carpet was a charcoal gray. Connor sat down in one of the large black leather chairs that were perfectly spaced around a large square black wood table.

Hamlin took a chair opposite Connor and a large folder on the table seemed to materialize.

"Ham, according to the NSA report you sent me, it is all confirmed, the thought sharing capability is available to the general public, yet no one talks about when it was launched." Connor said while pulling himself closer to the table.

"Connor, I know. We have been seeing the same disconnects, but what I really wanted to share with you are the results of our hardware and device testing. I think you will agree there is more to this than we originally expected. I have asked Julie Vo, one of my lead researchers to brief you on the results." Hamlin motioned to a woman waiting just outside the glass door.

An attractive Indian woman in a white lab coat entered the room. Julie walked to the front of the conference room, picked up a small remote control sitting on the table and punched a quick series of commands on the touch screen and the glass walls darkened, the lights dimmed, and the front wall of the conference room morphed into a large presentation screen.

Hamlin nodded to her, indicating she can begin her presentation.

She softly cleared her throat and then began "The experience phones are extremely advanced tech, almost to the point of something we have never seen before. Their design and manufacturing output are unparalleled. Our testing has focused primarily on the operation of the experience phones and their interaction and utilization by the end user. At its most basic operating level, the phones are advanced quantum interface devices that have the ability to recognize and translate the most minute electric impulses in the brain into parsed data streams that can be shared. Each of these data streams in essence is a thought. The phones use standard mobile and wireless platforms and networks to transmit these data streams to other users with the experience phones which translate these data streams back into electrical impulses thus creating a bilateral interface with the recipient's brain."

Julie paused and waited for any comments. Connor hesitated and then responded "Julie, this is consistent with the development and testing that was done at the Banner lab. It has become relatively easy to replicate and create these bilateral interfaces that translate both the thoughts to data streams and to create a machine code to control external equipment. My primary concern is about how rapidly the tech has promulgated and their usage patterns. I am, quite honestly, unsure of the accurate timeline of how this has developed and gotten into the general public so quickly."

Julie nodded and continued with her original line of discussion "This was actually one of our primary questions as we went through our testing. We observed and verified that there is a specific chemical reaction in the brain for people using the experience world. The usage stimulates the frontal cortex and resembles the brain activity of an addict. Specifically, the continued and prolonged usage of the experience world, can modify memories and recollection. Interestingly one of the primary responses is to reset the mind for people in the present and forget the past. It goes further than simply blocking those memories, for some reason, it actually overwrites this area of the brain memories and creates new happy memories. So, at its most basic level, the combination of a chemical dependency that allows people to forget their past and always feel happy creates one incredibly addictive situation.

Hamlin shook his head. "Connor. Unfortunately, it goes further, the experience phone user can lose their temporal reference, and these experience phones can rewrite the brains timelines on memories and learning. So, to answer your first question, we are not sure how long this has been in place, this temporal effect may actually have impacted the ability to know the actual start of the experience world. Incredibly frightening, if you really begin to consider the ramifications. We will continue to work on it, but I'm not really sure how far this goes and how dangerous this could become."

Connor sat still, letting the enormity of the situation settle in. He was confirming his conclusion that the experience world was larger and more dangerous than anyone could imagine. The ability to rewrite people's memories and change what an entire population was thinking was incomprehensible.

Connor left a short time later. Julie and Hamlin were now alone in the conference room. "Jim, did we go too far with Connor?" Julie asked. Hamlin shook his head slowly. "Not sure we could have done anything differently. We are in uncharted territory here and he needed to know everything we know. He's one of my closest friends and will help us figure this out."

"I know it is just so difficult to understand and process." Julie replied looking down at the table.

"Keep working on it. We will figure it out eventually. To be honest, I am so glad you are here. I know it has only been a few short months, but your work has been invaluable. I am so pleased and happy you are on the team." Hamlin took Julie's hand while he spoke.

Julie didn't hesitate "Maybe we both need to blow off some steam. How about you meet me in the empty office in 15?" Hamlin's face was transformed into a knowing smirk. Julie continued to hold his hand and stroke his fingers, like a tiger toying with her prey.

CHAPTER
15

The second assassin stood above the three men who knelt on the cold muddy ground, gagged, their hands bound, and burlap bags covering their faces. Each sobbed or groaned softly, knowing this cold, wet field was where their individual life journey ends. They had been without food and water for eighteen hours and their diminished strength added to their despair and recognition that there would be no salvation. Each man had a throbbing headache and their legs and arms were stiff and numb.

The assassin visually checked her gun, silently, and waited for the first man to react. She stood perfectly still and calmed her breathing waiting for the inevitable. She relished this part of an execution, the moment at which each man realizes that their only option is to run and for the briefest moments hope to escape. Her heartbeat rose slightly in anticipation, she knew one of these men would move soon, it always began and ended the same way.

It was two hours ago when each of the three men awoke, gagged and bound on the cold floor of a cargo van, their last memories had been getting into their cars to head to their analyst jobs at the Pentagon.

The assassin coated their door handles with a petroleum based neurotoxin that quickly absorbed into the skin, causing immediate unconsciousness. The assassin watched each man from afar, and when they touched the door handles, they slumped to the ground. She simply drove over and picked up the bodies, throwing them roughly into the back of the van. The targets didn't know why they were kneeling in the cold mud, but each had surmised it was related to their role in the NSA.

Each man worked in a specialized research group that was investigating the connections and similarities between global technology products and companies. They had recently finished their report and were preparing it for release. The three who were scheduled to be executed focused on the new experience phone hardware and network.

The younger Korean man on the left had confessed to the assassin one night at a popular Georgetown bar, after one too many beers and her low cut blouse, that they were close to connecting the dots on the complex web of interrelationships, and expected that bringing their individual research together would yield a roadmap for the person or persons behind some of the most advanced technological advancements over the last decade. In his words, the research pointed to one entity that was pulling the strings and that potentially all of the technology was leading to some inevitable and planned result.

The assassin had laughed off the conjecture of the analyst and moved onto other topics. When she returned to his apartment later in the evening and after the analyst passed out, she quickly hacked his computer and identified each of the other team members of the research team. Due to the compartmentalized secrecy of the research, she was able to confirm that only the three kneeling before her today were aware of the full extent of their work. The assassin was immediately instructed to eliminate the threats within two days.

The assassin returned from her thoughts as the man furthest to the right of the three began to turn his head and attempt to listen if anyone was still standing behind him. She hadn't guessed he was going to be the sprinter. This could become fun. What if all three decided to run at once? She felt an electric thrill that this may turn out to be more of a game than she originally anticipated.

After a few moments, the man on the right struggled to stand and began stumbling away from the others. The assassin allowed him to take ten steps, then aimed and fired three shots in quick succession, hitting him in the back and head. The shots were perfect and the man's face was blown outward as he fell forward in the mud with a dull thump.

The other two sat motionless, unsure of what had just happened. They moved their heads from side to side to locate where the shots had come from and she could see them mentally figuring out their odds and next move. The assassin patiently waited to see how long it took for the next man to move. In her experience, both men would go simultaneously and head in opposite directions. She was counting on this and let her breathing slow and waited, the exhilaration building.

Two minutes later, both men, passing some subconscious cue between them, stood and began to run away from each other. She waited for five paces and then she started walking toward the man heading to the left. She paced him for twenty yards, keeping her peripheral vision on the other target. She holstered her gun and pulled out a long serrated hunting knife. Coming up from behind, she made a deep long cut along the back of his knee, severing the tendons. The man fell forward into and writhed in pain. She looked over her shoulder and saw the other man increasing his speed. Moving with a practiced and experienced hand, she kicked the man on the ground to his stomach, kneeled down on his shoulders, and pulling the burlap bag, raised his head and slashed his throat deep enough that she felt the bone. The blood covered her hands and arms. She stood up and stuck the knife in his back and began running for the other captive.

The man heading in the opposite direction began to sprint, sensing the opportunity to escape. He was working his hands behind him in an effort to free his wrists. The assassin was momentarily surprised by how quickly the man was moving and she immediately took an intercept path to cut him off. She maneuvered to stand directly in his path and raised her gun. As the man was within two paces, she said, "Boo"

The man froze in his tracks, trying to find the source. She walked forward and placed the muzzle of her gun against the burlap bag and his temple. "I win" she said and pulled the trigger.

The assassin dragged the bodies back to the natural stone crevasse near where each man was originally kneeling. She rolled the bodies into the gap and watched as each tumbled down into the darkness below. She knew that animals and decomposition would get to each of the bodies long before they were ever found.

Smiling and content, Julie stripped off her bloody clothes and put them into the small fire she had started. Standing completely naked in front of it, she reached to the sky and throwing her head back laughed a deep throaty primal laugh. She was completely energized, there was nothing like taking a life. The finality, the closure, the power was completely intoxicating. She jumped up and down as the adrenaline slowly wore off and she was coming down from the high. It started to drizzle as she cleaned up and got back into the white cargo van to change and head back to DC. Mission accomplished.

CHAPTER
16

Lucas, Connor, and Alexis sat on their balcony looking out at the Pacific as the evening sun was setting over the ocean. They faced the water staring at the wide blue ocean below.

Connor was the first to talk. "Hamlin determined that there is an actual physical response from the use of the experience phones. The experience world stimulates the user's brain and creates a chemical reaction similar to that of a drug addict. In addition, the chemical reaction can overwrite a person's memories and leave only happy feelings in their wake. It's a recipe for disaster. Think about it, we have a generally available technology that anyone can buy that has the potential to create an entire population of addicts. Literally and figuratively we are now addicted to information and the experience world."

Alexis shuddered at the thought "It is really unbelievable. A technology that can create an addiction is what we are talking about. There's been research over the last several years where we've seen early signs of this in video games and young children, but nothing as pronounced. Is it just me or does this all seem too convenient? Almost like this was engineered or designed to have this effect?"

Lucas smiled and chuckled before speaking "Funny you should bring up the concept of a conspiracy theory. Over the last several days, I chased down the various connection points emanating from Li, the mysterious co-worker of Connor. All of these connections lead back to the Indian company Dakarta, based in Delhi. Dakarta is a virtual rock-star group of scientists that have been involved in some of the most lucrative and successful military technology and consumer inventions in the last decade. Like most great companies there is one man who has put his stamp and personality on the company. Unfortunately, for us, the personality isn't one that works well with outsiders. Dakarta is owned and controlled by a mysterious man named Ravi."

"Just Ravi, no last name? Never heard of him." asked Connor.

"Yes, no last name. Actually I haven't been able to find out much about him. Apparently he is scientifically brilliant, has a shrewd sense of business, and is able to fund an international network of corporate espionage with no morals or ethics." Lucas replied.

"He sounds like a great role model," Connor quipped intrigued by this development.

"Actually, he is revered in India and has become somewhat of a national treasure, like an actual and metaphorical darker version of Bill Gates" Lucas continued "As you know, the Indian government is infamous for looking the other way when they are dealing with successful Indian entrepreneurs. Big money runs the county. Ravi is similar to other business leaders who brought considerable wealth and jobs. The wealth has given him considerable access and privilege, and he is not a person to be challenged."

"Thanks for the background, but I'm struggling to make the connection." asked Connor.

"Interestingly, it appears that Li has been communicating with Dakarta for some time. Not only recently since she has been in your shop, but even before when she was in China. She really gets around, by the way, she was in at least ten countries in the last eight months based on my trace on her ip addresses.

Anyway, Ravi and Dakarta were instrumental in the design and manufacture of the next generation wireless chip used in the new TG phones and earpieces. Apparently he controlled every aspect of the manufacture, which is somewhat unusual for a high volume chip that would be used in a mobile phone. Each chip has a manufacturing cost of several hundred dollars. Apparently, Dakarta is providing these chips at a loss to TG."

"Which means?" Connor replied urging his brother on.

Lucas continued to roll. "Dakarta, Ravi's company, manufactures the chipsets for the TG phones. The TG phones are the only phones that create this un-intended consequence. The TG phones are capable of allowing people to control electronic equipment and communicate with their thoughts. The TG phones create a user addict that rewrites memories. To Alexis' question, there is one person behind all of this - Ravi. So my inclination is that he knows why and how the experience phones do what they do."

Connor slumped into his chair and stared out at the ocean for several minutes as he absorbed the final pieces of the puzzle from Lucas. Looking back up, Connor asked "So, to net this out, there is someone working on my Banner team that has a mysterious background and is connected to the Indian company which makes this new technology, which by the way was supposedly only discovered several weeks ago and is now out in the general public and allows for addictive mind control?

"Yep, pretty much sums it up." replied Lucas

Alexis interrupted "Unfortunately, the real question is what do we do now?"

Connor and Lucas looked out at the sunset and considered the alternatives.

CHAPTER
17

A light scratching was the only sound in the dark cool room. A thin honey colored naked man was seated at a desk with his elbows and forearms resting on the edge while his neck was bent to put his face very near the surface. He wrote with small precise movements, his pencil flying over the paper. His arm and shoulder muscles were rippled and strained. He couldn't write fast enough to get the words out. A line of perspiration rested on his forehead and across his back. His focus was unwavering.

As strange as the desk scene appeared, the room itself was even more of an unusual sight. It was a perfect stainless steel cube. No visible seams were present. The only opening was a door that sat directly behind the man. The coolness and symmetry of the room cast a stillness that was unique. The room was completely sound and surveillance proof. A perfect cube; any dimensional variance was measured in single digit millimeters.

The scratching from the desk continued, the man writing constantly. His thoughts spilling out onto the pages that now began to cover his desk.

The sole occupant was also the sole designer of the room. He was involved in every aspect of the room's construction. He drove the design, developed a new stainless steel forging method, and supervised the installation of the room. The construction crew that completed the installation met a peculiar end; each of the men and their families died tragically shortly after its completion. The authorities never knew of the room, and no one ever made a connection between the untimely deaths and the room's construction. No records existed.

The only person alive in the world who knew about the room sat naked writing on a stainless steel desk.

His focus entirely on his work in front of him. The only connection to the outside world sat in the upper corner of the desk, where sits a small earpiece.

The man wrote in excruciating detail. Five sharpened pencils lay at the top of the desk in a perfect row. The man leaned close to his paper and continued to write.

Today the newspapers discussed the death of the young Indian athlete from Delhi unable to find medical help after a tragic accident in her sport she sought help from the government family friends no one was able to assist would I have assisted if asked should I have been asked why did she decide to end her life she was a national champion for India brought them medals and honor they heralded her to the world they used her image people looked up to her she was a national hero the government liar said he hadn't heard anything when asked about her death he acted as if someone had missed a bus on a weekend if we could only know what he really knew if the aggrieved family only knew what he really knew the government is forever locked in an endless loop of bureaucracy and sustaining the status quo our opportunity lies in connection in togetherness in harvesting the true natural wealth of our human resources...

This went on continuously, the man observing daily events, discussing India, referring to others, writing constantly. Inside the room, the man was nothing. He had no identity. He was a man possessed by daily events, consumed by the pressures of the world, an antenna, something that observed the conflicts built upon lies and deceptions. He was an observer, a participant in the world's chaos—he studied it, worshiped it, despised it. Inside the room, the man knew only what his mind created.

Outside the room, the man was one of the most successful and well-known people in India. His face and name were known throughout the world. Media appeared about him on a daily basis, schoolchildren studied his biography. He was known as Ravi.

Ravi was a study in contrasts, a brilliant scientist, a ruthless businessman and a zealous believer in peace among all nations. His meteoric rise to the top of the microchip industry was the stuff of legends. A true rags-to-riches story. Ravi began his life like many other Indians, poor and uneducated in a farming community. The youngest of the family, he showed exceptional intellectual abilities at a young age. He was able to talk with a fourth-grade vocabulary at age 2. He excelled in music of all types and was able to do complex algebra by his 5th birthday.

A now famous anecdote that is taught to young Indian schoolchildren tells how Ravi's father took his young son to the headmaster of a respected school 15 kilometers from their home. Upon arriving he requested a meeting with the headmaster to present Ravi's qualifications and beg for a position for him in the upcoming class. They waited patiently for several hours for the headmaster to return for their impromptu meeting. As the hours dragged on, Ravi, being a young and precocious boy, became restless and began combing through the headmaster's impressive book collection that ringed the office waiting area.

Noticing many texts on mathematics and computer science, the young Ravi sat down among the books and began to read. He read like a much older child, his face near the page, his concentration complete.

The Headmaster returned. He wore the high collared jacket preferred by many college professors, and carried himself with an air of practiced superiority. The legend continues that this educated man begrudgingly listened for a short time to Ravi's father to describe his son's unique talents. The headmaster, visibly sighing, heard a similar story hundreds of times before from other parents convinced their progeny was destined for higher education.

The headmaster glanced disapprovingly over to the young boy whose face was buried in one of his books. "Why don't you bring your son back in a couple of years when he would be more capable of understanding the beginning classes fitting his age such as coloring, counting, and nap time."

Ravi's father, a proud and calm man, realized that he wasn't getting anywhere and was prepared to leave when a small voice interrupted his departure.

"Sir" said Ravi, addressing the Headmaster, "do you not believe I can do the things my father said I could do?"

The headmaster looked down at the small boy addressing him from the bookcase, amazed by the audacity of this country simpleton. "No, son, I don't think you are material for my school."

"I see," said the young boy, moving toward the headmaster, his arms behind his back. "If I were able to do something to show you what I know, would that change your mind?"

"My boy, I don't think you can convince me." The headmaster made a dismissive gesture and began to head into his office.

"Well, how about we both do a problem from this book?" Ravi produced a book from behind his back. He held up Hollinger's treatise on geometrical challenges "and see who gets it right."

"My boy, don't waste my time. I believe it's time for you to be on your way." The headmaster continued his progress back to his office.

Ravi looked to his father and said "I'm sorry Father. I guess the headmaster isn't as accomplished and learned as you thought?"

The headmaster turned quickly at this comment and glared at Ravi. "What did you say, you insolent child?"

"I am sorry you weren't treating us in a fair manner. I thought you would be at least willing to see if I can do a math problem." Replied Ravi.

The headmaster was startled by the boldness and nerve of the young child, the impetuousness of the tone, and the challenge masked under the surface. He decided he would teach this backward farmer and his coddled son a lesson they soon wouldn't forget.

"If you insist, boy, I will indulge you in a little mathematics lesson," continued the headmaster. "You can show me your math skills. Let us simply lay the book down and open it at random. We will then complete the first full problem on the page. Do you understand?"

"Yes," Ravi answered simply.

The headmaster purposely lifted enough pages to take him to the end of the text for the more difficult questions.

He opened the book and found a problem that caused him to smile inwardly, thinking that this young barefoot farmer would be scratching his head for years to figure this out. He turned the book around, allowing the boy to look at it. The boy read the problem for a short time and then walked back to the bookshelf, where he started to write on a piece of loose paper. The headmaster smiled to himself and looked down at the book to begin thinking through the question.

He was just finishing reading the problem when he heard the young boy say, "Sir." The headmaster looked up from the book and expected the young boy to begin crying or asking for help or any number of surrenders.

"Yes, can I help you?" the headmaster replied condescendingly.

"I am finished. Here is my answer," stated Ravi handing the paper over.

The headmaster smiled and reviewed the young boy's work, again expecting some colorful drawing or blocky writing. Instead he found very precise writing much clearer than would be expected of a boy his age. The proof was written on multiple lines. The headmaster frowned, realizing he needed to review the answer in the back of the book.

There was complete silence in the room as the headmaster leaned close to the book and continued to look between the paper and the book. After several minutes, the headmaster looked up with all color drained from his face.

"How did you do this? You just solved this problem faster than anyone I have ever known." The headmaster looked back and forth between the father and son, his tone accusatory.

Ravi just smiled at the man, clearly pleased with himself. The headmaster was amazed by the child, clearly thinking he found a child prodigy. Apparently this boy had been studying geometry for some time.

He sat bewildered. "When did you learn how to do this geometry?"

"Oh, that," said Ravi. "I learned while I was sitting listening to you and Papa talk about your school."

Ravi excelled in his studies and attended university at the age of thirteen. During his second year of university, he was introduced to the Kashmir conflict by Professor Govil, an outspoken radical, who believed that the Kashmir situation was an insult to all Indians. Ravi, brilliant, but at an impressionable age, became Professor Govil's most avid pupil. He devoured books on Kashmir, reading the biographies of the Indian leaders and convincing his parents to take him traveling to the region.

During one trip Ravi was taken by a young girl who was in the Village of Jhabla. During their discussions, Ravi committed that he would make it his life's work to remove the stain of Kashmir from the Indian nation and reunite the country.

It was only until recently that the final piece of his plan came into place. His board of directors, his company leaders, his relatives. No one knew what he was thinking. He paused from his writing and looked up. Very soon, very soon, he thought.

He returned to his writing. He began to rewrite his plan, a plan he had devised years ago, now finally close to being achieved.

CHAPTER
18

Connor smoothed his hair for the fourth time as he sat facing the legendary television host, Harry Moran, waiting for the interview to start. The studio lights were harsh and he felt like he was squinting across the desk. Connor was an expert at facing the camera, but today he found himself out of sorts and more nervous than he could ever remember.

Harry arrived moments ago and engaged in some lighthearted banter about California politics and college sports and now sat engrossed in reviewing the interview notes and preparing for his questions.

The producer gave the all clear sign and the studio lights were dropped and all talking and noise was hushed. The producer began the countdown "in five, four, three, two, and " then, in a rather exaggerated fashion, pointed at Harry.

"Good evening ladies and gentlemen, I am your host, Harry Moran. Welcome to my corner of the world. Tonight I am pleased to bring you one of our frequent guests and one of the new luminaries in the scientific world. I am joined by Connor Shaw, a noted scientist and television show host, who has challenged our conventional thinking, and in the words of many "has made science cool again." Not since the space program in the 1960s have we seen such interest and focus on scientific achievement. The public's appetite for knowledge is unquenchable. Connor and several fellow scientists have become iconic personalities and they have achieved a celebrity status."

Harry and the camera turned to Connor. "Connor, nice to see you again."

Connor flashed a winning smile, easily settling into this element, his nervousness gone. "Always nice to be seen, Harry"

Harry leaned forward on his elbows that were now sitting on the table. "So, Connor, it seems like whenever you are on the show you talk about some new form of technology that promises to change our world. I have to admit that most times your predictions have been accurate and the topics we discussed have gone on to become household standards. So, what's new in technology and what should our viewers take notice of?"

Connor leaned his elbows on the table, matching the host's posture. "Well, to start, we are all in a time of massive change within the areas of theoretical physics. The findings by several top labs about the existence of particles that travel faster than the speed of light has thrown the foundation of theoretical physics into a tailspin. Fifty years of theories changed in literally an instant, and we are seeing several leading physicists establishing new groundbreaking ways to look at our world at its most basic and elemental levels."

Harry interjected, "Connor, I, like many of our viewers, am fascinated by this news, but what does it really fundamentally change for the average person?"

Connor smiled a knowing smile. "Absolutely, positively, nothing. It makes no difference today to the average person. But what if this new line of thinking allows us to better understand the space/time continuum, and in several hundred years changes the way that we manipulate particles and energy across time and space? Now, that could be mind-blowing."

"Yes, it could" Harry said, "Connor, let's move into something more pragmatic, if you will, something that there has been considerable chatter about namely the experience phones and this newly developing experience world. What do you think of all of this?"

Connor was prepared for this question and chose his words carefully. It was imperative that he build a logical and reasoned argument. "Harry, the experience world is like nothing we have ever seen before. It is a monumental leap forward in our ability to communicate, and I would argue changes the mores and human social condition virtually overnight. Think about it, a few months ago, the concept of a place where people could share their innermost feelings, experiences, and actually sense what the other person is thinking would be considered pure science fiction. Today, there are tens of millions who are connected to the experience world and who are actively engaged in doing just what I described. To put this in perspective, we have seen an entirely new way that humans experience the world and each other. Nothing ever existed like this in the past."

Harry responded, "As always, a perfect summary. I am one of those folks that has had a chance to connect to the experience world and it is absolutely amazing. However, there are rumors and reports of issues and concerns with the experience world. Can you comment?"

Connor was ready for this volley. "Sure, I heard from many fellow scientists that they are uncomfortable with how quickly this technology has made it to market and how prolific it has become in such a short time. As a scientist, our experience is that advancements come very slowly and incrementally. Very rarely do you see a massive leap forward without others knowing about it or at least discussing it. The fact that this came from literally nowhere makes scientists uncomfortable."

"What specifically are they concerned about?" asked Harry in his trademark way.

Connor didn't miss a beat. "Advancements that come rapidly without the benefit of testing and review make scientists nervous because we really don't understand how or what has driven the innovation. Think about it like this. We are operating a world where we understand the rules, and these rules have been developed and refined over a very long time. At times these rules haven't been easy to develop, but everything operates according to those rules. One morning we all wake up and the rules have changed. No one is really sure why the rules have changed, they just did. We now need to learn how to operate under those new rules, and we don't understand the consequences if a rule is broken or what the change really means. For instance, let's assume that one day we all wake up and we can fly. Everything else remains the same, but now we can fly. Think about what that would mean and how, as a society, we would need to rework our rules and laws."

Harry was driving to a point. "That's an interesting analogy and I understand your point. One of the other interesting byproducts of the experience world is how many people explain that they are now connected to each other in a way that they never experienced. Can you comment?"

Connor responded, his pace quickening "Actually, I think it's a very interesting element of the experience world. I would argue that we have the capability to create a truly global, greater consciousness that many religions have been pursuing for thousands of years. When we are all operating in the experience world, we are literally all connected. We are a part of one massive level of consciousness. We have broken down the final barrier in human relationships by not connecting one to one, but many too many. Its potential is mind blowing."

Moran pushed further "What can a greater consciousness yield?"

Connor replied realizing where he was going with the line of questioning. "That's the big question, Harry. Does the ability for us to have a connected greater consciousness allow us to work better? Will we be able to truly understand the motivation of our enemies and friends in a way that will create a more peaceful world? Or on the other hand, if you really knew what the other person was thinking, would it become a darker, more dangerous world? I'm not sure I can answer any of these questions, as only time will tell. But the one thing I can say, unequivocally, is that we are now closer than we have ever been before. The question is, how will we deal with this intimacy?"

Moran nodded knowingly and paused with a moment of silence.

Connor called an audible, and before he even knew what he was doing, he continued talking. With emotion fueling his words about being beat to the discovery he felt like lashing out. "There is one other item that I feel compelled to mention. I believe there is considerable risk with the experience world. As I mentioned earlier, inexplicably this discovery came out of nowhere into the general public. My lab team was working on this area for many years and did considerable testing around the operation and usage of this type of technology. One observed result is the ability for the experience phones to create a chemical dependency in the brain of the user and potentially reorder our thoughts and memories. Now, I recognize that his sounds preposterous, but we all know that the human mind works in mysterious ways. We need to be very careful as we are in uncharted territory here and I'm not sure any of us know what will happen as this continues to expand and create the network effect."

Moran recognized that Connor had just gone off the prepared outline and was making a claim that could have massive repercussions. He immediately saw the opportunity to drive ratings and interest, so he pushed forward with a typical probing question, already knowing the answer. "So, Connor, are you actually saying that there is a risk of harm to people by using the experience world?"

Connor replied, going all in with his comments. "Yes, I have personally witnessed that when a network is established using the technology and protocols of the experience world, there is a risk to all of the connected users. The use of the experience world could create an addictive dependence with potentially harmful physical or mental consequences."

Moran stoked the fires "I must say you are quite emphatic about the risk. Why haven't we heard about this from anyone else. Wouldn't this be an observed result as this technology was developed? Shouldn't our government have some knowledge or feedback about these potential issues?" Moran pushed sensing an interesting angle for a story.

Connor quickly saw Moran was simply stirring the pot and looking for him to double down on his statement. "Harry, that is an excellent question. I have no idea why you haven't heard about this potential risk from any other sources. All I can say is that hopefully people will consider that nothing is without risks.

And that they are informed consumers who protect themselves from this potential set of risks. Connor wanted to leave it hanging, and his media training kicked in, always turn the question back on itself when you are in an interview. "Maybe the best question is "Why haven't we heard about this from anyone else?"

"A very, very good question," replied Moran turning to the camera "Connor Shaw, thank you for your time today. As always enlightening and entertaining and leaving us with some big questions. We are going to take a short break and we will be right back with Senator Arnold Schwarzenegger."

The studio lights dimmed and the show cut to commercial. Harry leaned back in his chair and looked at Connor. "Nice job today. You are really a natural although you surprised me at the end. What was driving that the sky is falling revelation?"

"To be honest, not really sure. Maybe it's a feeling of responsibility or duty to let people know about the risks." replied Connor while wondering to himself why he actually made the statements and starting to regret not being more discrete.

Moran laughed, a deep hearty gut laugh before responding. "Connor, the day when you are thinking about your fellow man is the day I leave the business. Face it, for people in our business, the world revolves around us and when someone takes away the spotlight it's not fun. First rule is don't lie to yourself. See you around." Moran left the stage and headed out of the lighted area.

Connor looked around. The production crew was gone and he was suddenly alone on the stage staring at his reflection in the darkened monitor as he reflected on Harry's comments and wondering if he was right.

CHAPTER
19

The four figures stood again in the nondescript white room at their required check-in. The shadow man stood in the middle of the three operatives and began to control their thought streams and pull everyone together.

Report.

We have eliminated the analyst threat at the NSA. Their bodies will not be found for years if at all. The toxin has degraded and each simply appears like they have disappeared. We continue to control the primary scientific channels. Risk is mitigated.

Connor Shaw and Banner may require a change in strategy. Not able to fully predict his next move and reaction to the research. His recent television interview was working exactly to plan when he went off the deep end on the risk to the users of the experience world. Our monitoring shows the experience world risk was quickly becoming a common thought across the experience world. In response, we have refocused the thoughts on the Greater Consciousness concept on a broad scale to fight the negative thoughts. Early signals show this is eliminating the experience world risk thoughts and is becoming one of the primary thought schemas across all of the experience world. Connor Shaw is acting uncharacteristically non-ego driven and his psychological profile did not predict his reaction would become selfless. We will have another approach and report back on next steps.

He is a risk. We will need to move quickly if he is not cooperating and supporting our model. What about our other puppets?

Adam is controlled. His greed makes control simple.

The Scientist is working to plan.

The Indian may be moving away and down his own path. We need to monitor and respond if required.

Nothing to worry I have built a failsafe into the application infrastructure.

Finally, Connor's twin brother Lucas is getting deeper in the experience world. We have a challenge in determining if it is Connor or Lucas at times since they are identical twins and their thought signatures are almost identical.

We are fine. No worries. Keep up the activity. <Feelings of content, superiority, success swarm about the room>

Now my friends, I have done a little experiment this week that will demonstrate the full power of the experience world. I have made it my mission to change the opinion of the holocaust and the Nazis. I have been selectively planting ideas across all areas of the experience world about the little known societal benefits that Nazi science has provided. These are wholly inaccurate and untrue, but I have planted the thoughts that modern medicine would not have its current advances in organ replacement and stem cell research if not for the valiant efforts of several Nazi scientists during the war. Since I planted those thoughts there has been a groundswell of positive news and conversations about the Nazis. Just think about it — if I can convince the world that the Holocaust didn't occur and the Nazis are misunderstood, what can stop me? <Swelling feeling of pride and self-confidence, feelings of power and dominance, images of Smiling Nazi in SS gear, patting the head of a little Jewish boy, laughter> Continue your check-ins.

Experience Pod 333.16.917

Grace Baptist Church sat comfortably off Michigan Avenue, her white clapboard exterior sparkling luminously in the early morning sun, her windows shining clean and spotless, her cross rising to the sky like a gold beacon calling the faithful. She was a regal centenarian, resembling an old-timer reclining in a rocking chair and watching the world go by.

She had witnessed 80 years of the cyclical decline and rise of the city that surrounded her white picketed fence yard. Today she was one of the country's oldest black churches and one of Chicago's most recognized and influential institutions. Over the last 75 years through her large green doors walked Kings and Queens, Presidents, Senators, and Mayors, all hoping to share the aisles of the old wooden church and experience her magic and pay homage to permanence and the power of her faithful.

The Grace, as she was called throughout the city, became a powerful and influential voice in the Chicago area. She was one of the original and founding churches of the National Baptist Convention, today the largest religious organization among the African-American community with over thirty thousand churches and six million members. Her progeny were many and accomplished. Political careers were made and lost within the Grace. She had raised a long line of reverends that went out to the world to spread the faith and belief that they had gained in her halls.

Today, like every other Sunday for the last 80 years, the congregation was a sea of colors and moved in a rhythmic motion. The music carried the prayers of the faithful and contrite. Participating in the Sunday mass sat the four charter members of the hired help ladies group. They sat comfortably just off the aisle in the second row, adding their colors to one of many threads in the colorful Sunday quilt.

LaShaunte, the largest of the four, was resplendent in a bright purple two piece outfit and a bright purple hat. Her bulk sat sandwiched between Carol and Halle, who framed her purple statement with their own statements in baby blue and light yellow. Next to Halle, sandwiched between the end of the pew and her light yellow flower, sat Mia. She wore a dark blue suit and conservative blouse. Her appearance, more like that of an accountant leaving the office after a hard day, contrasted with the vibrant colors of the other three.

As the women sat on the old wooden pew, they swayed together to the music, moving with the flow of the room.

The gospel music at the Grace had seen the best. Tommy Dorsey and Sallie Martin were early Sunday service participants. Willie Mae Ford Smith was a regular who worked on many of her earliest recordings. Today, the thirty person choir, their green robes accented with yellow, sang "'Til the Storm passes by" in perfect harmony. Reverend Desmond Goff sat off to the right of the choir, his smile evident from the rear of the church. He was a tall and powerful built man, attractive to both men and women, and cultivated the power to influence others like a constant gardener. He sat on the edge of his chair and was turned towards the choir, a sea of green and yellow, and moved as if he was barely able to contain himself in his chair. He was singing as loudly as the choir, matching the vocal talents and the movements of the group. He looked like a spring ready to release, ready to shoot from his chair and let the energy of the movement carry him away to the heavens.

The choir built to a crescendo sending almost visible energy into the air and everyone in the congregation felt a chill run through them. The music ebbed and flowed with its own heartbeat. The choir sang as one voice, exulted to the heavens, its power growing as the song neared its joyous end. The congregation packed into the small church was a sea of movement as it added its energy to the power of the music.

To an outside observer, it would appear that every aspect of the worship came together as well as if it had been choreographed by the most accomplished Broadway veteran. There was an energy in the room that pulsed and flowed, as each member experienced, in their own way, the power and celebration of God.

LaShaunte glanced over to Carol to catch her attention. She held out her Dakarta earpiece, motioning Carol to put her earpiece in to have a quick "thought-talk," as the ladies liked to call their new discovery.

The choir music built to another crescendo as Carol and LaShaunte' put in their earpiece. LaShaunte felt the familiar feeling of the electrical wave, as their minds were connected.

In their mind's eye, the four ladies were now sitting in the same pew at the Grace, similar but dramatically different, as the pew sat in the clouds. The sun was shining and the beauty filled their thoughts. The thought streams swirled in warm hues, moving rhythmically with the music from the choir. Each of the four women would reach out and touch a thought stream and connect with the others. They were sharing an experience space that represented a heavenly and spiritual world. Sunlight streamed from every direction and in the distance angelic figures darted among the clouds. The women's dresses had now become flowing robes of the same colors.

Carol, we are blessed by the Good Lord. We are humble servants in the Almighty's grand plan. The Grace is amazing. The choir sounds absolutely heavenly, Reverend Desmond is inspired. Thank Heaven for little miracles and our phones. Can you believe how he works the crowd? Absolutely, I agree. I was especially taken by the majesty and energy of the congregation.>

Halle and Mia, afraid they were missing something, quickly put in their earpieces and connected to the "thought-talk" and immediately appeared in the Heavenly scene in their mind's eye.

<Carol replied they were just discussing the beauty and power of the sermon. Everyone agreed. Images of the congregation again.<warmth filling their minds, swelling feeling of pride and

love> The next song is beginning, how beautiful. <they all heard the next song begin and experienced the emotion flowing from the choir's voices.> it reminds me again of the power of our Lord and His grace and love. <Agreement all around, absolutely, continued feeling the swelling of pride in the chest.> The power, the power of Jesus. Looking at the cross that now had bright light coming from behind the cross. Everyone locked their vision on the cross. What—what, is that?

At the exact moment Mia finished her thoughts and looked up at the crucifix, the four women sat upright as if simultaneously shocked, their backs straight and their eyes all grew large. Halle's entire body became rigid, her legs shot forward and her back arched, her head started shaking uncontrollably and she fell towards the first row. At the same instant, LaShaunte started yelling, screaming at the top of her lungs, as Carol slumped back into her chair, and promptly passed out, her head hitting the wooden back of the pew with a resounding thud. Blood began to trickle down the wooden seat from a gaping cut in the back of her head. Mia, however, sat transfixed, her eyes were locked on the cross above the altar, a smile was planted across her face, she looked at peace, while her friends' distress surrounded her.

Reverend Goff whipped his head toward the scream and recognized it as fear. His heart dropped into his stomach, as his mind went through a thousand possibilities of why someone was screaming during the service. The sight he beheld he would remember for the rest of his life. In the second row sat four women. One women, he recognized her as Mia, looked as if she had been frozen in a state of ecstasy. Her face was turned upwards with a beatific smile, her eyes were turned to the cross. He thought of Caravaggio's portrait "*Conversione di San Paolo* - The Conversion on the Road to Damascus," where the young Saint Paul was transfixed at the love of God. The other three women, however, looked as if they had just returned from Hell. One women shook with an uncontrollable seizure, her head and arms flailing wildly. The second woman was slumped backward as if the life had been sucked from her. Her neck was turned at an awkward angle as her head rested on the back of the pew. Her tongue hung from her mouth like an overheated dog. The third and largest woman, the reverend vaguely recognized her as LaShaunte, screamed uncontrollably. She looked absolutely terrified, her face contorted into a horrific yell, her eyes bulging. The Reverend Goff looked to where her gaze was focused and realized she was looking at the cross. Reverend Goff sprang from his chair, moving toward the women.

At the same time, the music died, and the energy in the room dissipated, fading away into the heavens from which it came...

SECTION TWO

PROMULGATION

CHAPTER
20

Emily wasn't accustomed to waiting this long for an appointment. She had arrived at ten o'clock for her morning meeting with Adam MacArthur and had promptly checked in at reception. It was now close to 10:20 and she was getting to the point where she had memorized the entire Tribe messaging reel and could recite the next screen before they appeared on the flat panel displays.

A voice woke her from this daydreaming. "Emily Holmes, Mr. MacArthur is ready for you now," the receptionist called out from behind her minimalist desk.

Emily stood up quickly, grabbed her bag, and headed for the elevators. "Please take the elevator to the fourteen[th] floor. Tess, Mr. MacArthur's secretary, will meet you there," said the young lady behind the desk.

As Emily stepped off the elevator, she was greeted by an attractive young black woman. "Ms. Holmes," said the woman with a slight nod of her head, "I'm Tess, nice to meet you. Right this way, please."

Emily followed Tess across the plush carpeting toward two large black doors. Tess leaned forward and opened both doors at the same time, flooding the dimly light reception area with bright natural light.

Emily blinked as her eyes became accustomed to the light. As she looked into the office as she momentarily caught her breath. The view was amazing. She felt like she was standing at the edge of the horizon, hovering above the Pacific Ocean. Floor to ceiling windows made up the back and side walls of the office. There were no window frames visible and the polished floor added to the optical illusion of stepping into the sky. She had immediate thought it looked like heaven. It was one of the most impressive offices Emily had ever seen.

A large modern glass and steel desk was at the end of the room. Slightly to the right of the desk sat four black leather chairs and a small glass table. The room was stark and exuded a sense of power.

Seated behind the desk, framed by the vast blue sky, was Adam MacArthur. He was motionless staring at his computer. Adam didn't appear to hear them enter his office. Tess cleared her throat and said simply, "Adam." At this he immediately looked up at Tess with a direct and angry stare. It flashed away into a slight smile when he saw Tess was accompanied by Emily. "Excuse me, Mr. MacArthur, this is Emily Holmes from Banner Corporation."

Adam stood up from his desk while Emily closed the distance between them. He reached across the desk offering his hand. "Emily, it's nice to meet you."

Emily gripped his hand like a vice. "Adam. Nice to meet you too."

Sitting back down, Adam motioned to the leather chair in front of his desk. "So, Emily, what brings you here today?" Adam said curtly.

"First, thanks for taking the time to meet with me and congratulations on building Tribe. You are the first to truly commercialize the experience world. It seems I can't go anywhere without seeing your face on a magazine or newspaper." Emily replied hoping to break the ice.

"Thank you. Coming from a fellow scientist that is especially meaningful. It's been a busy time for Tribe and me." Adam flashed a brilliant smile, looking very pleased, Emily wondered if he was flirting.

"So Emily, I'm sure you didn't come all this way for small-talk. What can I do for you?" Adam continued rather quickly.

"Actually, I wish this was pleasant, but I need to talk with you about research and testing we have been doing on the TG Dakarta phone. We have found some disturbing results and I sought you out due to your position in the industry. I was hoping you would be interested in what we discovered." Emily cut to the chase, figuring direct was going to be the rhythm of this discussion.

Adam turned to his current quarry "Emily, my pleasure. Can you start with a summary? We may need to coordinate with the proper people in my organization."

Emily paused and then began her summary. "Absolutely. As you may not know, Banner has been working on organic quantum interference devices and embedded microchips for several years. We were seeking to develop an organic based microchip that interacted with the human brain through a closer physical proximity. We have experimented with implantation of chips and use of wireless signals for communication. Needless to say when your discovery was announced, we were surprised by the speed and extent of your discovery. It's quite impressive that you were able to..."

"Thanks, Emily. I know the history. I was there." Adam cut her off with a dismissive wave of his hand. "I'm sorry. What is it exactly you wanted to discuss?" Adam stared at Emily challenging her.

"Right. Well, as I said. Even though we were surprised by your discovery, we quickly went into a mode where we wanted to learn from your work. We have spent time reviewing your report and doing our own testing on your microchip design." Emily stopped waiting for some recognition.

"Understood," Adam said simply.

Emily continued more strongly, seeing that Adam had just erected a mental wall, wondering if all brilliant scientists were so self-obsessed, "Well, as I have said, we conducted several controlled experiments and have generated some interesting results. One of the most interesting results is that your chip design was identical to the publicly available TG Dakarta phone and very similar to our prototype designs at the lab. Were you aware of that?" Emily asked.

Adam didn't miss a beat when he answered in an automatic tone " Actually, we have heard this before, and we did our own testing on the TG phone. As you know, most chip design today is very similar. We are all working with the same materials and somewhat, the same limitations. Our tests have shown conclusively that the TG phone chips are copies of our discovery. We have several lawsuits currently in process to seek injunctive relief and compensatory damages." Adam added with a flourish. "It's really a shame how the scientific world has become so competitive and cutthroat, don't you think?"

"Interesting perspective. So how can you explain that the phones already are in mass production. Wouldn't it have taken some time to reverse engineer the chips and get them into production?" Emily replied.

"Exactly my point!" replied Adam pounding the desk "It only goes to prove that someone stole our work while we were still in development of the chip and sold it to the highest bidder. We have several leads on who is responsible."

Emily continued unfazed and driving to her planned conclusion. "Well, notwithstanding the source of the chip design, I wanted to discuss the results we have seen in our testing. We have documented several instances whereby the chipset and quantum device can damage the human host, as it relates to memory and emotional responses of the cerebral cortex."

Adam finally seemed engaged and asked hesitantly. "I'm not sure I understand."

Emily spoke slowly "In the right circumstances, the electrical impulse levels between the headset chip design and the host can create a frequency feedback which targets specific areas of the brain."

Adam sank deeper into his chair actually considering what he was hearing "I'm not sure I follow. Are you saying you have created results that create a physical danger to the user? That's impossible. We have never seen that in any of our testing!" Adam gathered himself as he began to get emotional when he saw his house of cards teetering. "Besides, I am not the manufacturer of the phone. I only provide the service."

Emily raised her voice slightly. "I understand that, but you are the person credited with the discovery of the phone chipset and, as you just told me, it has been copied. Isn't that accurate?"

"Of course," Adam replied dryly.

Emily continued, "If these frequencies are created, over time they may cause considerable brain damage to the user. The question is not if these can be created, but rather how and when will these frequencies be created. Did your team ever test the phone susceptibility to a virus?"

"A virus. What are you talking about?" Adam replied brusquely.

"A standard run of the mill computer virus. When a phone connects to an infected device or network, it propagates any virus at an exponential rate. We only know that it moves incredibly fast, and when coupled with the user network we have the potential for a very dangerous situation."

Emily finally had the attention of the pompous ass.

"The bottom line is that your discovery—excuse me, rather the TG Phone design—has potentially disastrous effects on the human mind. The membrane conducts electricity bilaterally, thereby opening up a conduit to the brain that could be used to pass electrical current back into the brain. If a virus was introduced which somehow created a specific frequency, the spike that would occur would be similar to electro-shock therapy. Think of it like an extremely focused and rapid lobotomy-like experience."

Adam blinked, clearly contemplating Emily's words. Gone was the calm demeanor that was there only a moment ago. Now he looked like a caged tiger ready to lash out.

"Are you suggesting that there is physical risk from the discovery and the experience world?" Adam replied in a low threatening growl.

Emily felt the change in the room as the tension spiked. She had just crossed an invisible line. Taking a deep breath, she answered "Actually, no I'm not suggesting that there is a risk. I am telling you that there is a risk. We have reliable and valid test data that shows there is a considerable risk to the users of the TG phone and your chipset design."

Adam smiled and like a switch was pulled his calm reassurance returned. "Emily, I'm sorry, but you are mistaken. We have done thousands of hours of testing, and I am more than willing to share the data. Can we schedule time in the next couple of weeks when you and I can meet with my team to discuss these issues? I appreciate your feedback and would like to schedule a follow-up to look into this further."

Emily finally exploded as weeks of being subverted and patronized finally became too much. "Absolutely not. We don't have time to go into this later. Something has to be done now. I am tired of getting thwarted by everyone I talk to about these issues. You are responsible for this just as much as anyone. Your membrane and the chip you designed generates the same testing results as our rejected membranes. It is dangerous to the user."

Adam composed himself and shifted slightly forward. He spoke slowly and deliberately "Again. I appreciate your bringing me this information, but you have to realize we have done considerable testing on the product and experience pods. All of our testing has shown both to be completely safe. You must know that we have something nearing 400 million Tribe users today and have not received any reports of problems. So, unfortunately, you are mistaken. Actually, sorry, I mean you're wrong." A condescending tone came into his voice. "Maybe you should go back and talk to your boss Connor. You can run some more tests and he can go back on his television show and read his teleprompter. Oh, by the way, his greater consciousness comment on Moran was brilliant."

Emily's head cleared and she unloaded on this jerk "Screw you, you fraud. We both know that you had nothing to do with this discovery. I can't prove it, but you are simply the beneficiary of extremely good fortune. Also, I fully expected that you were probably going to react this way, so I just wanted to tell you that we will be releasing our complete testing and report to several media outlets tomorrow, It should be very clear to the general populace that there is a very serious danger." Emily replied while reaching into her bag and removing a thick report. She placed it on the desk just out of reach of Adam. Adam leaned forward but didn't touch the report. He stared at it for several moments.

Emily continued motioning to the report "You may want to review this. We have documented every test and result from our experiments. I will give you the summary version, if you don't have time to read it. This report states that Banner Corp., a highly respected global scientific research and development company, has evidence that the microchip and membrane combination that you discovered, and that also miraculously exists in the new TG phone, poses considerable danger to the users brains. The effects include brain damage and memory loss. Furthermore, the structure of experience world only compounds this risk."

Adam didn't respond. He just sat staring. Emily continued even more forcefully. "People have the right to know about the dangers of para-networking and the experience world. It is our obligation to inform them. Also, I am sure some of your 400 million members will be impacted by this report. My hope is that they won't end up as victims, but as readers." Emily stood to leave. The meeting was over.

Adam picked up the report and threw it down with considerable force and exploded from behind his desk. "Get out. This meeting is ended. I can't believe you would come in here making such preposterous claims. Who do you think you are?"

Emily turned to leave as Adam continued to yell, "You can expect to hear from my attorneys. I am going to lock you down so tight, this report will never be released. You won't be able to take shit without me knowing. You hear me, you bi…"

Emily quietly closed the door behind her and walked to the elevator bank. Tess sat at her desk with a look of complete surprise. Emily smiled and said "Tess" as the elevator doors closed knowing that she had just unleashed a firestorm with her conversation and realizing her initial thoughts of finding a kindred scientific spirit were unfounded.

———

Adam sat back roughly in his chair and took several deep breaths as he swiveled to look out the windows. A thick marine layer was rolling in and the sun was blocked out by the thickening cloud cover. The weather was matching his mood. Not more than a few weeks ago he finalized the agreements for taking his company public and reaping the benefits from the windfall. He had been riding high since that conversation, and the company results kept coming in to reinforce the success of the impending equity event.

Now, however, he was unsure of everything. The bankers had been nervous after the tragic death of Sam Ford, but Tarun had calmed everyone down and the plan was back on track. Now another problem has surfaced. Taking advice from his executive coach to always know more about the person you are meeting than they know about you, he had some of his people do some background checking on Emily Holmes prior to the meeting. This research showed that Emily was a brilliant research scientist that was working on human microchip interaction for a considerable time who was published in multiple science journals and was considered the rising star in the organic computing and quantum interference fields. She was credible.

Adam recognized that his discovery had thrown the entire field into chaos. Adam chastised himself for losing his temper. One of his basic rules of business was to never make it personal. However, he couldn't help himself when he heard what Emily was suggesting. People being damaged by his invention, it was ridiculous. Adam told himself that his team had tested it and didn't see any issues arising from the integration.

Adam caught himself. He knew full well that there wasn't any real testing of the discovery. He had fallen into it and he convinced the rest of his team to follow him to fame and fortune. Most of those people now worked at Tribe and were clearly waiting to cash in. He had a really big problem that he needed to deal with and he knew exactly what he needed to do.

He connected to the experience world and used the back-door protocol that gave him the universal umbrella access over the entire experience network. He had become especially good at planting the thought fragments into the experience world, primarily as a way to increase the number of customers. He now, however, was about to use his access to get retribution against Emily Holmes and her boss Connor Shaw, who no doubt set her up to talk with him. He was going to make sure that both of them would never be able to have any ability to impact Tribe and his success.

Adam leaned back looking at the tendrils of fog closing around the palm trees in the park across the street and smiled as his thoughts began to flow.

CHAPTER
21

The traffic moved like it was a living organism. It ebbed and flowed in a sea of colors, sounds, and smells. Almost every imaginable type of vehicle occupied the narrow dust covered road and they conducted a deliberate and delicate dance with each other on the way to their destinations.

Kunal Kinslay straddled his dusty blue scooter, his sandaled feet resting in the loose dirt, as an especially large brightly painted truck lumbered through the intersection, making any forward movement impossible. He watched as various men, all wearing lightly colored clothing and turbans hung out of the green and red cab waving their arms wildly, willing people to move out of the path of the steel behemoth. Kunal waited among hundreds of others as the truck brought the traffic to a standstill. His scooter quickly was surrounded by even more people, pushing forward, anxiously waiting for the congestion to clear. The truck finally moved on and the group bolted ahead again but was immediately slowed by a white tourist car that, seeing its opportunity by riding in the wake of the truck, cut in front of the line of waiting vehicles. For Kunal the stops and starts of the commute became routine. Each day he slowly wound his way through every imaginable delay that was found on this hot dusty road.

As he neared the city center, the roads improved and the traffic thinned. The morning heat was rapidly increasing as the sun continued its ascent into the early morning sky and the heat began to bake the pavement rolling off in waves. He didn't want to be on the road any longer than necessary, for early June in Northern India was a brutal time of year. The temperature could range from 35-45 Celsius and anyone sane or educated tried to stay out of the sun for most of the day.

Kunal came around the long sweeping round-about leading into Consulate Row, thereby entering the final stage of his journey. His destination, the Indian Institute of Technology, was only a few more kilometers. The IIT schools were the most prestigious science and engineering schools in South Asia. Gaining admission to IIT alone was an incredible accomplishment, a fact which Kunal's family never failed to remind him. Kunal had just started his junior year at IIT Delhi and was currently focusing his studies on advanced metallurgy and superconductivity. He was one of the top students in his class and was a favorite with his fellow students and teachers.

He pondered his upcoming experiment as he parked his scooter in front of the Ravi Science Center. IIT was the only school where the namesake of the building was also an emeritus professor. Kunal took a great deal of pride in that Ravi himself had encouraged him to conduct these experiments.

Energized by his thoughts, he jogged up the stairs to the second floor to his computer science classroom. He glanced at this watch. He still had two hours before his first period class, more than enough time to complete his experiment.

After a series of initial experiments with the new mobile devices, Kunal formulated a plan to test his hypothesis on a larger scale. He discussed his hypothesis with several of his fellow students in his advanced physics class. Through the influence of Ravi, he assembled the four top physics students in the room to participate in his experiment.

They all sat in the first row of the classroom, looking somewhat uncomfortable to be in the same room with their sworn competitors in the ultra-competitive grade and class standings race.

Each of them held the newest TG phone in their hands. They had all been briefed about the goals of the experiment and they waited patiently for Kunal to define the parameters and start the test. Kunal dropped his backpack on the desk and sat on the corner of the desk facing the four physics students.

"Gentlemen, thank you for joining me this morning. As I have discussed with each of you individually, we are going to conduct an experiment that I believe will yield some unique results." Kunal paused and held up a sheet of paper "This my friends is a series of equations that describe the space- and time-dependence of quantum mechanical systems. These equations are central to the theory of quantum mechanics. These equations are what we are going to work with today. I propose that we will be able to combine our talents to solve these equations in a very short period of time."

Just as Kunal finished, the classroom door opened and Ravi walked into the room. The other students all caught their breath, for other than Kunal, none of them had ever met the legend.

"Don't stop on my accord" Ravi said smiling and looking to each of the students "I am only here to be a quiet observer. Please continue"

Kunal swallowed, now nervous with the audience. He turned back to the four men sitting quietly "Let us start. We are going to conduct this experiment using the phones you are each holding in your hands. As unbelievable as it may sound, these phones allow users to share their thoughts. I have experienced this myself on numerous occasions. In each experience, I have been able to see how the users can integrate their thoughts and share a unique experience. I have also personally experienced the by-product of linked minds in accelerating my own thought process and allowing me to quickly learn and solve problems. As a result, the little device you hold in your hands will allow us to integrate our collective brainpower, essentially networking our minds into an incredibly powerful and fast parallel computing engine. We are all math and computer science majors which has afforded us specific and unique training and experience. My belief is this by harnessing this like-minded approach we will solve this equation in a fraction of the normal time. Are you all ready?" Kunal glanced briefly at Ravi, then put the pen down and walked toward the line of students.

The students all looked somewhat unsure of what was going to happen next and waited to be prompted. Their eyes darted between Ravi and Kunal.

"Please insert your earpieces and we will begin. Oh, I almost forgot one final caution before we start, when we connect it will at first be quite disconcerting, expect to be somewhat uncomfortable with the connection and the flood of images and thoughts you will first experience. I assure you this is all normal. I will control the experience pod and will get us to a collaborative and comfortable space where can all work together. Are you ready?"

Ravi leaned back in his chair and began to smile and watched the young men take their first steps into the experience world.

Ravi would let them get accustomed to the experience world with some math problems then he was going to join in to frame a problem around superconductivity and superinsulation. He reflected while he watched the students in their physical space interacting with their minds' eye. Superconductivity was first discovered by the Dutch Physicist, Heike Kamerlingh Onnes in 1911. A quantum mechanical theory characterized by zero electrical resistance and the exclusion of an interior magnetic field, superconductivity occurs when a material is cooled below its critical temperature. This phenomenon allows an electric current flowing in a loop of superconducting material to persist indefinitely with no power source. The theory and the testing of superconductivity is well-documented and many breakthroughs have been realized by leading scientists.

Ravi wasn't concerned with superconductivity. Rather, he saw the real opportunity as the inverse of superconductivity, the super insulator which has almost infinite electrical resistance. Conceptually, a super insulator, when paired with a super conductor, could form a battery that would hold a charge forever. Also, super insulators could theoretically reduce the heat loss from electrical equipment to zero, thereby improving current battery life twenty-fold. The opportunity for solving another condensed matter physics challenge would yield tremendous praise and recognition to the university and to the professor.

The students all turned on their phones and inserted the earpieces. Within several seconds the students all became very relaxed, their shoulders slouched and their eyes obtained a far-away and unfocused look.

As Ravi watched the room, he became fascinated by the body language and the appearance of the group. At first, he could see each student working on the problems in their own ways. Some looked down and immediately began writing furiously on their paper; others stretched back and looked contemplatively at the ceiling. However, slowly and almost imperceptibly, Kunal, the leader, continued his writing while the others began to assume very similar seating positions, with their arms folded on their desks and their heads slightly bowed. Kunal, however, moved forward on his chair and was writing faster than Ravi had ever seen someone write. At first, the questions were changed at a 30 second interval, but as the room fell into its strangely silent state, the leader accelerated in his ability to solve the problems. As the group neared the 12th question, they were answering questions at 10 second intervals. Coming to the final question, the difficult magic square challenge, the pace quickened and moments later, Kunal shouted "Finished" as all the participants broke from the experience pod in unison.

The silence of the room was broken as everyone took a collective deep breath and removed their earpieces and shut off the phones. The room, which not 15 minutes earlier had been a collection of random students, now appeared as a group that had known each other for years. Everyone was smiling and looking about, clearly proud of their performance.

Ravi went through the results with agonizing detail. Reaching the end of the paper, he slowly looked up at the room of the young students. He believed that this group would soon learn what it was like to discover something that would truly change the world.

He slowly rose and cleared his throat. "Students, I have to admit you have truly surprised me. I provided you with twenty of the most complex mathematical equations, and I fully expected we would be here for hours working through the answers. However, you were able to answer each question correctly and in the amazing time of eleven minutes and forty-three seconds. I have to say we are definitely onto something here…"

CHAPTER
22

Connor, Emily and Li sat in the patio of the Soho Club on Sunset Boulevard. It was early evening and the club was full of Hollywood elite sitting and drinking and milling about the space. The room had an expansive view of the entire Westside. Connor was already nursing his third drink and he had a nice buzz going but couldn't shake his black mood.

Emily felt bad about the recent developments and Connor's obsessive behavior and wanted to cheer him up. "Connor, come on, shake it off. You need to forget about it. Don't take it personally. Shows are cancelled all the time. You will be back on in no time with a different network. Don't sweat it."

Connor stared at her for several minutes before replying "Thank you for trying to make me feel better, but in this case it's different, something else is going on. Tell me when does a show with top ratings get cancelled mid-season? When have you ever heard of any network canning the current shows that are ready to air? I royally messed up here by opening my big mouth on Moran. This experience world is the worst thing that ever happened to me. I was beat to the finish line on the discovery, lost my television show because I spoke up, and now will probably lose my job at Banner. If I didn't know better, either my luck has just run out or someone really has it in for me."

The three were quite unsure of how to respond. As the conversation paused a young well-dressed man came up to the table.

"Connor, I'm Dave Sheridan from WME. Sorry to hear about the show. Let me know if you ever want to talk maybe I can help you."

"Thanks," Connor said dejectedly.

The agent continued, "I also spoke to Fred Taylor who worked extensively with your Dad…"

Connor looked up sharply and focused on the agent "You know, it's probably a good idea that before you come over and kiss my ass and ask for a meeting, you do some research and ask around to better understand my relationship with my father. In the simplest possible terms so you can comprehend, my father is dead and rotting in the ground. Any affiliation or reference to him is a very bad thing."

"Sorry, I didn't know.." replied the agent taking a step back.

"Time for you to go. We are in the middle of a conversation." Connor waved his hand dismissing the young man.

"Fairly harsh, Connor, you don't need to take it out on everyone else." said Emily

"Not really that harsh, he's the first of many working the room. They are all sharks with thick skin and looking to steal me from CAA due to the show cancellation. Remember, they make a lot of money when they represent someone working and getting paid. The only person we won't see tonight is my current agent. Just watch."

"You wallowing in self-pity now?" replied Emily.

"Of course, isn't that evident" replied Connor weakly smiling.

Li interrupted with an officious "Can we change the subject?"

"Sure" replied Connor as he downed his drink.

"Actually, no we can't change the subject." replied Emily "Connor, since I spoke with Adam at Tribe and your now famous television revelation, I have asked the team to refocus the analysis on confirming the chemical interaction and the thought reordering. We need to learn more about what's actually happening." Emily waited for Connor to catch-up as the alcohol was hitting his system and she fully expected him to blow up.

Connor slowly turned his head met Emily's eyes "I agree and I know. Remember, I mentioned all of these dangers to the general public when I taped my most recent interview."

"Telling the truth is hard. But, regardless you did exactly what you should have done." Emily interjected "I did the same with Adam and that has brought us some new legal troubles and absolutely nothing else. This is serious, very serious. We have confirmed the dependency and ability to reorder memories and thoughts. You were right."

Connor looked down and shook his head.

"I'm sorry, but I have to disagree with the two of you" Li interrupted clearly frustrated "You are both operating in a world of conspiracy theories and conjecture here. It just doesn't make sense for us to sound alarm bells about danger and viruses without truly understanding the situation."

Connor ignored Li and continued on replying directly to Emily, "Just what we need, a system that could create a massive damage to connected users with no controls and no limits. I hate it when I am right."

Li became visibly agitated observing the exchange. "Emily and Connor, I'm sorry, but you both have to stop this line of discussion. This has already cost Connor his television job and I think you are both being sore losers. My vote is to look at the membrane and determine how it can help our own research. How can we take advantage of this discovery to further our other projects. How can we use this to further our project and objectives?"

Emily glared at Li and responded directly to Connor "Li is wrong. There is an issue here and we need your leadership to investigate it. We cannot ignore this risk and I hate to break it to you, but you are the only one who has ever said there is a potential risk. You are obligated to figure this out and help. You have to keep working on this problem. You need to be visible and vocal. You need to keep fighting for what's right."

"I'm not comfortable with the word obligated, if you know what I mean". Dusk settled in across the outdoor patio as the three sat in silence. Connor fought the growing realization that Emily was right and he needed to continue to do something about the risk of the experience phones. He reluctantly accepted that he was actually in the best position to deal with the potential problem but he still wasn't sure why he really wanted to help.

Experience Pod 411.11.411

Press Release

CNN.COM – TG Phone becomes highest seller in history

April 6 – TG, the world's leading technology company, today announced that the new Dakarta phone is the highest selling phone in the history of the mobile phone industry. Simon Prowse, CEO of TG, made the announcement in front of the company's new manufacturing plant in Delhi, India.

"We have already sold 440 million units through the first half of this year" Prowse stated "and we have orders for another 350 million already in place. This phone promises to revolutionize the mobile phone industry and make good our claim of creating the first true world phone. We are also pleased that the phone is supported by every mobile phone network provider."

Prowse claimed the Delhi plant is capable of producing 50,000 phones an hour which would make its annual production at close to 330 million phones.

The new phone, manufactured in India, has quickly become an international best seller. The technology allows for the phone to be used in all markets, and it is compatible with multiple mobile phone carrier systems.

David Baron, editor of Global Wireless News, believes this is only the beginning for the next generation of TG phones. "It has become true phenomenon in terms of its sales and usage. We have never witnessed one specific piece of hardware that has become so prevalent, so fast."

CHAPTER
23

Emily hadn't liked Li from the first moment she met her. The incident at the Soho Club was just one of many examples. There was just something about her that didn't sit right. Chalk it up to women's intuition. She recognized it could have been her competitive spirit surfacing, as she had been the alpha female in the group, but after a couple of weeks, Emily realized that it wasn't caused by any of her insecurities. Li wasn't genuine. She couldn't place what it was exactly, more of a feeling that she was pretending to be something she wasn't. So her skepticism and caution was aroused when she bumped into Li at her spinning class in Santa Monica. Emily was fairly certain that Li lived in Pasadena, a good thirty miles from the studio.

"Emily, hi, how are you?" Li asked, coming over after class to Emily's bike.

"Great, I didn't know you spun at Revolution," replied Emily hesitantly.

"I usually don't. However, I read a ranking of the top studios in LA, and this was at the top of the list, so I had to try it out." Li was wearing a tight spandex midriff top and black workout pants. Her figure was visible and Emily noticed she was in incredible shape. Emily was still sweating and catching her breath from the workout, while Li looked completely relaxed.

"Do you want to grab a coffee?" asked Li.

"Um, Sure, why don't we walk over to Pete's," Emily replied while packing up her things. "I need to use the restroom. I will meet you there in a couple of minutes."

In the restroom, Emily impulsively pulled out her phone and sent Connor a text. "Met Li at Revolution. Wants to take me for coffee. Do you really know Li?"

She felt better after she sent the text. A distant memory from childhood from her mother telling her to always let people know where you are going suddenly resurfaced. Strange timing, she thought as she left the bathroom.

Li sat on one of the outdoor tables facing 14th Street and had two coffee cups in front of her. She reached over and lifted the farther cup as Emily approached. "Caffe Latte work for you?"

"Thanks. That's perfect." Emily sat, taking the cup, and took a sip.

"So, tell me a little about yourself, Li. I don't really know anything about you," asked Emily.

"Well, not much to tell. I was raised in China to middle class parents who valued education and worked to put me through school. I attended Columbia on scholarship and graduated in three years and went immediately into graduate school. Once I completed my degrees, I went back to China to fulfill my commitment to the Chinese military. I then began working in a variety of high-tech and bio-tech firms, which eventually led me to Banner." Li finished then took a quick drink of her coffee. "So, what about you? What's your story"

"Somewhat similar to you, I suppose." Emily replied, surprised she was opening up "My parents realized that I had an interest in math and science and decided to allow me to pursue the subjects. I attended Stanford, and like you, did my graduate studies immediately after my undergrad. I then met this headstrong young rich kid Connor Shaw who told me all about his big ideas of making science cool again and how he could use his Hollywood connections to get a show, and the rest I guess is history."

"I'm sorry, but I have to ask, are you and Connor together?" Li asked.

Emily laughed a deep laugh. "Of course not. Never in a million years."

Li looked surprised "Really, you just seem so close and you have all those years together. I just assumed."

"Li, I'm gay. I am not interested in Connor other than being his friend and colleague. I care for him deeply but not in any other way." replied Emily matter of factly.

It was Li's turn to laugh. "Oh my God, that is too funny. I'm sure you don't know this because I always hold back because I'm not sure how people will respond, but I'm also gay. I've been holding back with the team. It hasn't always been easy for me, and in my past people haven't been so accepting."

Emily almost smacked her head when she realized this was what Li had been hiding, the barriers melted away as she immediately felt a lot better about her. After their confessions they ended up spending the afternoon together. Things moved fast and later that day they were back at Emily's apartment. Emily was surprised, but she agreed when Li asked if she could take a shower.

Emily sat on her bed and to check her phone. No texts or response from Connor. Tossing the phone on the nightstand,

Emily stretched out on the bed and put her hands behind her head to relax. She heard the bathroom door open and saw the steam from the shower roll out and crawl up the wall.

Li stood with a towel wrapped around her torso. "Sorry, I took so long. Do you have some clothes I can borrow? I don't want to change back into my workout clothes."

"Sure," replied Emily "but first, why don't you come over here first?"

Li moved to the side of the bed, looking down at Emily and smiled. "I was hoping you were going to ask."

Li dropped her towel and sat down next to Emily and kissed her. Li removed Emily's top and bra, and in a matter of minutes both women were together on the bed. Li's hands caressed Emily skillfully, causing her to relax and begin to lose herself in the moment.

Li leaned closed and whispered in Emily's ear. "I'm sorry I have to do this. I really liked you."

Emily barely had time to process as Li shifted quickly off the bed. She picked up the laptop sitting on the nightstand and swung it hard at Emily's head. It struck her squarely in the face and immediately broke her nose. She started gushing blood down her chest as she raised her hand to her face to defend herself. As she was reacting, Li raised the computer again and tilted the computer so the edge hit her squarely in her left eye. The force embedded the computer deep into the socket. Emily screamed as the pain coursed through her skull.

Emily tried to fight against the pain and struggled to roll off the bed in the opposite direction. Li anticipated her move and jumped on her torso as she was rolling to her left. She delivered three quick hits to her right ear and then rolled her on her back. Emily sat dazed as she looked up at a naked Li. Her mind couldn't process violence of this level and her situation. She was terrified as he watched her move to her right.

Li reached out to the nightstand and grabbed the heavy steel light. Lifting it high, she brought it down on the top of Emily's head. She heard a sickening crunch before she passed out.

Li jumped off Emily as she lost consciousness and went for her gym bag sitting in the corner. Reaching into her bag, she unzipped the inner lining and pulled out her SIG Sauer P250 taped to the bottom of the bag. With practiced hands she chambered her round and returned to the bed. Her face impassive, she shot Emily, while still unconscious, three times in the head at close range and twice in the chest.

She tossed her gun back in her bag, pulled on her pants and sweatshirt and left from the back door. As she headed down the stairs, she put in her earpiece and connected to the pod.

In her mind's eye, she was standing in an ornately wood paneled library. She stood before a large table where an older, austere-looking Indian man was wearing a red smoking jacket and his hair was slicked back from his forehead. The thought flow started immediately

Emily is dead. Vision of Emily lying on the bed with red blood flowing and staining the white sheets. This will slow down Connor Shaw. Good, good. We can accelerate on Adam now and building the network. You work beautifully.

CHAPTER
24

Venice, California, has always been a destination for the unique and free-spirited. In 1890, wealthy businessman Abbott Kinney launched a grand vision to re-create Venice, Italy, in Southern California. His idea centered on creating a uniquely American experience with canals, gondolas, Venetian styled buildings and a rich cultural tableau. From its very beginning, Venice became a magnet for the free-spirited and forward thinking. Pushing the boundaries in Venice became commonplace.

It was therefore no surprise that the first Experience Fest would be taking place in this iconic city. The previous month, Huffington Post, the venerable barometer of current public issues and scandals, ran its cover story on the Experience World. There was a complete and thorough review of the experience people and the current phenomenon of para-networking, which was described as "the ultimate in thought, feeling and experience sharing." The blog featured four influencers from around the country that all were early adopters of the experience world and were recognized as leading the way for the "inevitable growth and profits" that were coming out of this new world.

Adam MacArthur received the primary billing, as the scientist turned entrepreneur whose discovery had made this all possible. Adam was compared with Bill Gates as a visionary, to Steve Jobs as an ultimate salesman, and Brad Pitt for his Hollywood good looks. The article propelled Tribe's memberships and creation of new experience pods.

Also profiled was Connor Shaw who has moved from his celebrity television status to the new icon of the anti-experience world movement. The article was pointed and directed at Connor, the outsider, who many considered misguided and flat-out wrong about the Experience world.

The Venice boardwalk was a sea of movement. Experience followers milled about near the stage, just opposite the Boardwalk facing the ocean. Two enormous video screens flanked the sides of stage while a video loop ran of Tribe's corporate video. The police were already creating a perimeter and adding more officers as the crowd quickly grew.

Connor Shaw stood on a small retaining wall that overlooked the crowd. He wasn't entirely sure why he had decided to come down to Venice for the Experience Fest. Part of it was certainly professional interest, as this was the first opportunity for most of the experience culture to come together. Connor told himself that it would be a good environment to observe the users outside of the lab. Another part of Connor wanted to see what he was missing.

Connor noticed someone moving through the crowd toward him. He turned to see Alexis climbing up on the retaining wall. He was both surprised and momentarily confused at the same time.

She looked at him and simply said, "Hi".

"What are you doing here?" Connor said without taking his eyes off her.

Today, her dark full hair was pulled into a pony tail, and she wore a black sweater with a wide collar that accentuated her collarbones and skinny blue jeans that made her seem taller. He had to admit, she looked good.

"I was looking for you. I called around and your office told me you would be down here," Alexis replied "I want to talk after this, if you can."

"Um, sure," said Connor. "I have to admit this is unexpected. Where's Lucas?"

She didn't answer directly. "Let's see what this is all about first," Alexis replied cryptically, motioning to the stage.

A microphone was turned on, and "Cinnamon Girl" by Neil Young started to play. A guy in an all-black outfit ran out on stage to warm up the crowd.

Raising his hands above his head, the speaker leaned into the microphone and said in a low gravelly voice, "Welcome to Experience Fest!" The crowd roared with anticipation.

"Ladies and gentlemen, I'm Atticus Young. And yes, I am experienced"—there was an explosion of applause—"and I am happy to be here today as the first-ever honorary chairman of Experience Fest!" The crowd continued to roar with approval as the energy level began to build.

Young continued, "Now I'm here to officially get this party started, so are we all ready for the Experience!" The crowd roared and began to move together, stirring up the energy.

"Today I am joined by several people who are going to educate, entertain, and enlighten you over the next several hours. I recommend that everyone link up to the experience fest pod, as we are going to be going in dual mode reality and para-world." The crowd inserted their earpieces.

"First, I would like to welcome the distinguished members of our Experience Fest Sponsors Committee. Joining us from the world of entertainment, a man who needs very little introduction, please join me in welcoming Jeb Stone." A disheveled dark haired man wearing baggy non-descript clothes, evidently Jeb Stone, stepped forward and waved to the crowd. The crowd replied responded with shouts of 'Clinton," the recent movie by Stone that glorified the corruption and decadence during the two Clinton presidencies.

Young continued, "We are also pleased to have with us the newly elected Venice Mayor, Robert Harrelson." A balding thin man wearing earth tones stepped forward and waved to the crowd. Apparently a favorite of the Venice residents, a chorus of "Woody, Woody" started through the crowd. Harrelson stepped back and patted Stone on the shoulder and turned back to the crowd.

'Thanks, Woody. Next, we are pleased to have with us banker and technology visionary, Tarun Patel, the man behind most of the advanced technology companies in the last twenty five years." A tall older Indian man walked onto the stage and waved to the crowd.

'And last but not least, we are extremely pleased to have one of the shining stars in the business world, the man whose support is the reason we are all here today. Fresh from his various cover shoots, please join me in welcoming Adam MacArthur, the CEO of Tribe."

Adam materialized from behind the stage and sprinted onto the stage, waving to the crowd. The crowd went wild and surged forward, wanting to share in his energy. Adam definitely looked the part of a successful entrepreneur with a tight black T-shirt and designer jeans. Even from his perch atop the small retaining wall, Connor could see that Adam shone with the luster and charisma of a movie star.

Adam shook hands with all the others on stage and leaned forward to say something to the honorary chairman. Young laughed and Adam took the podium. The commotion of the crowd continued and Adam stood with both hands resting lightly on the sides of the podium. He smiled to the crowd, waiting for the noise to subside.

"Ladies and gentlemen, welcome to the first ever Experience Fest. I recognize a lot of old friends in the audience today, and I welcome all the new friends I'm about to meet. Before we go any further, I want to give a shout out to our experience fest pod."

Adam paused and the entire crowd went silent and went into their minds eye. It was both surreal and terrifying how quickly it happened. A moment later, Adam was back. "Whoa, a lot of people in the pod. So, as we start the festival, I wanted to spend some time and talk about the para-networking phenomenon and share with you some very interesting recent developments and advancements.. As many of you know, I am the CEO of a little company we call Tribe—" Adam was interrupted as the crowd erupted with cheers, and various chants of "Tribe!" began to echo through the crowd.

Adam raised his hands asking for quiet. "Folks, we started our company with a simple idea – to allow people to connect and share their common experiences. We believed that there was an unfulfilled need that we all have – a need to connect – a need to feel that we are a part of something greater – that we belong. This concept has really taken off. We have witnessed for the first time a greater consciousness that can be achieved when we are all connected at this primary level. We are building something great here – we are building something that will transcend business and become inextricably linked into each of our lives. I am happy to announce that this morning was a milestone for Tribe and for our experience economy. This morning Tribe surpassed one billion members."

The crowd roared with approval. Connor sighed heavily, realizing that the growth was much larger than he had anticipated. Seeing his shoulders slump, Alexis leaned over and said "Scary, isn't it?"

Connor caught a whisper of her perfume. "You have no idea."

The crowd noise subsided and Adam continued. "While these are impressive numbers and we continue to see the good that is being created by our experience world and the experience pods, there are some dark clouds on the horizon. There are many critics who don't think that we have created something valuable. They see it as something that must be constrained, controlled, something that needs to be regulated. There are also fellow scientists who are attempting to lessen the importance of this discovery and present erroneous findings in an attempt to discredit the value we are creating. To these people I say – you can't stop the inevitable – you can't stop progress – you can't restrict the power of our collective experiences!"

The crowd applauded and cheered as Adam stepped away from the podium and waved to the crowd. He was working them into a frenzy.

Alexis leaned over to Connor and said, "Had enough? I think there is a coffee shop around the corner."

"Sure. Just down the street behind us at the corner of Main," Connor replied, deflated by the experience.

"Well, how about telling me about your experience world over a cup of coffee?" Alexis asked. "I've seen enough and I would like to talk."

As they both stepped off the retaining wall, they didn't notice the entire back row of the crowd turn in perfect unison and watch them leave.

———

Connor felt better once he put distance between him and the crowd. Alexis walked to his right, neither of them ready to talk as they both walked in silence. The silence wasn't uncomfortable; it was as if they both needed to clear their heads from what they just witnessed.

As they walked in silence, people would stop and watch them pass. They didn't notice the reaction they were getting from the people on the street, many would stop mid stride and turn and watch. Once they were past, the people would resume their previous activities, not aware they even stopped and stared.

Connor and Alexis entered a coffee shop and went to the counter to place their order. The barista, a Haitian girl, looked frazzled as she pushed on her touch screen repeatedly in the back of the store. Connor could hear someone asking repeatedly if "that" made any difference, at which point the young barista said a loud 'No.'

Looking up from her terminal, the young barista brushed her hair from her forehead. Her eyes flashed with recognition upon seeing Connor, and she smiled. "Sorry, the computer is out. Seems like we got some stupid virus, it keeps shutting down. I can't place any orders."

Connor replied, "I'm sorry, can we still buy two cups of coffee – nothing special."

The girl looked over her shoulder. "No problem – with this stupid computer acting up, it's definitely on the house."

As the girl was getting the coffee, Alexis turned to Connor and said, "Sorry for surprising you back there. I needed to talk and thought this was the easiest way to get to you."

"You could have just called me," replied Connor as they walked to an empty table.

Alexis paused "I'm really worried about Lucas. He is obsessed. You know him better than I do. It seems like this whole experience world is changing him and our relationship along with it."

Just as Alexis finished her sentence, Lucas burst through the door. The hanging bell banged loudly when he slammed the door open. Everyone turned and watched him frantically enter the store. Lucas scanned the room quickly spotting Alexis and Connor. He ran to their table and grabbed Alexis by the arm, pulling her up he spoke to Connor "We need to go now. Don't ask any questions, we need to leave."

Connor looked at his brother unsure of what to make of this "What are you..."

Lucas cut him off "Not now, we need to leave now" Lucas dragged Alexis toward the door as Connor followed. The coffee shop got very quiet as they moved to the door. Connor glanced back and stopped in his tracks as several people got up from their tables in perfect unison and began moving to the door. He was reminded of puppets moving together from an unseen hand.

Lucas grabbed his arm and pointed him to his car which sat idling in front of the shop. They both got in and before the door was shut Lucas was driving away.

"What the hell is going on?' yelled Alexis, clearly concerned and scared by this behavior.

Lucas looked in the rear view mirror and accelerated through a stop sign driving erratically.

Connor joined in "Lucas, what is going on here. You are scaring us"

As Lucas got on to Ocean Avenue and headed north he seemed to relax. He turned to Connor and Alexis and for the first time they noticed he was wearing the headset that connected him to the experience world.

"I'm not sure how to say this, but I think I just saved both of your lives. So maybe a thank you would be in order?" Lucas said matter of factly.

"What are you talking about? Have you lost your mind?" Alexis said becoming more distraught.

"No, I definitely haven't lost my mind. In fact, I am thinking more clearly than I have in a long time. I have been spending a lot of time in the experience world and I have been watching some interesting trends and signals. I have been working under the hypothesis that the experience world operates on two different levels. When someone connects to an experience pod, they are clearly conscious, but they are interacting with others through their thoughts. They are seeing and experiencing the pod through their mind's eye, which interestingly enough, much like the experience phones, isn't fully understood either. The human brain has the ability to have a perceptual experience in the absence of true visual input. This creates the mind's-eye phenomenon. All of this processing occurs in the higher cognitive processing centers of the brain that interacts with the thalamus, which acts like the traffic cop in processing all forms of perceptional data. Therefore, the users mind is working in a new way in that it is balancing and sharing its internal cognitive functioning with others when connected."

"While I appreciate the medical explanation, can you tell us how any of this relates to you saving our lives?" asked Connor.

Lucas continued unfazed ignoring his brother "I also believe that there is a lower level, the subconscious, that is also affected in the experience world. It is at this subconscious level that I have seen a series of interesting patterns emerge. I have confirmed our earlier suspicions that there is someone or something that is interacting and influencing at this level, at a point where people don't even realize they are bring influenced. I believe this level can override their consciousness and control people. Someone is controlling the minds of everyone connected to the experience world."

Connor interrupted "I can't believe it. How did you figure this out and how did you find us?"

"Well, I have been tracking these spikes in the experience world when there is a concentration of thoughts around a particular subject. It's fairly easy to track these thoughts when they are so concentrated. Being concentrated makes it even easier to jump in to the swarm and see what it's all about. This morning, the concentrations were primarily around the Experience Fest, which makes sense, and there was a tremendous traffic with all the people present. I was floating through these thought streams when very quickly they changed. It was clear someone was influencing the entire group and when I jumped in I realized that there was one thought that was permeating. The thought was to find you and Alexis and eliminate you." Lucas finished as he merged onto Pacific Coast Highway.

"Eliminate us? What are you talking about?" Alexis asked.

"I meant what I said, the thoughts were looking for you and trying to locate you. They wanted to silence you, to get rid of you. Clearly someone is after you and I'm not sure why" Lucas finished with genuine concern.

Connor was about to respond when he was interrupted with a series of text messages. His heart dropped when he read the text

Emily is dead. She was killed in Santa Monica. Call the office now.

He shut down. He couldn't process. How could she be dead. Was all of this true?

Alexis saw Connor's reaction and asked, "Is everything okay?"

Connor barely heard her, as all at once, the pieces began to fall into place. Lucas was right. The weight of the situation descended on him and he caught his breath.

He looked back at this texts and realized that he missed one this morning from Emily. His heat dropped. Emily told him she met Li for coffee. Emily's instinct was to tell Connor and he missed it. He missed the opportunity to warn his friend about his concerns with Li from Lucas' research. Something never sat right with him about Li, but he had pushed it aside. Now he began to understand.

Connor looked dazed and had a faraway look in his eyes. "I'm not sure. But we need to get my office. Emily is dead."

Alexis and Lucas sat and drove in bewildered silence.

CHAPTER
25

Lucas and Alexis dropped Connor at his office. When he arrived he found several team members congregated in the bullpen. They were trying to figure out what happened to Emily. Everyone was visibly shaken from the news and consoled each other trying to understand the tragedy.

His head was spinning as he tried to sort it all out between the revelation by Lucas and the death of Emily. It didn't process and he was especially bothered by the text from Emily, apparently right before her death. He wondered if he should go to the police.

He spun his chair around and glanced toward the window to his right. He looked back at his reflection in the darkened window. He looked haggard and run-down. He still couldn't believe Emily was dead. He realized that he loved her at that moment. He never told her. In all those years, he never reciprocated. She was probably the best thing in his life and he let her slip through his fingers. He was a fool.

As Connor sat lost in regret, Li entered the office. He instinctively tensed when he saw her. She greeted several people and exchanged conversations before coming over to see Connor.

She wore a pair of khaki shorts and a tight-fitting blue polo shirt. Li's relaxed demeanor turned to a look of frustration when she saw Connor leaning forward on his chair.

"What are you doing here?" Connor asked pointedly

"What do you mean? I came here as soon as I heard the news about Emily. I was hoping to find you here." Li responded taken back.

"Well, you found me," Connor said brusquely.

Li pulled up a chair and sat down to face Connor. "I am sorry about your loss. I know you and Emily were very close and had worked together for many years. I can only imagine how hard this is for you. I have also been thinking over the last several days, and we need to talk. The entire team is all worried about you and your obsessive fixation on these goddamn experience phones. We are hearing rumors from a variety of sources about your erratic and dangerous behavior. People are talking about your wild ranting about these phones and the so-called danger. To be honest, Connor if I didn't know you, I probably would have called management and told them you are crazy. Connor, this has to stop now."

Connor chose his words carefully when he responded. "When did you hear that Emily died?"

Li's pupils widened slightly. "Um, I don't know. Probably a couple of hours ago"

"Who told you?" asked Connor

"I think it was Carol. She sent out an email and called. Why do you ask?" replied Li tensing ever so slightly.

Connor responded, keeping his eyes on Li's face, "No specific reason. I guess I am mourning my friend and still can't believe that she was brutally killed. It doesn't make any sense."

Li relaxed and stood up and came over to put her arms around Connor. "I'm so sorry to hear that. I never really spent any time with Emily, but she seemed like a really smart, dedicated person. I am sorry for your loss."

"Thank you. If you don't mind, I would like to be alone." Connor replied while he pulled away from her.

Li slowly walked out of the office. As she reached the mechanical doors, she pushed her hair back over her ear, exposing the earpiece she was wearing.

Connor recognized and understood that the stakes had changed. He was a part of something much bigger and more sinister and Li was a critical part of it.

A plan began to form in his head as he left the office and said his goodbyes to the team. He needed to find Alexis and Lucas.

Experience Pod 771.33.458
Opinion – When have we gone too far?
Los Angeles Times - May 8

I heard the hype and got the background on the "Baby and Me" doll from Bay View Toys in San Francisco, It was the hottest selling toy in the US and became an overnight phenomenon when it was released. It is billed as the first toy that utilizes the experience world for an interactive and immersive experience.

I was skeptical about the claims that the doll actually created its own "thoughts" which were pre-programmed responses to external stimuli.

Children across the country link into their dolls to experience the doll's feelings as it has its basic needs met. In addition to the thought engine, the doll had advanced animatronic and vocal capabilities that enabled the child to teach the doll to talk and play. Across the US, it was the "it" toy and sold out instantly when it arrived in stores.

I tried the doll and realize that we have crossed a point in our existence of no return. Gone are the days of imagination, of playing and dreaming of lands never realized or kingdoms in our mind. Our children are now being linked to a robot and sharing its feelings. Children are now being told what it feels like when a doll isn't "fed" or "changed." The impact of this experience is monumental.

How do we learn but through trial and error, self-discovery by an understanding and empathy for the other person. We are taking all this learning away and linking directly to a computer program to teach our children.

It's a dangerous world where we are all taught to have the same feelings and responses. Variety and imagination are lost and we are becoming no more than responses to external stimulus.

CHAPTER
26

Connor sat outside Pinks as he waited for Lucas and Alexis. He wore sunglasses and a baseball hat pulled down low. Behind his shades he watched the steady stream of people move from the counter, their trays filled with hot dogs and fries. Many glanced at him, doing the long stare, he wasn't sure if they recognized him from television or if it was the experience world looking for him. It was creepy. Either way, I look like crap, he thought. Good luck.

Alexis and Lucas finally arrived and sat down across Connor at an old wooden picnic table.

"How are you?" Alexis asked, showing genuine concern.

"I'm not good. You both need to listen to me," Connor said in a low voice barely controlling his emotions. "I think I know who killed Emily and I believe Lucas that there is something much bigger and dangerous going on here. It's almost too much to believe, but I think we are in real danger for our lives."

Lucas and Alexis sat quietly, each knowing what Connor said was true.

"Right before Emily died she sent me a text which said she was going to coffee with Li. I didn't see it until after she was killed. The last person she saw was Li. For a while, something has been nagging me about Li even after Lucas had identified her experience world activity was off the charts. I did some checking on her at Banner. I spoke to a Chinese human resource director and she tells me Li's entire family was killed in China right after she left for the US. Li never mentions it and acts perfectly normal. It doesn't add up. I don't believe Li is who she says she is. I believe that Li killed Emily and she wasn't the first person she killed. I spent the last day putting all the other pieces together. Do you know that Banner's head of security was killed three weeks ago? Seemed like a nice guy when I met him, but apparently he was into some kinky stuff. Did you also realize that one of the bankers funding Tribe died in a fiery car crash two weeks ago? Since I went out on a limb and suggested there was a risk in the experience world, everything has changed. The final piece of the puzzle is that Emily spoke to Adam MacArthur at Tribe. She gave him our report on the risk of the experience world. I know I sound like some conspiracy theory nut-job, but I think everything is connected. People are being killed when they get too close to the truth about this discovery, para-networking and the experience world."

"You know you're right." Lucas responded with a defeated look on his face.

"Yes, we are all right." Connor responded earnestly. "People are being killed who pose a threat to the development of the experience world. Anyone who is in a position, either by job or influence, to expose the truth is in danger. We are all moving down a path towards some fateful end, and someone or some group is indiscriminately killing people that could impact the experience world development."

"So what do we do?" Alexis asked wondering if there was any solution.

"To be honest, I don't know. What we do know is that the rules are being rewritten in business, social interaction, education, science, entertainment, you name it. I have to believe that someone or some entity is behind this all. Think about it. What if this is all some master plan that has been developed over several years?" Connor began to talk faster the pieces falling together "At this point, all we know is there is a real personal danger to the three of us. We know the truth about the experience world and I have already been out publically talking about the risks. We are a target and yet we need to warn the public. We need to stop it."

"I have an idea that I've been ruminating on for a while." Lucas interrupted. "I think I know how to shut it all down. To stop it at its source. It's a long shot but it might work. I need to spend some time with some other folks to figure this out, but I think it's possible."

"You think we can stop this? How?" Alexis asked even more confused.

"I'm not ready to answer that yet, because I'm not entirely sure. Just need some time to figure it out. I think there's a technical and programming hack that could end this craziness." Lucas responded confidently.

Connor and Alexis began to understand the implications of their discussion and path forward. "I guess we have nothing to lose." Replied Connor.

"No, we have a lot to lose, more than any of us can imagine." replied Lucas.

Experience Pod 567.21.523
Anarchy Limited LMI

The fastest growing and coolest spot in the Experience world was Anarchy Limited and it was now the largest experience pod in existence. The anarchylimited model followed a similar format to other experience pod communities. The primary difference was that the world created an entirely immersive experience within their individualized virtual world. The anarchylimited experience world became a lifestyle with user contributed content that covered everything technology from video games to local concerts and clothing and overnight was a national brand for the young, hip, and tragically cool.

The collective rebellious nature and ideology of anarchylimited became a burning activism against any form of organized business. The members of Anarchy Limited coalesced into a smoldering movement of contempt and anger against corporate big business, government and profit-making.

In bitter contrast, and ironically, with the growing ideology of anarchylimited, the founders were making millions of dollars as they offered sponsorship for several of their sub-experience pods. This arrangement allowed for members of various companies, primarily the movie and video game companies, to join experience pods, and promote their products and services through thought sharing.

This new form of marketing and promotions opportunities were completely unique and incredibly powerful. The experience marketers would enter the pods and listen into the reactions as they introduced their thoughts and feelings about their products. The feedback came in fast and completely unfiltered. It provided unadulterated and tremendously powerful market research as the marketers captured the actual thoughts and feelings. It immediately became the holy grail of marketing.

The first experience marketers were subject to limitations where the collective thoughts of the pod caused these marketers to reveal specific deficiencies or problems with the products they were promoting. Because of this, several of the product companies started training their experience marketers to think about only specific positives of their products, to guard their emotions, and to avoid other thoughts while they were bombarded by others in the pod. The successful experience marketers, or "ice-men" as they were called, quickly became a hot commodity in the developing experience world.

anarchylimited also became the primary host location for experiential parties. These parties allowed any member, regardless of their location to "jack-in" to an experience party. The experience parties became one of the most popular new areas, quickly competing to become the hot weekend party. Every Monday, the ranking for top party by number of experience participants was released, which became the most watched and coveted statistic for the anarchylimited members.

The Mountain Boys Experience Pod, based out of Wheeling, West Virginia, put together their plan to go all out in an attempt to win the top weekend spot. Kip and Tommy Stewart, computer science students at Wheeling University, designed a party that they were convinced would create the wildest experience party ever by combining visual, auditory, sensory, and technology elements to create a completely new experience.

To put their plan into action, Kip and Tommy borrowed a friend's apartment and signed up for three new credit cards. In addition to the standard experience party roles of the nerd, the drunk, the slut, the clown, the gay, the dope head, and the frat party boys, Kip and Tommy created their coup-de-grace with a sensory overload chamber. Their idea was simple. In addition to all of the people participating through the experience world, they would assemble twenty of their closest friends and surround the party-goers with a completely immersive real-life sensory experience.

The sensory overload chamber's walls, floor, and ceiling were completely covered with flat panel displays. These displays were all run into a video server that pushed multiple signals out to 90 individual monitors. The floor was covered with a special clear plexi-glass that allowed people to walk around with the floor monitors underfoot. In addition to the monitors, the room had a state of the art sound system that ran multiple channels to different zones, and cameras were also installed that allowed the actual visual experience to be captured. For Kip and Tommy, the key was that no matter where anyone is in the room they will be receiving some form of sensory input. The final piece was an amplifier for the cellular signal, so that the experience in the room could be shared at the same intensity as if everyone was there.

The invitations for the party were delivered across all available channels: party for the experienced.

Saturday

9:00 pm

158 East Cove, Apt. D

anarchylimited.lmi/mountainboys

Kip and Tommy sat in the apartment at 8:45 pm, each working on their third drink of the night. Kip, normally the more reserved of the two, sat at the end of the couch with his legs bouncing nervously. "Dude, do you think this is going to work? I mean, this is going to be the party of the year, right?"

Tommy looked relaxed. "Dude, chill out, it's cool. Everything's worked out. Everyone will show. We link in to Anarchy and it will take off. Just like we planned."

Kip turned his head to look at the ceiling. "I'm not sure, our sensory room is over the top. What if something breaks down and our play list tanks or we don't get the video signal?"

"Dude, chill out, do you hear me. Chill out now. You're ruining my buzz." Their attention turned to the door as four partygoers fell through the door into the apartment.

Within the hour the entire apartment was filled with people. Music was blaring and the alcohol and drugs were flowing. The party was already the top weekend party draw on Anarchylimited and the news spread quickly. Members started jacking-in at a rapid rate. By 11:00pm there were close to 400,000 people throughout the world all connected and experiencing Kip and Tommy's party.

At 11:30, Kip and Tommy knew that they were on the way to creating the experience party of all parties. Kip pulled himself off of the pod and went to find Tommy. Tommy was hanging over a blonde girl who sat reclined on a chair, clearly connected to the experience pod; she was vaguely aware of Tommy's probing hands. Kip pulled Tommy away from the girl and the pod. Once his head cleared he agreed that they needed to turn up the experience. Kip reconnected to the pod while Tommy went to increase the sensory output and amplification.

When Kip connected, he found himself in a massive grassy field with thousands of people in every direction. He stood on a natural mound in the middle of the field and everywhere he turned he saw people. This was mind-blowing. The sky changed colors and vaguely followed the beat of the music, which while all different, somehow came together in synch. He saw experience flare-ups where new groups would join and for a moment he would be in their original experience world. He saw a group of five men flash into the experience world, all sitting in leather Barco lounger chairs. The chairs dissipated as they all connected to the party and assimilated into the grassy field background.

Kip began to see multiple thought streams that moved throughout the crowds like snakes of color. He caught one and immediately got lost in a thought stream of people thinking about their first time doing hallucinogenic drugs. He began to experience the similar

*colors and feelings that everyone was sharing, for one moment he
was in the thoughts of a 16 year old girl who was getting high for the
first time. He felt her worry and concern that she might get caught.
He dropped his hand and lifted it into another thought stream
where he jumped with a group experience sharing accidents they
witnessed. This triggered Kip to remember this kid from high school
who crashed his car into a tree and went through the windshield.
He remembered the blood streak that started at the window of the car
continued across the hood and then was sprayed onto the tree. This
thought caused the others to remember some of their own experiences
of car wrecks, which caused a guy from Wichita to lament the loss
of his first car.*

*As Kip started to ride this last experience wave, he felt like he was
physically shocked. He jerked upright, as his thoughts took on a new
clarity and relevance. He immediately felt a sadness like he never
felt before, as a wave of depression washed over him making him
feel like he was drowning in his emotions. He caught a memory of
a smell of fresh cut grass, and someone remembering a baby crying.
This heightened awareness was disorienting. He was thinking in
imagery and he could taste, smell, and feel everything. He became
nauseous as the effects continued to increase. Everyone else riding
the experience wave was feeling the heightened awareness.*

The spike in the amplification caused the group of
guys originally in their Barco loungers to be momentarily
disconnected from the experience party. They were in the
midst of sharing an experience wave of someone at the
party having sex with two girls. As the amplification level
was increased, they all momentarily lost their focus, became

199

confused, and lost connection. The five ninth graders blinked quickly as they looked around the room. One of the boys who sat spread eagle on the floor screamed, "That was awesome" to the group as they all scrambled to reconnect to the pod.

The actual party-goers in the sensory overload chamber began to deteriorate. Two young women began to feel a tingling in their arms perfectly timed to the beat of the music. The effect made them feel like the beat coursed through their body and they were becoming the music. Their breathing became synchronized with the beat of the song. Their vision was going back and forth between their mind's eye and the apartment. They couldn't control what they were seeing.

In another corner of the room, Tommy sat transfixed by a video of a beating heart exposed during open heart surgery. He watched and felt the heart beating; his own heart matched the perfect cadence of the heart in the video. The physicians administered a drug to slow the beating heart. As he watched, his own heartbeat slowed. Tommy felt his head becoming heavy and he began to lose feeling in his legs and arms. He began to lose his vision and then blacked out as his head fell forward and hit the glass coffee table.

Several people lay watching an especially lurid and explicit porno movie. Like the other unwilling participants they began to experience the physical reactions of the participants in the video. The group writhed and moved, acting out the scene in their minds.

Everyone was quickly being drawn into their own private heavens or hells, as the word was spreading across Tribe about this amazing experience party. People began to connect to the party in ever increasing numbers. The Tribe system administrators saw an incredible spike in connection activity. Later during the ensuing investigation, it was shown that the system administrators first recorded the spike in connection at 11:42pm EST. The numbers began exponentially expanding as nearly thirty per cent of all registered Tribe experience pod users switched to the party.

In the room, Kip began to feel as if he was being crushed. All of his thoughts were cascading through millions of different experiences. He began to lose track of all that he was experiencing, and began to get a tremendous throbbing headache that moved down his neck into his chest. At some basic survival level, Kip's mind recognized that there was something tremendously wrong, and it attempted to rid itself of the oppressive weight and pressure he was experiencing.

His body was losing the battle, as his vision began to fail and he noticed a peculiar smell, almost as if he was standing in the midst of an orange grove. The smell was overpowering. His vision cleared momentarily and he looked around the room and saw people collapsing, falling into each other, leaning against walls, sliding to the floors. His mind made a final effort to will his arms to disconnect from the experience party. As he reached up to remove his earpiece, he blacked out and fell forward, hitting the wall and leaving a bloody streak as he slid to the floor.

At 11:49pm, Tribe recorded a massive system spike that momentarily reset everyone's connection. The experience party went offline and everyone connected was returned to a disconnected state. Tribe shut down for three minutes. The Mountain Boys experience pod did not come back online that evening.

The following morning, three police officers from the Wheeling Police department responded to a call of loud music from a party at the Riverbend apartments. Neighbors complained the music had continued all night and no-one was responding from the apartment.

The apartment manager opened the door and stepped aside to allow the police to enter. Before they could enter the apartment, they were overcome with the smell of urine and musty stale air. The police officers drew their weapons and entered the apartment. Throughout the room people were strewn, looking like dolls thrown out of a petulant child's toy box. No one was moving, and the only sound was the loud pumping music coming from the other room. The police moved through the apartment and counted 41 people. The officer's first impression was that they were facing a mass suicide. However, after checking for pulses, they realized that there had been some kind of a horrible accident as everyone was alive but unconscious.

As Kip was lifted on the stretcher his eyes fluttered and he looked up at the paramedics. He croaked, "What happe.."

"We have one awake over here," shouted the paramedic to the police.

"Don't talk, kid, we need to get you to the hospital." The officer placed a thick hand on his chest to calm him. "Party" was all that Kip could manage before he slipped back into unconsciousness.

SECTION THREE

DISSIPATION

CHAPTER
27

The Prime Minister of India, P.N. Chadabra sat back in his chair and carefully surveyed the room. The large white marble table extended out twenty feet in each direction from center, its massive weight and permanence contrasting with the diminutive dark skinned men sitting around the table. The men in the room represented the often fractious power bases in India. Chadabra was still amazed that they had agreed to participate in a two day economic conference. It was probably too hot to golf he thought to himself.

At one end of the massive table sat a podium, where currently a man was droning on, not talking to anyone in particular. The Indian men surrounded the table, all sitting in different positions, some listening to the current speaker, others looking down, and others with their eyes closed. The Prime Minister chuckled to himself as he thought this wasn't too different from what he expected. Even the most powerful are drowsy after lunch.

He continued to survey the room looking for something of interest to break the monotony. He looked up at the ceiling and sighed. He sat within a cavernous marble room with 30 foot ceilings layered with multiple marble tiles. Each wall was covered in marble, and the entire back of the room was framed by massive windows looking out to manicured gardens. It was early afternoon and the light filtering in through these windows illuminated the room in the warm glow of a Delhi afternoon.

The room fell silent as a man named Chandankar stood stoically at the podium. Slowly every head in the room turned toward the front of the room and waited for him to begin. "Gentlemen, I am most honored to present to you, my esteemed colleagues, one of our national treasures, who has single-handedly led our scientific progress and created millions of jobs for our citizens. He is with us today to present his findings from a recent experiment he conducted in the State of Gurgaon. Please join me in welcoming Ravi."

The room erupted in applause as every member shot to their feet, all drowsiness and disinterest having left the room immediately. Ravi bounded onto the stage shaking Chandankar's hand as he strode to the podium. He started with a flourish. "As most of you are aware, we have been fortunate enough to have attracted some of the leading technology companies into our beautiful and most prosperous state. With these trend-setting companies we have seen several scientific advancements over the last several months. I am pleased to report that we have made tremendous progress with our discoveries for the glory of India." He paused for effect, looking around the room.

"Today, I want to highlight one such example. One of the greatest scientific challenges of the latter half of the twentieth century has been the riddle of superconductivity. The theory of superconductivity has promised to change the world's approach to and usage of power. Superconductive materials promise to provide tremendous benefits in the ability to reduce and improve the production and distribution of electrical power. But that is only half of the challenge. While the scientific community has already created superconductors, a challenge remains in super insulators. A super insulator would allow a charged superconductor to hold its power forever. The creation of a battery that would never lose power, the promise of new microelectronics with no heat loss, the opportunity to conserve power and reduce the world's energy consumption is the benefit of a super insulator.

"But enough of science lessons. Gentlemen, it brings me great pleasure to announce to you a recent breakthrough that will revolutionize the world to firmly establish India's superiority in the scientific field. I am pleased to announce that our Gurgaon scientists have discovered how to create the first super insulator that is stable at normal operating temperatures. We are the first to achieve what no one else in the world has been able to develop."

The room erupted in applause as the enormity of Ravi's announcement set in. Looks of astonishment and joy crossed everyone's face as they realized what this meant for the Indian economy. Prime Minister P.N. sat in an awed silence, completely amazed by the announcement.

The celebratory noise settled down and Prime Minister P.N. rose from his seat to address Ravi. "My dear Ravi, let me be the first to publicly acknowledge this amazing accomplishment, and to pass on my gratitude from the people of India. Your service to our India and the humble state of Gurgaon is unparalleled."

Ravi bowed slightly accepting the compliment and beamed with pride.

"But I have to ask Ravi, how were you able to make such considerable progress and overcome this hurdle?" Chadabra posed the question that was clearly on everyone's mind.

"Mr. Prime Minister, we used India's most valuable and plentiful natural resources, our people." Ravi answered simply.

The Prime Minister, not sure of Ravi's cryptic response, continued, "It goes without saying that our people were critical to this discovery. However, was there a specific reason for our success when so many others have faced failure?"

"Mr. Prime Minister, please excuse my truncated response. We created a massive neural network using new wireless experience technology, which allowed our researchers to link their minds to collaborate in solving these problems. Much of this neural network approach to research and development was pioneered out of IIT."

"So, you are saying, by putting all of these people together, we were able to crack one of the most challenging problems in modern science?" the Prime Minister asked wanting to understand.

"Exactly, our most plentiful natural resource is our people, and it is now our most valuable natural resource. This is only the beginning, Mr. Prime Minister, as we now can move to some of the other areas of genetic research and manipulation, pharmacological development, energy, and computers, artificial intelligence, drug engineering." Ravi paused momentarily and lowered his voice. "This was exactly what our Indian scientific community was seeking. We can utilize our greater numbers to propel us ahead in our intellectual property and discoveries."

The Prime Minister, not sure of Ravi's claims, nodded solemnly, recognizing that he needed to investigate the implications of these discoveries and their inevitable economic and social effects. He moved forward and shook Ravi's hand, knowing that he should keep him very close in the coming months.

CHAPTER
28

Connor and Alexis sat patiently as the boarding announcement finally concluded. They were on the late morning flight to San Francisco sitting in the second row of first class. Connor stared out the window as the last bags were loaded. His mind was racing as he thought about where he was going and what they were planning to do.

Turning to Alexis, he expressed his doubts and uncertainty "Do we know what we are doing? Maybe a better question is what are we actually planning on doing? I feel like Alice in Wonderland; I fell down this rabbit hole and the world is completely different. Do you really think we can actually stop this madness?"

Alexis put down the magazine she was flipping through and turned to look at Connor seeing that the normally composed and measured persona was gone and a nervous and worried man was emerging. "Well, actually, I think we are doing the only thing we can do. Remember what you and Lucas told me were some of the last words of Emily. Telling the truth is hard. You have to see this through and bring the people who killed your friend to justice. We need to see Hamlin and enlist his help. This is the only way."

Connor wasn't convinced since there was a part of him that was thinking that staying in LA and pretending like none of this happened would be the preferred route. "I know, but we are way beyond some theoretical lab discovery and being able to control the negative effects. There is danger out there and everybody is using it. What if we are the only ones who realize the potential impact and risks. What if we can't stop it?"

Alexis looked down at her hands folded on the top of her legs surprised that she was once again the controlled and rational thinker when dealing with the Shaw brothers. "You and I both know what we have seen and what your team has documented. We aren't wrong and we have to stop it. If you ask me how it will turn out, I honestly don't know. But all I can say is that we will have to try. I'm scared, actually terrified, but we have to be strong."

Connor turned back to the window, knowing she was right, but feeling even more anxious, thinking how he could get off the plane now and return to his safe and predictable life. As he watched the ground attendants, they all moved about in an ordered precision that only comes from many years of experience. He noticed that none of them spoke to each other. They all smiled and frowned as if they were all in conversation, but there was no way they could talk over the jet noise.

Connor leaned closer to the window and saw a glint of silver as the sun reflected off one of the ground crew's earpiece. The realization made his stomach drop. All of the baggage handlers and ramp workers were in the midst of the experience world.

As he expanded his view and looked at the other workers, he realized all of them were using the now ubiquitous headsets. It seemed everywhere he looked, people were in the midst of another experience while working on the tarmac.

As the cargo door shut and the plane prepared for take-off, Connor willed himself to relax. Finally returning to humor, he chuckled to himself at the ridiculous irony of his situation, for the first time in his life, he was acting selfless, thinking of others and taking action. Unfortunately for Connor, the only problem is that his approach had the potential to actually harm the world. Great time to begin to feel like he needed to make a difference.

Sitting two rows behind them, an attractive brunette held a folded newspaper in front of her and while it appeared that she was reading, her actual attention was focused on Alexis and Connor. She sat patiently running over her plan as she removed her earpiece and disconnected from the experience world. Rina closed her eyes, biding her time until the plane landed.

————

Adam MacArthur sat on a director's chair under the glare of the studio lights. The makeup artist continued her work on a last minute touch-up. Adam felt good. He loved having his ego stroked and recently he was being fluffed almost constantly.

Just outside of the lights to his right stood three figures in silhouette waiting for Adam. The tallest of the group, Jacqueline Adams, was a speech coach hired by the investment bankers to work with Adam on his diction and pace. Adam had improved markedly over the course of the last several weeks. He had lost his slight Long Island accent and learned to project his voice with the authority and cadence expected of a successful CEO. To her right stood Lonnie Carlson, Adam's executive coach. Lonnie had been working with Adam for over eight months. He was working through many of the behaviors and attitudes that are necessary for someone of Adam's soon to be status. The final figure cast an attractive profile in the low light. Gemma Sanders, the daughter of

Hollywood's famous acting coach, Leo Sanders, went through her mental list of the staging and acting directions she had provided Adam. He tended to move too quickly, and Gemma was working on making sure his actions looked measured and confident.

As his make-up was finished, the producer prompted Adam to take it from the top. Adam jumped into position, taking his mark, staring at the camera waiting for his cue and willing himself to relax his facial muscles. Adam heard the direction "action" and immediately smiled into the camera. His face brightened and his eyes sparkled, he looked the part.

"Ladies and gentlemen. Thank you for joining me here today. I would like to welcome you to the Tribe investors' roadshow. I am Adam MacArthur, CEO and President of Tribe. As many of you know, we have a full agenda this afternoon, and I am very excited to share it with you. So without further delay, let's get started."

Adam shifted his weight slightly and turned toward Camera #2. "I am here today to tell you about Tribe. We are planning an initial public offering later this year, and I would like to discuss with you our strategy, high-level financials, and most importantly our key and unique differentiators. Matthew Heyes, the Tribe CFO, will follow my presentation to review our detailed financials and other relevant financial metrics."

Adam glanced down and put his finger to his lips before starting again. "Like most great companies, Tribe started with a simple business idea. We met and improved an existing need in the marketplace with a new technology. Like eBay, Facebook, Google and Instagram, we identified a basic human activity and improved it through the use of technology."

"Our company, at its most basic level, simply allows our customers to connect. We all know that connection isn't anything new. A basic element of human nature is a need to connect with others, share our experiences and communicate. From the earliest cave dwellers, who shared their experiences with crude drawings to the social networking sites today, we are fulfilling the same need. But here's the good part. For Tribe this connection is like nothing ever before imagined or conceived. Our customers can now connect with each other in experience worlds conceived and built in their minds. They share their thoughts, feelings, their actual experiences with each other through each other's mind's eye. It is an wholly unique experience that never before existed in human history. People can now connect in entirely new worlds in ways never before possible. Think about our business, it is literally only limited by our customers' imagination. Tribe has developed a pay for service model that enables these like-minded customers to connect in their very own experience pods."

Adam turned back toward Camera #1. "As you can imagine, our growth has been considerable. We have seen consistent quarter over quarter growth in the 40-50% range. We have seen quick adoption in overseas markets. We expect a growth rate of 30% each year thereafter. We are currently on track to achieve $700M in revenues in our first full year of operations. Our business model continues to expand. Our traditional revenue stream of monthly user access and pod fees continues to be the core of our business. However, we are beginning to garner revenue from other sources. One such source is a pilot we are currently running with two video game publishers to conduct a new form of marketing. These companies are sponsoring experience pods that are aligned with specific interests and gamer profiles. These pods are free for users to join, and the companies obtain user access to conduct market research and also interact with the users in a very intimate manner. The companies have reported promising initial results, in that they are able to obtain valuable and reliable customer insight."

Adam paused and gathered himself for the final pitch. "This, however, is only the beginning. We believe that Tribe is poised to become the predominant global brand for the experience economy. With our continued investment into infrastructure, development, and marketing, we believe that we are establishing a successful and lucrative future."

"Cut!" The producer stepped from behind the camera, extending his hand to Adam. "Wow. Excellent job, that was the best I've seen. I think we are finished for the day. Good luck... when you finally do it for real."

Adam nodded and accepted the compliment feeling immensely self-confident and in control. His three coaches stepped from the shadows into the lights to offer congratulations and constructive feedback. Adam was surrounded as a young assistant from the public relations department stepped into the circle.

"Excuse, Mr. MacArthur, I have Joshua Coleman from CNN on hold. He is wondering if he can conduct a quick interview." The girl placed her hand on Adam's arm to get his attention.

The coaches all smiles encouraged Adam as he took the call.

Adam took the phone and walked out of the circle his exuberance feeding his confidence. "This is Adam MacArthur."

"Mr. MacArthur, this is Joshua Coleman, from CNN. Sorry to interrupt you but I was hoping to get your comment for a segment I am developing and also to ask you if we may be able to have you come into the studio for an interview with Harry Moran. "

Adam beamed. He was getting used to the spotlight.

"Sure, it would be my pleasure. How can I help you?" Adam responded confidently.

"Well, thank you, Mr. MacArthur. I must say that you have been very busy lately. It seems that your company and upcoming IPO are the primary chatter on the investment wires these days."

"Yes, we are very pleased with the media coverage. By the way, you can call me, Adam." He was becoming more smug by the moment.

"Very well, Adam, we are developing a three part series on the experience economy, and I want to highlight your discovery and company. I have done some detailed research and have a few questions. Do you mind if I ask you those questions?" replied the reporter.

"No, go ahead." Adam settled himself into his standard question and answer routine.

"Ok, great. Also, do you mind if I record this conversation?" asked the producer.

"No, that's fine. You can use it as you need to." Adam stretched his neck from side to side, ready to nail these questions.

'Great. Thanks. Let's get started. Adam MacArthur, are you aware of the recent incident in Wheeling, West Virginia, involving several dozen college students who were connected to your Tribe network?"

Adam was caught off guard and momentarily unsure. "Yes."

"Are you aware that twelve of those young adults are still in comas, and the remainder that have regained consciousness have filed suit claiming that a malfunction in the Tribe network caused their injuries?" the reporter said directly, his voice flat.

Adam realized that the producer was looking for controversy and was attempting to bait him into a scandal. He forced himself to relax. "Joshua, we have been investigating the incident, and our technology and legal staff is fully reviewing the situation. I have no other further comment on this subject."

"Adam, there have been several other reports recently that point to the danger of the experience world. Are you prepared to discuss the potentially damaging physical effects that can be caused in your experience pods?" the reporter continued pressing.

"No, I am not. Is this the primary theme of your questions this morning?" Adam asked perturbed.

"Yes, I am trying to understand why the negative elements of the experience world haven't been covered. I know specifically of several incidents that need better explanation." The challenge was evident in the reporter's voice.

"Well, maybe the issue is that you are digging where there is nothing to be found. This interview is over." Adam cut off the connection.

Adam left the studio in a silent fury, heading for his office. He was going to connect to the experience world, hunt down this reporter and kill his reputation and story. *There's your answer Mr. Reporter why the negative elements of the experience world haven't been covered.* Adam thought. *Because I won't let them.*

CHAPTER
29

Lucas stood in line at the Whole Foods on Montana Avenue and waited patiently for the woman in front of him to finish paying the cashier.

He was lost in his thoughts, mulling over the situation, thinking about his conversation with Hamlin, and his plan to stop the experience world. He had just disconnected from the experience world when his hunger became insatiable. He didn't have anything edible in his apartment, so he was forced to go out into the real world.

He felt someone looking at him so he glanced behind him and saw an extremely attractive Asian woman reading a magazine while waiting to unload her groceries. She was in amazing physical shape and her long black hair flowed across her shoulders. He immediately recognized her from his research for Connor. It was Li from Banner.

She looked up when she felt him returning her gaze and smiled saying, "Hi."

Lucas returned the smile and acting almost involuntarily extended his hand and said, "I'm Lucas."

The woman shook his hand. "Nice to meet you. I'm Sunny."

Lucas held her hand a moment longer and made a quick decision, remembering to keep your friends close and your enemies closer. "Would you like to get a coffee with me?"

"That would be very nice, Lucas," Li replied.

CHAPTER
30

Ravi tossed his newspaper on the stainless steel table and exhaled loudly. He just finished reading the series of articles on the PM's news conference.

"Unbelievable," Ravi exclaimed to the empty room, barely able to quell his frustration. "The Prime Minister and his illustrious cabinet can hardly contain themselves about the political value of this new discovery. They didn't hear a damn thing I said. This is the new world order, India can conquer all. Our people are the greatest natural resource."

"*I agree. It seems they missed the point.*"

"Seems they missed the point!" Ravi exclaimed his frustration and anger building to a near fury "That's an understatement. Simple-minded Neanderthals, they are focusing on me. Not the power of the discovery, how India's most plentiful natural resource, its people, can change the world. It couldn't be more obvious. They are unable to see this as a catalyst to drive peace, to reunite India with Kashmir. They are only motivated by their economic greed."

"*So what are you going to do about it?*" replied the calm and measured response.

"Well, I think I need to do something immediately. I think it's time for me to open the back door and take control of this situation."

"*It will only work if you take control*" agreed the voice.

"You're right. I need to take control."

"You need to take control now."

'Right. You are absolutely right. First, I will target the politicians and their families. We can easily obtain their experience tags and experience world connections."

"Yes, it sounds fairly straightforward. Why couldn't you control it all?"

Ravi forced to himself to breathe slowly to calm his heart rate. He rose from the table and began to slowly pace the stainless steel room, focusing his anger on the next steps.

"I can. I will. I can make these politicians understand the error of their ways. I will convince them that this technology is a gift. It's a gift to bring peace to Kashmir. The politicians will finally know what lies in each other's hearts. No longer can they hide behind a well-groomed façade. They will see that everyone wants peace for Kashmir. Peace is achievable if we put aside our petty differences."

"You need to make them understand."

"Yes, I will make them understand"

"You going to use the back-door protocol."

"Yes, of course. The back-door protocol."

"You remember this was written into the original design."

"Yes, the original design. The back-door allowed us to broadcast at a different frequency, at a much deeper subconscious level. This will be perfect."

"You will need to use our White Dove. You need Tribe."

"Yes, I will need to access the Tribe system to run the White Dove program. They won't even know they are in my experience pod. It will all work at the subconscious level."

"So you are going to use the White Dove?"

"Yes, of course. The politicians will realize that the experience world is the path to peace."

"We need to start quickly."

"Yes, we need to start very soon."

The conversation ceased as Ravi slipped on his clothes and left the empty stainless room.

———

Ravi sat at his office desk looking out over the Delhi landscape in the late afternoon sun. There was movement everywhere he looked: cars, bikes, people, animals. They all moved in a chaotic manner, but from his vantage point it all looked like a perfectly choreographed dance.

Ravi turned away from his windows and returned to the task at hand. It was fairly easy for him to access the Tribe user databases to create his list of Indian, Kashmir, and Pakistani politicians. He assembled a list that included some of the most powerful men in the two countries, from the Prime Minister, President, high-ranking Cabinet members, and supporting staff. It was an impressive list and managed to cover close to seven hundred and fifty people.

The White Dove program was ready to execute.

Even though all the pieces were in place, he sat and stared at his screen. His hand remained motionless, not moving to the keyboard to execute the program.

He went through his mental checklist. He had triple checked all of the code, he had tested it extensively and knew that it would work flawlessly. Yet he still lingered.

Something nagged at the edge of his thoughts. There was something that he had missed. His intuition was rarely wrong.

"What are you waiting for? "the voice returned

"Nothing. I am just going through it all one more time in my head. I want to make sure everything is perfect."

"You know it's perfect. Run the program and fulfill your destiny. Do it. Do it now."

Ravi pressed enter and watched as the program went through its experience pod initialization routine.

He placed the TG earpiece in his ear and waited as his experience pod was created in the Tribe network. In a few moments he heard the first voice, which was quickly joined by others. There was no consistency. Everyone's thoughts were random. No one knew that they were part of the experience pod. The program connected at a subconscious level, so the mind's eye phenomenon wouldn't be invoked. He chose to run the program at three in the afternoon, a time when most people were on their cell phones.

He watched the screen as the last member was registered and a notification popped that his experience pod was in place. The screen asked if he would like to run White Dove.

Ravi pressed enter.

At first there was no perceptible change. The voices were random and continued as they had before, each focused on their own world. However, within moments, Ravi recognized a barely perceptible change. The rapidity of the thoughts began to slow. It seemed like everyone was slightly distracted. The others in the experience pod began to recognize it. Ravi could see the confusion in their thoughts. Some people began to become afraid, not aware of the connection and the influences on their thoughts.

A strange feeling began to overcome Ravi as he realized that many of the minds began to comprehend the message that White Dove was projecting. He sensed a tightening in the experience pod as people began to resist and struggle with these subconsciously implied thoughts. Emotions began to spike as others betrayed their true positions. The key thought that continued to emerge was peace is possible in Kashmir. People began to agree.

As the thoughts continued to become focused, pressure began to build as everyone aligned on a common goal of peace, but the thoughts varied wildly on how to achieve this peace. In an instant, the thoughts scattered and turned against each other. Some believed the Pakistanis owned Kashmir by rightful title, and as the Indian politicians asserted their thoughts that they should own it, these thoughts began to collide, with Ravi seeing the spreading energy of the colliding thoughts. Confusion and anger spread rapidly.

Ravi had never personally experienced this level of determination and focus of opinions centered on any issue. Joined to the experience pod he was now riding wave after wave of indecision and anger. The thoughts came crashing into each other as the two sides were drawn tighter. The frequency and intensity of the thoughts became more pronounced. He was in the midst of a battle of the minds. Ravi began to feel he was losing control of his own thoughts and was being swept away into a churning sea of emotions. The hatred seethed as the sides continued to fight for dominance of their thoughts. Longstanding stereotypes surfaced, emotions boiled, as hatred, red and violent entered the emotional waves.

Ravi fought to gain control of his own thoughts. He wasn't aware of his physical being because he became completely immersed in the experience pod. In the physical world, Ravi sat at his computer his head slightly cocked to the right, as a small string of drool began to fall from his lips. One thought surfaced and fought for control; he needed to stop the White Dove program. It wasn't going as planned, it was going horribly wrong. Yet he was unable to move as images of violence cascaded through his mind. He couldn't regain control.

"You can't turn back now." the voice returned "this is your destiny, what you were born to do"

He was unable to move. With the voice still echoing in his head, he lost the last shred of his self-awareness and was swept into the swirling pool of thoughts. Within moments, his head hit his desk and he fell forward on his chair.

His secretary found him several hours later. He was lying behind his desk, curled into a fetal position. His eyes were glazed over and his breathing was shallow. All attempts to wake him failed.

As the secretary called for the doctors, she glanced at the computer screen. A text box showed a program with a picture of a Dove that was running through a series of commands. Within the application window, the words "Peace to Kashmir. You know what is right. Free Kashmir" looped on the screen.

The secretary reached down and shut off the monitor, but the program continued to run.

CHAPTER
31

Connor and Alexis exited the plane at the San Francisco Airport as Rina kept pace a few steps behind. Connor ducked into the restroom, and coming out accidentally bumped into Rina. With a practiced hand and quick movement, Rina slipped a small package into Connor's computer bag back pocket. Connor glanced at Rina, and a hint of recognition passed, as he apologized for the collision. Rina acknowledged his apology with a smile and continued walking out of the terminal.

Connor found Alexis waiting across the walkway holding her phone in her hand "Connor, sorry. It looks like my phone is out of power. Can I borrow your phone to call Lucas?"

Connor reached into his bag—and felt a paper bag that wasn't there before. He gingerly opened it and his face went white.

'Alexis, I think we have a problem." Connor looked around to see if anyone was watching them. Alexis followed Connor's gaze, not sure of what he doing.

Connor turned back to her, "Listen to me and don't act strange." Connor held out the paper bag. "Take this and immediately get out of the terminal. Go as quickly as you can and get it as far as possible away from people."

Alexis laughed. "What are you talking about?"

Connor grabbed her arm and implored her, "Listen, I will explain later. Just take this now and get out. I am going to start walking slowly to the cabs. I will meet you outside."

Alexis pulled away from him. "Connor, you are making me nervous. You are acting all paranoid. What the hell is wrong with you?"

Connor merely handed her the bag and walked away. Alexis was amazed. Considering the circumstances, she started walking towards the exit. As she walked, Alexis's curiosity got the best of her, and she glanced into the bag. She gasped when she saw what was inside. It looked like a small explosive device. She immediately knew that it could be remotely detonated. She quickly rolled it back up and sprinted for the exit.

Alexis hurried out of the terminal, made an immediate right and at the end of the curb tossed the bag into a flower bed that wasn't near anyone. She turned back intent to catch Connor as he exited. As he exited, he met her eyes and with an almost imperceptible nod he motioned to his left. Alexis followed his eye and saw an attractive women watching them walk.

Connor leaned over close and said "When the explosion occurs stay close. We need to get out of here quickly. She thinks I still have it. I expect she will detonate it when we get into the car and drive away."

About two minutes later, just as they got into the Uber and it was pulling from the curb, they heard and felt the blast. Smoke rose from the flower bed at the end of the walkway. Chaos erupted as everyone began running for their lives

"Get us out of here" he said to the driver.

The driver nodded and accelerated quickly pulling away from the curb and joining the mad scramble leaving the airport.

'What the hell was that all about?" she asked, barely able to contain herself.

"To be honest, I really don't know. I think someone was trying to kill us again. It was that woman that I motioned to. She's involved in this and placed the explosive into my bag. Had I not reached in, we would be dead now." Connor replied, looking around the general vicinity.

"You have to be kidding me." was all Alexis could respond.

"Someone knows what we are planning and is trying to keep us quiet. I never thought it would come to this. We have to get to Hamlin. He can help us."

Alexis became flushed. "I am starting to get really scared…"

Connor leaned close to Alexis and whispered, "Listen, we have to be careful. You never know who is listening to us." Nodding towards the driver.

Alexis nodded looking like she was living through a bad dream.

"Unbelievable. You were lucky to get out of there. What is this world coming to… Mr. Shaw, just confirming you are heading to 199 Fremont. Correct?" asked the driver over his shoulder, his eyes in the rearview mirror.

"Yes. Thank you," Connor replied automatically.

Alexis and Connor settled back in their seat. As they drove from the airport, the emergency vehicles were streaming in as people poured out onto the sidewalks as they ran from the airport. As their car cleared the airport and merged onto the 101, they both noticed the rhythmic head bobbing of the driver. Their initial thought was the driver had a perceptible tic. However, at closer inspection they saw the recognizable form of the silver earpiece. The driver was participating in an experience pod while driving.

Connor looked at Alexis and shook his head. Alexis sensed Connor's frustration as he began to move forward to ask the driver to disconnect from the experience pod. This time Alexis reached out and gently placed her hand on his arm. 'Don't bother. You don't want to rile up anything, now do you?"

———

Rina stood off to the right of the exit door and leaned on the glass window, people continued to stream from the airport screaming and running for their lives. Rina was calm because she knew there was no more explosives or danger. She almost missed Connor and Alexis getting into the black car, but she caught its tag and was now connecting to the experience pod. She walked to the parking garage as she connected to the experience world.

She found herself standing in a large warehouse. The space was so massive that she couldn't see either end or the side walls. Across the top of the walls small paned windows let in the light creating shafts of light across the concrete and dirt floor. In the distance, she saw a figure materialize and walk toward her. The figure was shadowed, and even when he walked through the light he remained dark. He had the outline and shape of a tall powerfully built man, but he was shadowed so none of his features were visible

Her thought stream, swirling in blues and reds reached out to the man <we have a problem.>

<I know> the man's thought stream was short, staccato and black.

<It didn't work. Somehow he got away. He is smarter than you think.>

Rina began to see other figures, almost transparent walking toward her in the warehouse. It seemed like her reality was starting to merge with the experience world.

<Impossible. It is not him. It is you. Simply put, you failed me. How is it possible that a television celebrity can outsmart you. Maybe you're not as good as your reputation pretends. My dear.>

Rina's thought stream turned black and red, and although she was controlling her physical response, her thoughts gave sway to the fury that she felt. <What do you want me to do?>

<What I hired you to do. I want you to kill him. I don't want him talking to anyone else. Where did you last see him>

<He got into a black car and headed out of the airport tag 345 YTRF.>

The shadowed figure looked away. <There it is. I will handle this. Don't do anything. I will contact you if you are needed>

The room vanished and she returned to the airport.

Experience Pod 122.34.569
Afternoon Chat with Norah Whitney

Norah Whitney, recognized as one of the most influential and powerful forces in television, had provided her audience with an entertaining and educational experience for the last eighteen years. Her long running television show was responsible for establishing the careers of many current media personalities. With slightly over six million viewers per day, she held sway in the hearts of minds of the largest consistent television viewing audience.

The next in a long-line of these neo-celebrities stood backstage staring unceremoniously at her shoes. The associate producer, wearing headphones and holding a battered tablet, watched the stage. Dr. McNichol calmed her breathing and waited patiently for the sign.

Dr. Nancy McNichol was a published author and renowned child psychologist working on early childhood development and communication. She toiled away for many years in her Chicago private practice, quietly building her reputation and following. Recognized throughout the medical and educational community as an expert on children's cognitive communication development. She was a regular speaker at the APA conventions.

Her book, "Children are Always Listening" became a seminal work on childhood communication and the role parents have in understanding and responding to the communicative needs of the developing child. The book became one of Norah's personal favorites.

Norah had enthusiastically announced the recent birth of triplets, Melissa, Melinda and Melodie. She regularly shared some of her own parenting challenges and accomplishments.

According to Norah, Dr. McNichol's book was a breakthrough in communicating with her daughters. Even though she had been rehearsed, coached, and briefed, she felt like she was going to shake right out of her new Mahalo Baliks.

The producer turned and motioned Dr. McNichol to the stage. "You're on."

Dr. Nancy McNichol walked quickly past the producer and entered the lights. After moving with practiced grace across the short expanse she hugged Norah. They both sat down as Norah flashed her world famous grin.

"Smart and sexy, I do say. Doctor, you look great today!" Norah opened the conversation.

"Well, thank you, Norah," returned Dr. McNichol. "I left my standard therapist outfit at my office. I love getting dressed up for your show!"

The audience greeted Dr. McNichol response with a flurry of applause, for she had an uncanny ability to immediately endear herself to large groups of people. The cameras panned the audience focusing on many mothers holding their children, all looking forward expectantly to the upcoming session.

"Listen to you" replied Norah still smiling "brains, beauty, and wit, what a deadly combination."

Norah leaned forward and rested her elbows on her knees and continued. "So tell me, Nancy what do you have planned for us today?"

"Well, I am going to demonstrate something I have been working on regarding early childhood communication patterns. As many of you know, we have recently witnessed the development of incredible technology that allows us to share our thoughts and innermost feelings to create and share experience worlds."

Norah sat back in her chair and smiled. "Yes, I know all about it. Some of my staff brought me one of these new phones and we connected to an experience pod. I can tell you, it was one of the most exhilarating and disconcerting moments of my life."

"Yes, we have heard about some of these experiences during our research," replied Dr. McNichol, "however we have found one common concern comes from the extended nature of the experience pods. Many times people are interacting with folks all over the country or even the world. Apparently, this causes some of the disconcerting feelings you experienced, Norah."

Norah nodded, letting Dr. McNichol continue.

"As most of you know," she said while turning more fully to the camera and audience, "I've spent my entire career studying the link between cognitive development and communication. My writing and research has studied the subject in defining communication through the then available verbal and non-verbal mediums of speech, sign-language, body-language, and touch."

Dr. McNichol clasped her hands together and sat forward on her chair. "Well, today, I am happy to be here with you as we take a step into the next avenue of childhood communication, thought-sharing between mother and child."

With this announcement, the audience erupted in applause. The camera panned the audience filled with the beaming faces of mothers and their children. Dr. McNichol and Norah stood up and walked downstage to stand immediately behind three chairs and three baby high-chairs.

Norah beamed at the audience. "Today, my producers have randomly chosen three mothers and their children to participate in our demonstration. Is everyone ready?"

The audience responded with a resounding roar of applause. Norah soaked in the response and smiled. "Then let's get started." She pulled out an envelope and opened it for effect. "Can Gail and Harrison Turner come on down!"

A blonde mother and her young baby boy shot up from the second row and made their way to the stage. Norah hugged Gail Turner and pinched the chubby cheek of Harrison. Dr. McNichol directed them to the first set of chairs.

"Next," continued Norah, "can Maria Sperling and Maggie come on down!"

A dark haired, fair skinned mother and her daughter stood up from the back of the audience and carefully made their way down the aisle. They were also greeted by Norah and asked to sit in the second set of chairs.

"And last, but not least, can Mindy Robinson and Marcus come on down!" A light skinned black lady and her little boy stood up from the front row. Mindy jumped with joy at being chosen which caused Marcus to smile from ear to ear. The audience saw the reaction of mother and child and joined in with applause.

As Mindy and Marcus got situated, Dr. McNichol walked in front of the chairs and faced the audience. "Now that we have our volunteers, let me tell you what we are going to do today." Dr. McNichol scanned the room. "First, I'm going to help these three mothers to communicate with their children through their thoughts. Live in front of this audience we are going to allow these mothers to connect with their children like never before."

"And the best part," continued Norah, "is that you all are going to listen in!" As Norah finished her sentence, several young assistants appeared and began handing out the TG earpieces to the audience.

"And just because I like you so much," continued Norah, "I'm going to let you keep the phones when we are all done." The crowd let out a collective gasp and more applause followed.

Norah turned to the camera. "We have supplied the entire audience and our volunteers with our own private experience pod. I am going to turn it back over the Dr. McNichol, who will walk us through our exercise"

Dr. McNichol stood behind the three volunteers on the first riser. "Thanks, Norah. First we will all need to connect to our private network. When you try this at home, you will need to configure your private experience pod for you and your child. For today, we have pre-configured everyone's phone for the same network. Let's keep in mind that everyone in the audience is on an observe-only mode. Our volunteers and volunteer babies are on full participation mode. Volunteers, please place your earpieces in your ears and we will be ready to begin."

The women moved in unison as they inserted their earpieces.

"Ok, let's begin," Dr. McNichol continued as she paced behind the three women. "Gail, Maria, and Mindy, please join me in the experience pod."

The four women immediately found themselves standing in a bright and warm room. It was an empty nursery school classroom. The tables had been pushed back against the large multi-paned windows that lined two of the walls. The other walls were covered with various children's art projects. Dr. McNichol stood in the center of the room as the women all became comfortable and acknowledged each other in the room.

"Ladies, we are now connected to the experience pod. Does everyone feel okay?" said Dr. McNichol.

She was greeted by nods and smiles around the room.

"We will now connect to our children and bring them into the experience pod. You need to remember that small children have a hard time discriminating between their mind's eye where we are all sharing now, and reality. It isn't an uncomfortable situation. Rather, they don't have the same boundaries that we maintain," Dr. McNichol continued. "Let's get started."

The women in unison inserted the specially designed earpieces into their children's ears.

"I will show you and your children a series of images. I want each of you to focus on your children and their reaction to these cards. Once you have recognized their reaction, I want you to think about your reaction to the images and blend it with your child's thoughts. These images will become "thought-starters". Let's try one first and see how it works."

The three children now existed in the experience pod. Their forms were somewhat blurred and lacked depth, but it was apparent they were now in both worlds.

Dr. McNichol held up an image of a dark green Christmas tree with brightly covered lights and several presents surrounding the tree. The babies all saw the picture and reached out to the photo, showing their recognition. The mothers stood behind the babies and smiled as they sensed their baby's thoughts. After several seconds, Dr. McNichol lowered the photo.

"Gail, what did you experience?"

"Well, at first, I felt Harrison's excitement when he saw the tree, and then I was bombarded with a series of images from our house last Christmas. Harrison was very happy and he began to think through several of the toys he had received. He fixated on a yellow dump truck that was always a favorite. When I realized he was fixating, I joined in with his thoughts and told him how much I liked that truck and how he was a big boy when he played with his yellow truck. He liked the thought that he definitely felt like a big-boy when he played with his truck. It was amazing – I was actually communicating with my baby," finished Gail she began tearing up.

"That's fantastic," said Dr. McNichol. "Did all of you also have similar experiences?"

The other two women nodded. "Anyone care to comment on their observations?"

Mindy nodded as Norah brought her a microphone. "Norah, it was amazing," said Mindy "I saw in my mind's eye exactly what Marcus was thinking. It was almost like I was experiencing Christmas for the first time, again."

The camera caught several women nodding and smiling in agreement. Norah turned to a gray haired lady sitting in the front row. "Now I understand that you are the grandmother of Marcus. What do you think of all of this?

The older lady rose unsteadily to her feet and wagging a finger at the stage said, "Well, to be honest, if we had this stuff when I was raising Mindy, I bet I could have avoided a lot of late night worries and headaches."

The audience exploded in laughter and applause. Norah hugged the older lady. "Well, let's see what's next. Dr. McNichol, what else do you have up your sleeve?"

"Well," replied Dr. McNichol, "I would like the audience to now share in the communication experience with our three volunteer mothers." Dr. McNichol motioned to the audience. "Can everyone please turn on your earpieces and join us in the experience pod."

The audience responded as the camera panned the room showing people turning on their headphones and placing them in their ears. Everyone's eyes quickly returned back to the stage. In the experience world, the audience began to fill the nursery. The room expanded as more people connected.

"Excellent," intoned Dr. McNichol. "Now I will show our babies some images and I want everyone to focus on their thoughts so we can share what they are thinking."

Dr. McNichol first held up a picture of a puppy. The three babies simultaneously smiled and wiggled in their chairs showing their recognition of the dog. Likewise, the audience latched onto the happy thoughts resulting in a collective smile. In the experience world, the thought streams floated around the room, in and out of people, looking like a contained and moving stream of colored smoke. The audience reached out and connected to the thought streams as it weaved among them.

Dr. McNichol next held up an image of all different types of candy. This generated a more animated response as both the babies on stage and several babies in the audience began babbling incoherently. The entire room was now clearly connected to each other's thoughts. As the camera panned the room, it was met with almost identical expressions of happiness across the members of the audience.

"Ok, everyone now I think we have the handle on this. Let's stir things up a little bit." Dr. McNichol turned toward the audience. She put down the picture of candy and held up a picture of a large tarantula spider taken in extreme close up. The babies on the stage let out a short gasp, and then Maggie, the middle child, began to scream uncontrollably. As she was screaming the mood of the room changed instantly.

Maria, Maggie's mother, began to scream as she first picked up on her daughter's thoughts. Her fear was immediately caught by the audience and several women began to scream while the other children looked terrified.

The camera continued to roll and the scene in the audience grew worse. The audience began to move in several different directions as people stood up quickly, as if they were shocked. Many of the audience members pulled their earpieces out of their ears and fled toward the doors.

The babies on the stage were all screaming as Harrison turned bright red. The three mothers rushed to remove their own earpieces, and they quickly moved to their children. Even after removing the earpieces the children continued to scream uncontrollably.

This entire reaction took no more than 25 seconds. The cameras continued to roll as no one realized what was happening. A producer in the control booth finally realized what was happening and quickly cut to commercial. The room continued to disintegrate. The audience was all moving at once. Women fell over chairs and stumbled forward falling down the risers. People pushed and shoved trying to get out of the studio as quickly as possible.

Norah was rushed back stage by security. Dr. Nancy McNichol was left standing in the center of the stage in an empty studio. Asking herself "What had just happened?"

CHAPTER
32

Adam sat at his desk, staring into the distance. In the experience world, Adam was in a flurry of activity. He sat before a control center construct that he had designed in his mind's eye. It allowed him to control and access the entire experience world and to connect to all experience pods instantly. He was currently focused on finding the newest group of users planting in their thoughts the need, and physical longing to bring their family and friends into the experience world. Marketing in the new world was so much fun.

To his left in the experience world, Rina had just joined him and was manipulating a group of Western Region users to purchase the newest tablet computer. Their newest client wanted to influence the market and through a series of undisclosed deals they were making millions from large companies. She was one of the best handlers at implanting thoughts that quickly grew into specific actions. He was amazed at how quickly she mastered her ability to influence.

Adam knew she wasn't physically present with him, as she had to make a trip to San Francisco to see her sick aunt, but he still felt her close physical presence. Previously when they traveled, they had "thought sex" which was surprisingly vivid and erotic. It was one of the highest frequency activities in the experience world and its usage was only growing. He sent a seductive thought her way to see if she would respond. Picking up on his thought, her blouse immediately became transparent and she smiled a mischievous smile.

As Adam prepared to send more thoughts, he began to feel a growing pressure in the experience world. It was similar to the feeling when a large object moves close and you feel its presence pushing the space around you. He turned his head in the experience world and saw a figure inexplicably walking toward him through the gray boundaries of his thoughts. He wasn't sure how this could be happening and sat mesmerized as the apparition began to take form.

He shook his head as the image of a shadowed man materialized. *<Adam I need your help>* The thoughts flowed from the figure, incredibly clear and powerful, completely black Adam felt breathless when he realized the power behind this man.

<Who are you? Why would you be here in my thoughts? <Images of aggression><confusion> immediately appeared.

<Stop asking questions. I control you. All of this <flood of images of entire experience world spread out across the entire view. Adam was overwhelmed. This is my creation. You are but the vessel I have chosen to extend and develop my world. You are mine. I own you. Do as I say.>

Rina sat transfixed in the experience pod, evidently experiencing the same revelation.

Adam tried to push back *<Who are you? How is it this possible? <confusion, anger, fear flowed from Adam as his thoughts swirled in a sea of colors. I don't understand. This was my discovery. This is my world. You had nothing to do with it.>*

<Red, powerful images, pressure, unbelievable pressure.> Silence. You are my pawn. You know you have done nothing that I didn't plan and put into place. You now need to listen to me and follow my every command. If not, I will kill you.> <images of violence, French subway, scientists in the field, Emily dying, Sam Ford being run off the road>

Adam's head throbbed massively. He felt his blood pressure rising and his brain felt like it was going to explode. On one level he was confused, but on another deeper level the pieces fell into place and he understood completely what had happened. The pressure was immediately released.

<Good. I see you understand. Now I want to show you something>

The scene changed immediately and Adam was in another experience pod. This time the image was of a pleasant porch on a large white plantation house facing a slow and meandering river. Several older women in large white rocking chairs were sharing an experience pod about growing up in the deep south. It was a pleasant and tranquil scene. Adam could smell, hear and feel what it was like to live in this time. As the shadowed figure walked up from the river with Adam to his left, the thought flow of the women all paused.

<Adam, pay attention.> The shadowed figure motioned to a pleasant looking matronly woman sitting second from the left in a billowy flowered print dress. Tremendous pressure built in the experience pod and Adam watched as the woman's appearance began to change. Her features twisted and her body began to collapse into itself. It looked like she was being crushed up by a giant unseen hand. In a moment a mass of color materialized

on the chair. No semblance of the woman remained. The other women sat perfectly still. No thoughts flowed.

The man turned to Adam. Adam could sense the pleasure and satisfaction emanating from him. He found himself smiling and pleased. *<She is dead. <Anger, seething hatred, violence, death> Her body sits in her home in Idaho already rotting away. Her mind has been crushed, mashed up and crumbled much like the form you see here All these other fools know nothing. In a moment, it will all resume and no one will ever remember she sat here in this chair or ever existed. Do you understand the extent of my power. Do you understand Adam MacArthur?>*

Waving his hand, the rest of the experience pod disappeared and they returned to Adam's control room.

<Now you need to fixate the entire experience world on Connor Shaw. We need to destroy him. Make him the most hated person in the world. Make everyone want to find him and kill him. Your job is to get rid of Connor Shaw. He wants to destroy everything we have built and our future as well><Images of power, success, pride> If you serve me well you will have a place in the new world order.>

Adam completely understood. He began to prod the experience world into a frenzy. He now understood that someone could control the experience world and physically manipulate the users even to the point of death. He involuntarily shuddered when he considered the implications on the global scale. But he did as he was told.

CHAPTER
33

John Owens had just celebrated his twenty-eight year anniversary as a black car driver in the Bay Area. During his tenure he had shuttled some of the world's most powerful, dangerous, and renowned people. CEOs, Senators, Congressman, and various tech insiders moved around the bay area like pawns in a giant chess game. John Owens always delivered them to their destinations. He had seen everything there was to see and do in a town car. He and many of his passengers viewed the Bay Area like a modern day technology utopia. People moved from company to company, creating and innovating a new world where technology continued to be integrated into almost every aspect of life. These young Turks were filled with optimism and energy and knew that they were changing the world.

Even though he hated to admit it, one day two months ago he woke up and realized his job had become boring and mundane. He found himself having the same conversation multiple times a day with his clients. In the old days, he could go on forever about a particular new company or invention. John loved the repartee; he would enter work energized and leave work refreshed.

Two months ago, he had lost his zeal for work. He became despondent and worried that he wouldn't be able to get his interest back even after a long vacation. And then one day, like a gift from heaven, John Owens was introduced to the experience world. Once he started using the experience phones, his old enthusiasm returned. He was energized by the experience pod and the thought conversations that he joined. He was amazed by the depth of analysis and subjects that were covered in the driver experience pods. He began to learn about novel subjects and information. He learned about foreign lands from the immigrant drivers. He was also educated on wines, good books, and of course, sports.

Today he picked up his clients from the airport and was heading downtown. He glanced back at the pretty young girl and the slightly older man. He recognized him from some television show. He was deep in an experience world conversation around the current European Union unification issues. In his mind's eye, a group of drivers sat around the main chamber of the United Nations and discussed the EU issues. A passionate Pole, standing behind the podium, was describing his countries' upcoming entry and the threat that the unification talks are creating for the European Union.

John had become very good at being in two realities at once. In his mind, he could interact with the other members of the experience pod while he also drove his taxi.

During a slight break in the Poles' thought stream John thought he had seen the girl passenger before. He glanced quickly in his rearview mirror to try to recall where he had seen her. As he looked at her, it dawned on him. He had seen her picture in the morning newspaper. She was a wanted fugitive from Southern California. The story described how she and her television star boyfriend went on a killing spree at a children's nursery school and were on the run and, apparently, they had just detonated a bomb at SFO and killed twelve people.

John was tempted to immediately stop the car. He remembered something he read that said anyone who had knowledge of their whereabouts was requested to immediately go to the closest police station. John discreetly locked the doors and windows. Since he was still on the experience pod, he stood up and announced that he had the two fugitives in his car. The pod erupted with activity; several drivers blinked out of existence and jumped into other experience pods. Others circled John and began relaying similar experiences with other fugitives. Several members of the pod began giving driving directions to the nearest police station, while another member said he knew an experience pod for the San Francisco police. One dropped out of the pod to notify the police that the fugitives were en route. One especially industrious member of the pod jumped back into the pod with an experience world correspondent from CNN who reported on the breaking news of the criminals' imminent apprehension.

The CNN reporter disconnected from the pod to the main news desk. It was especially disconcerting as the experience pod news desk was identical to the actual news desk and at times the reporters forgot if they were in reality or the experience world. Once the thoughts were shared with the news desk, a junior staffer jumped out of the experience world and called the San Francisco police to confirm the report.

This all took a matter of minutes. John Owens turned his Town Car onto Valencia Street and stopped in front of the Mission police station.

The car stopped quickly and the door was yanked open. A gun was pointed into the back seat. A policeman stared menacingly at Alexis and Connor.

"What's going on?" Alexis demanded.

"Please step slowly out of the car and keep your hands where I can see them." The policeman backed away slightly allowing them to move out of the car.

"What are you talking about? You've got the wrong people," Alexis exclaimed.

The officer's voice became more forceful. "This is the last time I am going to ask you. Please step out of the car, now."

Connor placed his hand on Alexis's back. "I think we should slowly get out of the car. Don't panic. We will get to the bottom of this."

Connor felt that this was simply a continuation of the pursuit at the airport and he wasn't feeling good about how this was developing.

Alexis calmed slightly and fumbled out of the cab. The officer backed away slowly, still aiming at Alexis and Connor. As they both got out of the car, three other officers quickly stepped behind them.

"Please place your hands behind your back," said the first officer.

Connor and Alexis complied as the men behind them handcuffed them. Connor looked up at the building and saw a light blue shield with white lettering. It said San Francisco Police – Mission Station. He was pushed toward the entrance.

Connor and Alexis stole furtive glances at each other, unsure what was happening, but knowing it was related to the experience world.

———

Connor lost track of time as he sat in the nondescript interview room. His handcuffs had been removed but his wrists still hurt. He had just finished his third interrogation since arriving this morning. Apparently, the police thought that Connor and Alexis were mass murderers that had killed preschool children in Brea, California and apparently planted the bomb at SFO. He was worried about Alexis. When he first heard the outrageous charge he laughed out loud. He thought he had entered some new reality show. His humor quickly faded as he realized that no one else in the room was smiling. In fact, many looked at him with barely concealed contempt and scorn. The police personnel began to question him in a methodical and measured manner. He was forced to tell them his whereabouts over the last several weeks, discuss his relationship with Alexis, and explain why he flew to San Francisco on short notice.

Connor repeated his answers several times. He even spoke about his fear about the implications of the experience society. He told them of his television work, his role at Banner, and his family history. One of the interviewers asked about his arrest as a teenager for computer crime. Connor calmly replied that he was a minor and no charges were ever filed. At one point, he thought something registered with the interviewer.

The door was opened and a huge man in a well-tailored suit walked into the room trailed by two officers. "Connor Shaw. I am Ari Peck with the NSA. You are going to come with me. Please rise and move toward the door."

Connor reared back from the imposing figure. "NSA. I demand to know what this is about. I have my rights. What is the charge against me?"

"Mr. Shaw, first, we aren't charging you with anything. Second, I would appreciate your keeping your comments to a minimum, as we attempt to get to the bottom of this. Please come with me." Ari motioned to the door.

"I'm not leaving. I'm not going anywhere until I speak with a lawyer." Connor sat back in his chair and crossed his arms.

"Sure, you can talk with a lawyer. First, you come with me and then we get the lawyer." Ari said his voice rising slightly.

"No, I'm not leaving until I get a lawyer" Connor said obstinately.

"Mr. Shaw, this is not optional. You are to stand up and come with me." Ari stepped forward and reached out to grab Connor's arm. The man seemed to expand and fill the entire room. The grip on Connor's arm was a like a steel vise. Connor stood up and held his hands out waiting for another pair of handcuffs to be affixed.

"That won't be necessary, Mr. Shaw. I trust you will behave yourself with me." Connor nodded, thinking to himself that there was no way he was going to pull anything with this giant. Connor was led out to the hallway, where he met a waiting Alexis. She ran up to him and hugged him.

"I can't believe this. They think we've done some terrible things. What is happening?" she whispered in his ear as she released her grip.

Connor shook his head. "The experience world is coming after us. I guess our trip evidently upset someone."

They left the police station by the back door. Ari stopped to sign some documents as they were ushered into a waiting black van.

Ari sat in the front passenger seat.

Connor interrupted the silence. "Excuse me, where are we going now?"

"We are going to see Hamlin" he replied simply.

Alexis leaned over to Connor and faintly said, "Don't worry, Hamlin will sort this all out."

Connor wasn't entirely sure, based on the last couple of hours. He wasn't sure anyone could help them out of this situation.

CHAPTER
34

The silence in the hallway was unnerving. Faces stared at Alexis and Connor as they walked through the California Department of Industrial Relations building on Golden Gate Avenue. This was actually the Northern California location of the National Security Agency and Hamlin's San Francisco office. The contempt was barely contained as people stopped and watched the procession. It was amazing that all of these superspies actually stopped to see the two of them coming down the hallway.

Rina stood behind two tall programming interns as Connor and Alexis headed to Hamlin's office. She couldn't move with all of the people, so she chose to remain in close surveillance. She didn't think they saw her face in the crowd.

Alexis overheard snippets of whispers: "they are the ones... what are they doing here...they don't look dangerous . . ."

Alexis was relieved when Connor nodded to an upcoming office. Hamlin's small staff spilled out into the hallway, apparently expecting their arrival. Everyone stood with their arms crossed and stared at Alexis and Connor.

They were ushered quickly into the office, not acknowledging any of the staff and were led into the large conference room. Heavy wooden doors were closed behind them.

"Did you see the brunette from the plane on our left when we walked in?" asked Connor.

"No, I didn't notice her," replied Alexis

"I rarely miss a pretty girl, and there she was. We should assume we are being followed," Connor said while sitting down in one of the conference chairs. "I hope Hamlin can help."

———

A few minutes later, the doors opened and Alexis and Connor were greeted by Hamlin. He shook Connor's hand and gave Alexis a hug.

"It is so good to see both of you. You look like you are holding up based on the circumstances." Hamlin tried his best to lighten the mood, but it wasn't working.

Connor's reply showed the gravity of their situation. "This is a horrible day. When we got off the plane at SFO a woman planted a bomb in my bag. Luckily we disposed of it before it was detonated. Then we were dropped off at the police station suspected of bombing a preschool in Southern California. Other than being completely terrified, we are both massively confused by what is happening and the fact that we have someone trying to kill us. Finally, I think the woman who planted the bomb on me at the airport was in the hallway as we walked into your office."

"Really, are you sure about the person from the airport?" Hamlin was genuinely concerned. "If she can get into the NSA that can mean only one of two things. Either she is with the NSA or she is better than the NSA. In either case, this adds another incredibly challenging element to this situation." Hamlin got up quickly and motioned them to another smaller room off the main office.

They followed Hamlin into a smaller wood paneled conference room. He requested that they sit in the plush chairs that surrounded a round cherry conference table. The walls were adorned with various pictures of Hamlin with technology leaders that spanned the last thirty years. This was clearly Hamlin's private sanctuary. Connor glanced around the room and noticed pictures with Larry Ellison, Marc Benihof, Vinod Kholsa, and Presidents of most of the major countries of the world.

"We're safe in here. This is a quiet room. Rare for the NSA. So, tell me what is happening. Why did the police pick you up?" Hamlin turned toward Connor and Alexis.

"Honestly, Jim, we have no idea. This whole trip is a bad dream. As I said it started when we arrived at the airport with the planted explosive and then ended when we got dropped off at the police station being charged with horrible crimes." replied Connor while mentally detaching himself from the situation and thinking about it rationally and clinically "I am confident that we are being followed and the experience world is being manipulated in every way possible to try to stop us."

"I spoke to your brother, and I know the reason for your trip." Hamlin replied "I am confident that some element of what you describe is accurate. I also agree that there is someone manipulating and controlling the experience world. They are trying to kill you."

Connor relieved by the corroboration, glanced at Alexis before unloading "I have seen the convergence of several seemingly unrelated factors and have discovered disturbing information about the new experience world. I believe that someone or some group is behind this discovery, and it is leading to something much bigger than just a new technology and business model. One of my friends and associates was murdered because she began to realize the connections between all of these experience world elements, and I also believe that others that can expose the truth have been killed. Both Alexis and I have witnessed the damaging physical effects of this technology on the experience world. The experience world is interacting with the brain in ways that haven't been fully tested and understood. The people behind the Experience world want to control the minds of the users." Connor hastily added, "I think someone knows we were on the way to have this conversation and ask for your help, and they are trying to kill us."

"Unfortunately, I have to admit that this doesn't seem too far-fetched in light of what has already occurred," Hamlin replied "but the real operative question is who is behind it and how do we stop it."

Alexis leaned forward and absently ran her fingers through her hair, speaking up for the first time since entering the room "The answer to the question about who is controlling it is driven by something as old as humanity. Greed and power. Simply greed and power. Whoever controls the people's minds and thoughts controls the world. Everything. Think about it."

Hamlin folded his hands under his chin. He took a few moments before answering.

"As I already said, I knew why you were coming to SF, and when we heard you were picked up, I asked Ari Peck to go and retrieve you. Like the both of you, we have been monitoring the experience world for some time now, and my research analysts have also come to similar conclusions." He nodded at Connor. "As we have previously discussed, we have also tracked several physical side-effects from the experience phones. These include seizures, brain damage, and comas. I know we are dealing with something that is extremely dangerous and that it is not yet ready for the mass-market. We are convinced there is danger and risk and we know that something needs to be done."

Hamlin turned to Alexis. "Having said all this, however, we don't have an answer. There is a unparalleled enormity to the challenge. We have daily briefings to review our work and findings. Would you like to sit in on this afternoon's discussions?"

Connor and Alexis nodded their agreement.

"Good" Hamlin stood up and headed for the door. "Make yourselves comfortable. We are scheduled to start the meeting in 20 minutes. But first I need to make sure we clear your names as suspects on the mass murderer charges. Peck is currently working with the media to make sure everyone understands it was a well-coordinated hoax. Seems like the NSA has some sway and influence as well."

Hamlin paused with his hand on the doorknob. "You'll be okay" was all he said as he gently closed the door behind him.

———

For the last twenty minutes, Hamlin has been questioning the results from the testing group and the tech review teams. The room was filled with scientists and analysts from the NSA. The scientists argued and discussed their results in an extremely animated manner.

Hamlin was the lion tamer in the middle of the room keeping the dialogue relevant and moving forward.

Once the dialogue had died down, Hamlin took the opportunity to introduce Connor "I would like to invite Connor Shaw, my friend and lead scientist from Banner Corp. to say a few words about the experience world. Connor has been leading research for Banner for several years on organic computing, and has done some investigation on the experience world. Connor, please." Hamlin gestured for Connor to come to the front of the room.

Connor walked slowly around the conference table, gathering his thoughts. He wasn't prepared to speak to the group and was still rattled from the morning. Turning to face the room, he noticed several recognized authorities and he had to fight back a slight feeling of nervousness.

"Jim, thanks for the opportunity to speak this morning. Much of the work my team has done is redundant to the testing that many of you have described, so it may make sense for me to discuss a byproduct of the phenomenon that I have personally experienced."

Connor left the podium and moved to stand in the center of the room. "This morning, as many of you may be aware, I was a mass-murderer." The room collectively inhaled, attempting to deconstruct his message. "I appreciate that we can all see it as a hoax, but just four hours ago, I was one of the most notorious and wanted criminals in the United States. Now, you should all ask, how could such a deception take place? How could my face get planted on every television in America?"

Connor paused, controlling his emotions. "The real reason is that it wasn't a mistake and while I'm clearly not a mass-murderer, someone has intentionally manipulated the thoughts of people to make them believe that I was a mass-murderer. We have all heard the old saying that perception is reality. Well today I lived it firsthand. Think about the implications if someone can bend the experience network. Someone can plant thoughts. Clearly, someone understood the paradoxical nature of millions of individuals, with their own thoughts and experiences, becoming one and quickly accepting a thought as fact. The experience world has the capability to influence the masses. It has the ability to make people think in altered ways. I would go as far as saying, if used like it was today, it could result in mind control."

The room was silent as Connor slowly walked back to his seat. Jim Hamlin took up his position at the front of the room. "Are there any questions?"

The room erupted again with dozens of voices all trying to speak simultaneously.

———

Connor and Alexis had returned to Hamlin's conference room. They had left the briefing when it appeared that the questions and discussions would continue indefinitely.

"Quite a day, huh?" Connor asked Alexis.

She absently pushed her hair behind her ear. "Yes, it still feels like some bad dream. I can't believe that someone is trying to kill us and that we were arrested, interrogated, and featured on CNN. You really know how to show a girl a good time." She smiled.

"I never said I was boring and introverted," Connor replied as he got up and walked to the window trying desperately to lighten the mood.

"I think we still have a long way to go. I'm not sure that the crowd in the other room is going to solve anything soon. I'm pretty sure the only thing we have accomplished today is to get more people aware of the issue, not necessarily solving the problem." Connor turned back toward Alexis and leaned on the window ledge knowing that nothing had changed and that whoever was coming for them is still coming.

"Connor, this is all too much. You forget that last week I was teaching a psychology class. I'm not really sure I have any idea why I am involved other than I want to help Lucas. I can't deal with the stress and want everything to return to the way it was." Alexis began to sob quietly, finally breaking down.

Connor went to her and put a comforting arm around her shoulders. "It will work out. We've gotten through the worst of it. We spoke to the NSA and Hamlin. They are already working on it. We will be able to head back to Lucas and Los Angeles tomorrow. We need to lay low for a while. Maybe all of us can get off the grid and go up to Mammoth?"

Alexis started crying harder. "You don't understand. The experience world is ruining my life. I can't handle it anymore. I can't keep running and hiding. It's overwhelming." Alexis said as she headed for the door.

Connor sat back in his chair and swiveled to look out to the San Francisco skyline. He felt confused and scared realizing what it felt like when the entire world was against you.

CHAPTER
35

Connor and Alexis sat at a small corner table at Boulevard on Harrison just off the Embarcadero. Hamlin was running late and called to tell them he would join them for coffee after dinner. Connor absently moved his food around his plate.

"I am physically and mentally exhausted," he said without looking up from his food.

Alexis stared at the top of his head and replied. "I couldn't agree more. It's like a bad dream."

A chair at the table was pulled out and the tall, attractive brunette from the airport and the halls of the NSA sat down across from Connor and Alexis.

"I'm Rina." she said with a deep voice. "Connor and Alexis, correct?"

Connor and Alexis tensed. This was the woman following them and trying to kill them and she now sat across from them casually smiling and looking like she was meeting friends for a drink. The server came over and Rina ordered a vodka tonic.

"What do you want?" asked Connor while uncharacteristically unsure of the situation, his confidence was fading fast.

"Want? Oh, no, I don't want anything. The question you should be asking is, what am I going to do?" she leaned in and stared into Connor's eyes. Her eyes were dull and flat and smoldered with aggression and anger.

"Ok. What are you going to do?" asked Connor, holding his beer bottle in his hand and slowly slipping his fingers up to the neck of the bottle.

Rina leaned further forward and lowered her voice and smiled "First, I am going to take you both out of here and drive you twenty five miles north. We are going to park at an old abandoned factory…"

Connor moved incredibly fast and swung the beer bottle hard at Rina's head. She reacted, by trying to duck, but she wasn't quick enough as the shattering bottle hit her left cheek and eye. Her arms swung up as she lost her balance and fell from the chair to the floor. She landed on her back. Connor was still moving and running on pure adrenaline, lifted the heavy table as he stood up and flipped it toward Rina on the floor. It flipped once and landed hard on her head with a loud and sickening crunch. Alexis sat dumbfounded by the speed of his reaction and stared at Rina's legs sticking out from under the table. She watched as one of her legs slowly moved and began to bend. Connor grabbed Alexis's hand pulling her out of the restaurant. People moved to help Rina on the floor. Shouts began as people reacted to the situation. Connor and Alexis slipped out the door quickly and sprinted from the restaurant.

The television droned on in the background as the Giants played the Pirates. Rina was pulled up and slowly regained consciousness.

The game was interrupted by a news bulletin. "This is Simon Borage for KRON Channel Four Action News. We are following the developing story of the case of mistaken identity this afternoon." The screen switched to two pictures of Connor and Alexis,

"Apparently, Connor Shaw and Alexis Mack were falsely identified as mass murderers on the run from California. They were brought into custody when they arrived in San Francisco. As we all know, they were cleared of these charges after the complex hoax was revealed."

The reporter continued, "In an interesting twist of fate, it appears that two individuals are now listed as persons of interest in the death of a family in rural California. CNN has learned of the grisly details from local authorities, and has confirmed with the Federal and State Authorities that these two are fugitives. They are labeled as sick and twisted serial killers. They are both considered armed and dangerous. If you know the whereabouts of either…"

"Connor, slow down!" Alexis pulled Connor aside to stand in a shadowed doorway several blocks from the restaurant. "What did you do? You just attacked that woman? Why?"

Connor couldn't believe what she was asking 'Why? She was the one from the airport. She was threatening us. Didn't you see the way she was looking at us? She was going to kill us? I could feel it. I attacked first because I didn't think we had much of a chance otherwise." Connor hoped Alexis realized the danger of their situation.

———

A short time later, Connor and Alexis sat in a darkened staircase next to a trendy restaurant on Mission. The valet car line was long with cars lined up three deep.

Alexis offered her phone and said "You need to call Hamlin. He was planning on meeting us at the restaurant."

Hamlin answered on the second ring. Connor immediately knew something was wrong. "Jim…" Hamlin interrupted him. 'Connor, listen, we have a problem, everything has gone haywire. The NSA agents are searching my house. They are going to bring me in for questioning. They believe that I am tied into a massive drug ring with some Mexican drug cartels. They also believe that I assisted you in some way to commit ridiculous crimes. I am standing in my bathroom right now and they don't know I have my phone. You have to get out of town. Don't use this phone anymore. I'm not sure what's happening, but it's like the whole town has gone mad." A loud banging and muffled voices could be heard in the background.

"Everything will work out. Get out of town. I will call you when this is all sorted out." The line went dead.

"What's wrong?" Alexis asked.

"The NSA is searching Hamlin's house. They are claiming he was an accomplice to our crime and that he was also involved in drug trafficking. He told me to get out of town. Alexis, we have to keep moving. Rina wants to kill us. Hamlin is being pulled into this as well. We have to keep going," Connor said while pulling her down the staircase toward the street.

"We can trust Hamlin," Connor muttered to himself as he stumbled along towards the last car that sat idling, an older blue Audi. He casually walked toward the car and looked in through the driver side window. The keys dangled from the ignition.

They got in, he put the car in gear and was out of the line a few seconds later. No one saw them leave and he figured they had at least a two hour head start before anyone realized the car was stolen. He turned right and quickly headed for the 101 back to Los Angeles.

Neither of them talked until they were comfortably cruising south. "Well, the good news is that we now have a car." Connor smiled as he looked over at Alexis, "The bad news is that fairly soon they will know we got out of town."

Alexis looked visibly shaken. "Keep driving for as long as we can. Don't stop for anything. We need to get back to LA."

Connor nodded in silent agreement. He stared at the road ahead trying to figure out where they were going.

Experience Pod 921.12.324

Justice Stephen Allan Watkins - DePaul University College of Law

Applicability of experience world testimony in criminal cases

Executive Summary

Developing case law is pushing the boundaries of testimony arising from and generated in the Experience World. Several legal scholars have argued confidentiality and first amendment rights are being trampled by several courts' use of the thought streams from the Experience World pods. The seminal case currently being argued in the Second District concerns the thought streams that a Chicago police officer encountered while participating in an experience pod for Bears fans. Apparently, the defendant's thoughts were exposed when one of the members of the group started a thought stream regarding the recent fatal beating of a Packers fan in the parking lot. The perpetrators were never apprehended and the Chicago Police were still investigating. The Defendant's thoughts disclosed that he was one of the men that killed the Packers fan. In a matter of seconds the Chicago Police officer knew all of the details and participants in the crime. The defendant argues this information is inadmissible as it was obtained without his consent and in a manner which violates his privacy rights.

The court is yet to rule on the admissibility of the evidence, however it is my opinion that this will set a new precedent in the way in which the authorities can obtain evidence and testimony. There should be no expectation of privacy in a public forum such as the experience world and the thoughts shared have no expectation of privacy.

My article will analyze existing case law and provide the foundation for the limitation of the first amendment as it relates to privacy.

CHAPTER
36

Adam had been continually connected to the experience world for the last fourteen hours. His body ached and his head was throbbing as he continued to plant the thoughts about Connor Shaw across the experience world. Unfortunately for Adam, an hour ago he realized he couldn't keep doing it. It was all becoming too much. He was accessing the deepest and darkest parts of the experience world thought streams. He would insert a thought and then watch it develop, inevitably going to some very dark places. He felt like he was physically overpowered in bad feelings and thoughts. He was having difficulty separating himself from all of the negativity. Instead of controlling it, he felt it controlling him.

While developing thought streams about the nursery school deaths, he stumbled onto a series of disturbing sexual and predatory thoughts from a pod in Chicago. He tried to switch to another thought stream but the black thoughts followed him and began to infect the other pods.

He finally extinguished the thought stream and disconnected from the experience world. He teetered as he shakily stood up and saw his disheveled reflection in the darkened windows. He stumbled across the room and splashed water on his face.

He realized now knew what he had to do. He had the courage to see it through.

———

Rina sat in the rented Ford with the police scanner on the passenger seat. She expected that Connor and Alexis would stay off the grid but that they would do something eventually that would get attract police attention.

She looked at her face in the rearview mirror. Her left eye was swollen and she had a large bandage across her cheek. She thought about the various ways she was going to get revenge on Connor Shaw. She settled on flaying his skin from the left side of his face while he was still alive. It was a very appropriate payback. Rina swallowed more painkillers and focused on the police chatter.

She finally caught the report of a stolen car from a valet line five blocks from the restaurant. As she put the car in gear, she memorized the license plate. She connected to the experience world accessing the experience pod for the San Francisco highway workers. She placed the car's description and license plate in their minds. She waited for recognition when they accessed the camera feed. They were now driven by some subconscious interest to find the car. She knew that Connor and Alexis needed to take one of the highways out of San Francisco. She was sure they were heading back to Los Angeles. Before she left she needed confirmation. She slowly headed south, hoping to get confirmation of her hunch.

———

CHAPTER
37

Connor and Alexis sat facing each other on the edge of two well-worn double beds. They had checked into the cheapest hotel they could find, gave fake names and paid with cash. The greasy kid working the counter didn't flinch, as he had undoubtedly seen this routine many times before.

The room gave off a curious combination of smells from stale cigarette smoke to greasy food and cheap perfume. They both leaned forward to speak into the pay-as-you go phone they purchased on the road. They had Lucas on speakerphone.

Lucas replied, "Yes. I'm here." He paused. "Connor, what's happening? Are you both alright?"

"It's been a crazy and unbelievable few hours. We have been targeted by a group that is trying to kill us. The experience world feels like a noose tightening around our neck. I'm not sure how large and deep of a conspiracy but it is clearly fueled by our enemy we are battling."

Lucas already knew and replied "I know. Everybody, and I mean everybody, is out looking for you. The experience world traffic is unbelievable about the both of you. Each of you is literally the only thing on people's minds. I have no doubt that all of this clearly being manipulated by someone."

Connor felt that he needed to talk fast. He was scared and needed to make sure Lucas understood what had to be done. He hesitated before he spoke, not believing what he was about to say.

"Lucas, I now agree with you. The only way we are going to stop this, the only way we are going to eliminate the mind control of the experience world is to shut down the entire wireless network infrastructure."

Lucas paused for several moments before replying. Then laughed out loud, "I know that's the answer, but unfortunately it's not that easy to shut it all down."

Connor replied quickly "Lucas, listen to me. It can be done. We need a global shut down. We bring it all down, reset the systems and stop the experience world. It is the only way we can do this ." Connor realized that he was desperate. He wondered if the situation was reversed what would he do. He immediately knew the answer and pressed on "You can figure this out. We were both good hackers as kids. Actually, we were great hackers. Think of what we accomplished on sub-standard hardware and dial-up modems. This is a new world. I gave it up, but I know you still chase the dragon. You need to create and release a virus that shuts down the entire network."

"I know." Lucas replied as he nervously paced the room.

"Lucas, listen to me. This isn't one of Dad's bullshit movies when we are at the "all is lost moment" and the heroes have one last shot to save the day. This is real. People are getting killed and seriously injured by the network. This is a real problem that we must solve. We must use the network against itself. We need to shut it down." When his brother didn't respond, Connor grimaced hoping he hadn't pushed his brother too far. He flashed back to when they were kids and when Connor would push Lucas to break a code and get through security. Lucas was always the better code breaker. He had an unnatural ability to get around any electronic barrier and figure things out. The only problem is the last time Connor pushed him they had both gotten into massive trouble that had changed both of their lives.

Hoping to steer Lucas away from these unpleasant thoughts, Connor cut the call short "I will to call you at our treehouse tomorrow morning."

Lucas sighed loudly discouraged by everything that was going on. "Treehouse. Got it. I'm already working on it, just need to accelerate everything based on what you just told me. Alexis, I miss you. Be safe." Then he abruptly disconnected

"Thanks," Connor replied to a dead line, he put his head in his hands staring at the floor.

"Do you really think we have a chance? Can Lucas help us? Could it really work?" Alexis said dazed from the situation.

"Maybe, I'm not sure, but we have to try." Connor looked up to see Alexis sitting up in bed. As he stared at her, he started devising the code for the new virus. He knew it had to work ; their survival depended on it.

———

CHAPTER
38

BBC – "This is Roger Neale reporting from Delhi, India. As you can see from the scene behind me, India is in a state of chaos, since last week's mysterious events. The majority of the political leaders of India and Pakistani were rushed to the hospital in various states of neurological trauma. Since then the countries have devolved into a state of anarchy. Roving bands of militia roam the streets preying on the weak. Entire sections of cities are burning. All civil services have been halted. The global business centers have closed and all commerce has come to a standstill. The armies of India and Pakistan stand poised on the brink of war. Over the last several days, this lack of leadership has crippled the political process. Early reports coming in are that a large portion of the leaders were found in comas and were diagnosed with having major brain embolisms. The remaining victims seem to have all suffered some form of brain damage from their experiences earlier in the week. The reason for these events is still being investigated. Suffice it to say, that in the absence of information, people come to their own conclusions."

The screen switched to a group of Indian men being interviewed. "This is the work of the Pakistani people. They have exploited our trust. They seek to reclaim the Kashmir region. They want to kill our officials and then attack us while we are leaderless. We will no longer stand for these overt acts of war." The group then broke into a chant of death to Pakistan.

The screen returned to the reporter, who was now hurriedly moving away from a scene where armed men were attacking a car and the passengers. The camera returned to the reporter once he stepped into an alcove away from the violence.

"The region continues to destabilize. Earlier today, Iran announced that they are siding with the Pakistani government against any aggression from India. Iran promised to back the Muslim nation with the full force of their military."

The reporter looked off camera before continuing. "We're not sure how this will turn out. The violence is escalating and no one seems capable of leading and returning peace to the region. Roger Neale for the BBC in Delhi, India."

———

Connor and Alexis stood at one of the last remaining payphones outside a small convenience store in Salinas. They huddled close to a heavy plastic receiver while calling Hamlin. Earlier in the morning, they had stolen another car from a Santa Cruz gas station and were crisscrossing the state using back roads in an effort to buy some time to determine their next steps. They drove for five tense hours until they reached the outskirts of Salinas.

The roar of the traffic was deafening and they strained to hear Hamlin when he finally picked up the call in his office. "Hamlin, its Connor and Alexis." Connor shouted over the noise from the highway.

"Yes, where are you?" Hamlin asked

"We are between San Fran and LA but that's not important. What is happening?" asked Connor.

"It's all been a big mistake. I have spoken to multiple folks here at the NSA and they all acknowledge that it's a hoax perpetuated by the experience world. Come in and we can place you in protective custody until we figure this all out." Hamlin replied in a cheerful voice.

"It still seems out of control from our end out here." replied Connor

Hamlin cut in "Remember when we were at Pepperdine and we had that whole issue about the genome splicer. Do you remember how much we questioned the results because we couldn't believe this was happening? This whole situation is about the same magnitude of misinformation. Come in and we will protect you." Hamlin continued.

"Ok, understood. So happy to hear. We will come to your office" Connor replied robotically as he clicked off the connection.

Alexis stared at Connor not sure of what just happened.

"Hamlin and I were never at Pepperdine together and we never worked on a genome splicer. He was warning us to stay away. We should assume that something is wrong" Connor said apprehensively.

———

Hamlin slowly placed the receiver down on the phone cradle as Julie kept the pressure of the gun on the back of his neck.

"I did what you wanted" said Hamlin while looking forward "now what?"

Just at that moment, his office phone started ringing again, the display showing reception.

"Do you want me to answer it?" asked Hamlin.

Julie raised the gun and hit him squarely in the back of this head. A dull crack was heard as he fell forward on his desk.

"No, I don't think that's necessary," said Julie as she stepped around the back of the desk and opened the door.

She quietly exited his office and discreetly put her gun into her jacket. She put in her earpiece and connected to the pod as she headed for the exit.

When she opened the office door she was met by three NSA agents who quickly subdued her tying her hands behind her back. She was roughly pulled along the corridor to the service elevator and was taken to the fourth floor. She was seated in an office chair that faced a massive man standing against the wall. The agents stood behind Julie.

"I'm Ari Peck. We are going to search your person to make sure you have no weapons." Ari nodded to the first agent, who went through Julie's pockets in an efficient and practiced manner. He came up with a variety of items including her gun, but the most interesting of which was the small Dakarta phone.

Ari held up the earpiece. "So I can assume this is your connection to the experience pod where you receive your directives."

Julie sat stoically, not responding.

"I didn't expect for you to respond. Let me just confirm a few facts and then we can get you on your way." Ari picked up a folder that sat on a table under the windows. "Your real name is Himani Govil. You are twenty nine years old. You left your family at age fourteen to join the Indian army. You excelled at advanced weaponry and had a knack for resolving difficult situations. You eventually joined an elite female secret military unit that officially was commissioned to deal with anti-terrorism activities. In your undercover activities, you realized that there was more money and enjoyment in being a terrorist, as opposed to catching a terrorist. As a result, you left the service ten years ago and have been freelancing, if you will, since that time."

Ari closed the folder and looked directly at Himani. "You are charged with espionage, misuse of classified materials, assault, and conspiracy to murder, quite a list isn't it?" Ari looked at the agent. "Please read her rights on the way to the transport." The agents grabbed Himani's arm and guided her to the door.

Raising his hand, Ari spoke up pausing the procession leading the operative out of the room "Oh, sorry, one other item. You do realize that when we catch your employer, you, and you alone, is the reason he will be exposed." Ari rose and walked over to her, stepping close to Himani. Leaning in he continued in a disgusting tone "For your sake, I think a trial is preferable to your employer's response when it's disclosed you are the reason we brought down the bad guys."

Julie's eyes widened and she turned pale as she was pulled from the room.

CHAPTER
39

Lucas was anxious. He was dealing with a completely incomprehensible situation and once again his brother was late. As he sat back in the creaky old leather chair, he stared at the ceiling. Lucas looked through the leaded glass multi-paned window onto the well-manicured yard. He was at their parents' house in Beverly Hills. Growing up, Connor and Lucas nicknamed their father's study "the treehouse" because of the wood paneling that lined the walls. The phone sat on a dusty massive wooden desk, a relic of their father's legacy.

When Connor finally called, Lucas felt like he needed to unload "Connor, I have been sitting here all morning, waiting for you to call. What took you so long?"

"Sorry, it's been a little difficult to call when we're on the run from most of the people in California." Connor replied sarcastically lightening the mood with his twin.

Lucas laughed out loud "I'm sure. We have a major destabilization going on across the globe. Have you heard about the situation in India and Pakistan?" Lucas asked.

"Yes, we heard this morning. It sounds like everything is starting to unravel just as we thought. It is like one of Dad's movies, but unfortunately it's true." Connor replied recalling his father at the strangest of times.

Lucas quickly shared the news with his brother. "The media estimates nearly 700 politicians suffered mental breakdowns and all are now in a coma. Somehow only the senior members of the political parties were effected. The country is moving towards a state of chaos with martial law declared with military control of all functions to follow. Do you realize that the experience world caused all this? Can you believe it?"

"Lucas, listen, we need to focus. We have to move faster. If there were ever any doubts that this is a dangerous situation, they are all gone. Hamlin has been compromised. We are on our own. It's up to us now."

"I know. I experienced it, remember." replied Lucas soberly coming back to the task at hand. "I'm really scared, and even though I have an initial plan and idea, I'm unsure of our ability to really stop all of this."

Alexis broke in "Lucas, we are all terrified and we only have one option at this point. We have to stop the network effect. If we don't the entire world can be affected by the experience world. Don't give up."

Lucas was silent for several moments as he fought back that jabbing feeling in the pit of his stomach. As he began, his voice remained calm. "I figured it out. I will create a virus that attacks the phone operating systems directly, and resetting the phone, essentially making it unusable. It will require a tremendous amount of programming to do this, but since we are only dealing with one Operating System on the Dakarta phone and one specific chipset, it is actually possible to write this program. I decided to use the power of the network to defeat the network. I have started to delegate the work to a large group of hackers who support our cause."

Connor felt a tremendous amount of pride for his brother and his courage. "Will we be compromised by this programming group. Do you trust them?"

"No, I don't trust anyone so I parsed out the programing into such small elements that I don't think anyone will be able to truly understand what we are building. I will handle the final compiling. We should be fine." Lucas paused and then continued with deep concern in his voice. "I have to tell you both, though, you need to be very careful. The experience world is singularly focused on finding you across every pod. You are the only thought stream that is flowing across the experience pods. They know that we are trying to stop them. So don't worry about me, just stay safe and off the grid. Keep moving and call me back in a couple of hours. I will continue working on the solution."

Connor disconnected quickly. He grabbed Alexis lightly by the elbow and urged her toward the door. His every instinct urged him to move quickly and get out of the store. He felt the pressure that was building around him, like a storm about to break. As he exited the door, it was too quiet and calm. He sensed that a change was going to happen quickly and he needed to move now.

Connor and Alexis quickly jogged across the parking lot to the SUV that they had stolen earlier in the morning. It was a big Suburban and something about its size gave him comfort. They were both absorbed in their thoughts and didn't notice the two women who sat in the rented Ford with the engine idling immediately across from their truck.

As they got into the car, the Ford' s engine roared to life and the car shot across the parking lot directly at their car.

Alexis caught the movement out of the corner of her eye and was able to yell, "Watch out!" just as the car hit their SUV squarely on the driver's side door, crumpling the door and smashing the window. Shattered glass from the window rained down in the truck as Alexis and Connor's heads were snapped to the right as the impact pushed the large truck several feet sideways.

Connor's eyes were momentarily blurred and he shook his head to clear the impact. His mind was racing ahead faster than his body and it was screaming at him to act now. "Get out of here." His arm finally responded, he jammed the truck into reverse and nailed the accelerator. The big V-8 propelled the SUV into reverse and it shuddered out of the parking spot, its rear wheels smoking and spinning.

As Connor was accelerating in reverse, he glanced at the Ford and saw both Rina and Li in the car. Immediately recognizing both, he knew they were going to kill him and Alexis. Time slowed as Connor watched Li draw a gun and lean out the passenger window to get a clean shot. She smiled a knowing smile. Connor was operating on pure adrenaline and reacted immediately by pulling hard left on the steering wheel while still accelerating in reverse. The SUVs back end whipped around to face the Ford just as four quick shots hit the tailgate, riddling the car. Connor threw the vehicle into drive and accelerated across the parking lot, jumping over a sidewalk and bouncing the truck into the street.

Connor and Alexis held on as the truck veered onto a small service road that ran parallel to the highway. They were accelerating quickly and he barely noticed the side streets and other cars that he swerved around while trying to outrun the pursuing vehicle. Connor's mind was focused on getting away. As he looked ahead and saw the overpass an idea formed. Connor looked over to Alexis, who was desperately holding on to the door handle with white knuckled hands. Connor didn't slow down as he yelled to her over the roar of the car, "Get in the back seat and sit behind me. Put on your seatbelt and hold on. I know how we can lose them."

Connor glanced in the rearview mirror and saw the Ford closing rapidly. The rental car wasn't able to match the speed of the SUV. Connor finally saw his opportunity slamming on the brakes and making a hard left turn beneath the highway overpass. He leaned over and opened the glove box pulling the contents onto the now empty front seat.

"Alexis open up these papers and maps and unfold the newspaper in the back seat and pile them on the front seat." Alexis hesitated not sure why he was asking. Connor yelled loudly when she didn't act "Do it now!" Alexis responded piling several papers and maps on the front seat as the chase continued.

Once Connor had the diversion ready on the front seat, he slowed slightly to allow the Ford to catch up and attempt to accelerate past him on the inside lane. He waited until the Ford was alongside when he reached down and threw the pile of papers out of the passenger front window . The papers caused Rina to momentarily swerve to the right away from the SUV. Connor saw his chance swerving hard to the right at the same time. He slammed against the smaller car pushing it onto the sidewalk.

His plan worked, as Rina didn't notice the large concrete post for the overpass above. Her reaction was a moment too slow and instead of nailing the emergency brake, she turned hard to avoid the collision. She wrenched the wheel but she knew it was too late. The car was traveling too fast and it kept moving forward. The front right wheel of the Ford hit the small embankment which lifted the car off the ground. With the wheels off the road and no traction, the car hit the concrete wall at a severe angle. Its forward momentum caused it to slide and smash into the concrete pole at a high rate of speed. The entire right side of the car looked like a beer can wrapped around the pole.

Connor slowed and watched the crash in the rear view mirror and heard the sound of the car being demolished. He accelerated away from the scene, knowing the vehicle was destroyed and hoping he had stopped Rina and Li.

In the car, Rina's airbag opened upon impact, and as driver, she lost consciousness momentarily from the impact. Waking up seconds later, the silence was deafening. She slowly shook off the impact and tried to move her body. Blood was flowing into her eyes and she tasted the salty warm mixture in her mouth. Her neck was sore and she was vaguely aware of several teeth falling from her mouth. She slowly turned to her right to look at the limp form of Li. The top half of Li's head was missing, but the bottom half looked nearly perfect. It reminded her of a Barbie doll that had its head sawed off. Li had been whipped out of the window and her head had collided with the concrete pole. Rina's training took over. She stumbled quickly out of the car and began to move away from the accident. She took off her outer jacket and ducked down the first alley just as the police came around the corner. She walked slowly to regain her composure and found a water spigot along a wall. She ran the water and washed her face and mouth. She stood up, spit out the blood and a few more teeth, and began slowly limping away. Her head and neck were throbbing with pain. She began to feel lightheaded. Automatically and without thinking she slipped on her earpiece to connect to the experience pod. As she joined the Experience World, her thoughts swirled around her like thousands of angry bees. She told herself the battle was now personal and she was going to make Connor and Alexis pay for this. As she made her way down the alley considering her revenge, she even managed a smile.

CHAPTER
40

CNN – Today China is under a shroud of secrecy as nearly all forms of communications with the country have ceased. The borders are closed, the airports, train and bus stations are all under military guard. There is no official statement from the government. The mystery follows a series of reports earlier today that people were becoming afflicted with a strange ailment that caused immediate unconsciousness while they were conducting their normal daily activities. This "sleep" flu as it was labeled was quickly followed by a large gathering at Tiananmen Square. Prior to the communications shutdown, the protesters were calling for greater freedoms from their government, many echoing the dissatisfaction in the early 1990s. We were seeing a tremendous numbers of people flocking to the cities immediately before we lost all communications. We will keep our viewers informed with any developments.

———

Ravi blinked several times as the light momentarily blinded him. His vision returned slowly and he realized that he was looking at a light fixture against white ceiling tiles. He slowly turned his head to look around the room. He was lying in a hospital bed. Turning his head to the right he saw various monitors and feeding tubes. He closed his eyes and tried to remember how he ended up in the hospital bed. He heard the door open and opened his eyes.

An older doctor and two nurses entered the room. They looked at the bed and immediately smiled as Ravi's eyes were open.

They flanked the bed as the doctor grasped Ravi's hand. Ravi croaked as he tried to answer.

"Ravi, how do you feel?" the doctor with the deep brown eyes asked.

"Not sure" Ravi replied almost in a whisper "Doctor, I don't remember anything."

The doctor's smile didn't waver, he patted his hand gently. "It's alright, it takes a while to adjust to coming out of a coma. You don't need to talk. Just take it easy and relax."

Ravi panicked and attempted to sit up "Doctor, what are you talking about? I don't remember how I got here. What am I doing here?"

The doctor looked into Ravi's eyes for a moment. He looked over to the nurse "Nurse, please provide the patient with 120mg of Valium. He needs to rest and relax. He is clearly distressed by emerging from his coma." The nurse nodded and left the room.

The doctor looked back to Ravi and spoke slowly "If you can understand me, you have suffered a massive brain embolism that caused you to enter a coma. You have awakened and will need to continue our treatment until your body returns to normal. The nurses will administer your medication and care for you. You must relax and let your body and mind heal. I will be back to check on you later." The doctor patted his hand before leaving the room.

The other nurse returned with medication. With the doctor gone, the nurses' demeanor changed. The nurses moved to opposite sides of the bed and began to prepare Ravi. The younger nurse asked the older nurse speaking Hindi "Is this really Ravi? His company employs most of my family"

The older nurse replied mechanically "Yes, it is. Unfortunately, he will never be the same. I've never seen such a bad case. If you look into his eyes you can almost convince yourself he knows what's going on, but it's all an illusion. They are never the same. Doctors always take the positive side of things. If you ask me its better when they stay in a coma, since it's easier to care for them"

"What are you talking about?" Ravi shouted which caused the nurses to jump back from bed. "I can understand everything you are saying and I'm feeling better. How dare you talk about me like that. I will have your family fired, do you hear me. " He realized that his words didn't come out as he wanted. He heard a guttural growl and almost doglike bark in their place.

The older nurse shook her head at Ravi and looked back to the younger nurse "These are the worse cases, the ones that get all belligerent and mean. We will have to watch this one and not forget to use the straps. We don't want anyone getting hurt." She roughly rolled Ravi on his side.

Ravi had a vision of the rest of his life, trapped inside his body, unable to communicate with the world, alone with his thoughts.

CHAPTER
41

Connor and Alexis sat in the back parking lot of a McDonald's just off the 5 north of Bakersfield. They both used a new prepaid phone as they spoke with Lucas.

Lucas spoke quickly and excitedly "We have made much progress in a short amount of time. I have developed a conceptual model that could theoretically disable the entire global connected wireless network. It would cover all geographies and networks. It's so dramatically simple, that I'm surprised it hasn't been done before. To be honest I'm becoming more convinced it will work. In the end, it's a very elegant, very simple, and very powerful program."

Connor urged him to continue. "So, what does it do?"

"It does two things. First it disables every phone that is powered on and connected to the network by targeting and destroying the specific chipset within each phone. There is software that is resident within each chipset that we can target and rewrite. So, if phase one works right, every phone connected to the network will be fried in a couple of seconds. But, it gets even better, before it destroys the chipset this little devil sets a program on the actual phone operating system that essentially runs every time a new chipset is installed. None of these phones will ever work again. Bada-Boom, Bada-Bing."

Lucas was on a roll and the old thrill of power and danger was returning when he described Phase Two, "As cool as that is, it is only the beginning, Phase two will commence and attack the network itself. Admittedly, this is trickier, but I am confident I can design a worm that resets the entire network by randomly attacking different domain name and experience servers. However, I'm not sure of the specific security protocol that will be enabled. My goal is to reset all networks by changing one digit in every single network address while also eliminating any record of the original addresses. It will take a while for everyone to figure out what had happened. In the end everything will have be to be reprogrammed and redirected. Since the address reset is entirely random, it will be impossible for the programs to be automatically reprogrammed since each will need someone to decipher the changes." Lucas finished.

"Sounds great," replied a smiling Connor amazed by his brother, "so what are the next steps?"

"Well, first this program needs to be completed and then compiled. Second we need to release this program inside a major telecommunication switching station. According to my research, it is difficult to get access to the network controls outside one of these hubs. However, if someone is physically inside the switching station, it will only take a matter of minutes to overwhelm the internal security and plant this bad boy on the inside."

"So, how long to finish the code?" asked Connor

"Twelve hours tops" replied Lucas "guaranteed. I have a bunch of hackers already plowing through the modular design and modular code."

"Really, only half a day? Seems quick. Do it. We'll call you back later to check-in," replied Connor as he disconnected.

"Do you believe that he can get it done and that no one will know about it?" asked Alexis

"No, I think he is underestimating the power of the experience world and their ability to keep information confidential. But it's the only chance we have. You know, Lucas has always been there for me and he hasn't let me down. I have faith in him." As he spoke Connor hoped he wouldn't regret his words.

Rina sat on a park bench in one of the many small parks in the downtown Los Angeles near Olympic Boulevard. She had just connected to the experience pod and stood in the same nondescript white room. Within moments, a figure materialized across the room.

He was wearing an immaculately tailored three-piece suit. He walked up to Rina as the thought streams began to flow.

<You are the only one left. The others are gone. <violence, aggression> we need to finish this and we are so close. We will stop Connor and Alexis. We will not let them hinder our plans and results. I know where Connor and Alexis are going. Join me and we will finish this together. Look up.>

Rina disconnected and walked to the street as a black Town Car pulled up. The driver opened the door for Rina and she saw Tarun sitting inside smiling warmly and holding his earpiece in his hand.

"We don't have far to go," he said as he motioned for her to get into the car.

The driver closed the door as the car headed south back toward downtown.

Experience Pod 556.78.112
My life in the kitchen

The group of restaurant owners convened their mind's eye experience pod in their minds eye at the iconic French Laundry in Napa. Each sat at tables and chairs that formed a loose circle. The members existed elsewhere but their thought avatars sat looking at each other in this virtual world.

I heard that Josie Jenkins sold her interest in Mastros yesterday. Who was the buyer? Yeah we heard that too. They sold to Levy Restaurants. (images of Levy restaurants flow through the experience pod, Chicago, Las Vegas) Did anyone ever visit Tru in Chicago? (images of dark rooms, sushi and dark leather chairs) Trotter once called Tru "a false restaurant if he ever saw one" Trotter is a purist – but what a chef – (images of kitchen table seating, several bottles of wine poured, chefs working on worktables) I loved his kitchen. One of the best workspaces in the restaurant industry. I heard that the family that was killed in California visited Tru the week before they were killed. Killers are still running free – just buried the family today. Why can't we catch them –(images of Alexis and Connor flood the experience pod) Anger emotions, red, have we seen these people – they should be dealt with swiftly.

The midwest.workingmoms.lmi experience pod convened each member's mind's eye in a Lincoln Park setting on a beautiful summer morning. The women all sat on blankets that were laid across the grass on a small grassy hill. The view of the lake was expansive. *>I am still amazed that the killers are still running free – just buried the family today. Why can't we catch them –(images of Alexis and Connor flood the experience pod) Anger emotions, red, have we seen these people – they should be dealt with swiftly.>*

The thought flows swarmed through the network, at each experience pod, the theme was always the same. Connor and Alexis must be stopped.

CHAPTER
42

Connor and Alexis sat in another roadside parking lot. Over the last several hours, they had kept moving via back roads. They were trying to avoid detection by staying off the grid and network.

Another prepaid phone sat between them as they listened to Lucas on speakerphone

"So does it work?" asked Alexis.

"Of course. Works as advertised. You just need to get it installed on a network and it will deliver the goods. This scary little program will bring everything down. I have dubbed thee, Apocalyptic" replied Lucas in a dramatic voice with a bad British accent. "I guess the only issue is that we need to seed the entire network with some idea or concept that will connect the most phones and users connected. I took a little poetic license and creatively weaved into our virus something I call a "thought conversation starter" that we believe everyone will notice. It should create enough distraction and interest to keep people busy while the virus does its work."

"What thought starter did you embed in the program?" asked Connor.

"Well, we let it out that Steve Jobs was found alive in Florida and was going to hold a press conference later in the day in the Experience world. He planned to share with everyone his reasons for disappearing for so long. We targeted our seeding with multiple groups at once, therefore exploiting the network effect" Lucas replied with a chuckle.

In spite of all the stress and danger, Connor and Alexis laughed uncontrollably for several moments. "You have to be kidding me, Steve Jobs was your answer to distracting everyone connected to the Experience world as the virus is launched. Amazing, absolutely brilliant."

"So, where do we need to go to plant the virus?" replied Alexis

"Downtown LA. Sixth and Wilshire." replied Lucas as he turned to access his computer. "I have sent you a text message with the address of the AT&T switching station. I have also sent the files containing the virus to your personal email address. You will need to download the file onto the computer so that you can run it locally. It's a fairly straightforward executable. The key is that you need to make sure you are on a computer that is physically inside the network firewall. If you are inside, the program will do the rest."

"Got it," Connor replied. "I am more concerned about how we get into the facility. Any help?"

Lucas replied, "We're working on it. Its apparently next to impossible to get in. Call back in 30 minutes."

———

The dark red Peterbuilt sat idling in the rear parking lot of the small diner parking lot. Benny Young leaned forward over his steering wheel to get a good angle to clearly see the two murderers. He was still jacked-in to the experience pod, and thoughts filled his head from other truckers and participants. He absently fingered the chrome .45 that sat in his lap. He originally bought the gun for just this type of situation. He always knew he was destined for something great and now he had his chance to bring down the murderers. He was lost in the experience world and was getting instruction on how to eliminate Alexis and Connor. He felt more alive and capable than he could remember. He floated in the experience world buoyed by the expectant and supportive thoughts that surrounded him.

Benny Young got out his truck and robotically walked towards the SUV. The chrome gun in his right hand reflected the sun as he raised his arm to a firing position.

Connor saw movement in his rear view mirror and screamed "Watch out," as he pulled Alexis to the floor.

A gunshot hit the back of the truck. Connor braved a look and saw the large trucker slowly walking toward them, his arm outstretched, firing a gun in an almost rhythmic way. Two more quick shots sounded as he closed the distance between them.

Staying low, Connor started the SUV and peeked cautiously over the dashboard. He threw the truck into reverse nailing the accelerator as they shot across lot. They rocketed out onto the street just as the man fired the final shot which shattered the front window. Connor sat up, shifted into drive accelerated for the highway.

Just as Connor began to relax, he saw movement from his left. An impossibly large white eighteen wheeler came plummeting across the median and aiming directly for their car. Connor pressed the accelerator and swerved onto the shoulder just as the truck missed their rear fender. The white truck careened off the road and plowed into a parking lot, throwing cars in the air as it ground to a stop.

Connor swerved back onto the road and looked ahead to an upcoming bridge. Three trucks formed a roadblock with three truckers standing in front of their vehicles simultaneously raising various rifles and handguns. Connor pulled the wheel hard to the left and shot across the oncoming traffic and down a side street just as the bullets hit the rear quarter panel. Connor accelerated and drove without regard. Several cars shot out across the intersections and barely missed his truck. He continued to accelerate as it was their only hope to get away. It looked like some unseen hand was throwing vehicles at them trying to stop their car.

He prayed that no one would come out on the street. Just as the thought entered his mind, three women ran into the intersection ahead. As they began to run toward his car at a full sprint, they fanned out to cover the entire road. He couldn't believe his eyes. They were sacrificing themselves as human shields to stop the car. He remembered his defensive driving course and drove directly at the woman on the far right. She was wearing shorts and a loose fitting floral print shirt, and looked winded as she continued to run at the car. He memorized every detail as he closed the distance in seconds. At the last possible moment, he swerved to the left, his right rear fender clipped the woman and sent her sprawling into the street. The other two women didn't pause but turned continuing their pursuit. The woman who he had glanced, rolled to a stop on the pavement and slowly began to pull herself in the direction of the car. He couldn't believe what he was seeing, as she was dragging her broken leg behind her continuing the pursuit. It was like everyone had become a puppet of some unseen hand in a pursuit to the death. Returning to the moment, he swerved across the front lawn of three houses and quickly wrenched the steering wheel back to the right and bounced back on the road.

He kept glancing at the GPS to find the on-ramp. He finally found the entrance ramp heading north, but just as he got on the highway, four more eighteen wheelers and several cars came careening northbound across the center median aiming for their car. It reminded him of a school of darting fish moving toward their prey.

"This is crazy. How do they know where we are?" Connor yelled to Alexis as he sped up hoping to get in front of the trucks and vehicles heading across the highway.

He passed the first and second truck, barely missed a collision with the third truck when we saw the fourth and the cars change their trajectory. They were learning as they employed the same fan formation the women had perfected in the street. They were coming right at him. Without thinking, he pulled the parking brake and threw the car to the left. The eighteen-wheeler tried to correct its angle with a quick turn. Connor and Alexis watched as the truck's weight shifted and its tires left the ground. It jackknifed quickly and slid across the remaining lanes of traffic taking out the other cars. The final car hit a large depression in the median and flipped on its roof.

Connor fought to steady their SUV and glanced at his dashboard at the GPS trying to figure out his next move when it hit him. He was staring right at it. He grabbed the GPS and threw it out the window and accelerated off the next ramp.

Coming off the ramp, Connor didn't slow heading directly across the street and went into a parking garage, smashing through the entry gate. He hit the brakes, wrenched the car into the first open spot and killed the engine.

Connor turned to Alexis. "Are you alright? We need to Get out of here now."

Alexis was visibly shaken and tears were running down her cheeks. She looked like she was close to becoming unhinged.

"Alexis. Come on. We have to move. We are getting close and they have the entire network going after us. They were tracking us with the GPS," said Connor, breathless and flushed. "Are you okay? Just try to relax and breathe deeply. We'll get out of this."

"Connor," Alexis replied, "I don't know if I can do this. They all wanted to kill us. Trucks barreling down at us, people running at us, people shooting at us. We hit that lady. Did you see that? She flipped into the air, landed on the pavement and then kept coming after us. This is madness. They were connected to the experience pod and were trying to kill us. Do you understand?"

"Of course. I know, I know," Connor replied. "I want to stop, I want to run and hide, to put this all behind us. The problem is, we can't. The only option is to see this through. We have to move now."

Connor got out and swiftly moved out of the garage. Alexis shuffled behind him trying to cope with what had just happened while suppressing the urge to scream with panic and fear.

CHAPTER

43

"You have to be kidding me?" replied Connor. Connor and Alexis sat in the back of a ride share car headed to downtown LA. Lucas had sent a friend to pick them up and get them to the switching station.

"Nope. You are going to need to talk your way into the facility," Lucas replied completely seriously.

"No way is this going to work. Do you have any idea what we have been going through. People are crazed and trying to kill us. Every single person who is connected to the network is being controlled and is trying to stop us. No way. It's impossible. No one is going to let us into a secured facility and then have access to their computers. How are we supposed to walk right in? They will recognize us. The entire experience network has been engaged and aligned to kill us." Connor rubbed his hand through his hair.

Lucas continued calmly, almost like he was talking from another time and place, "We will help you to fight the network effect. I have a few additional things up my sleeve that should be able to cause a diversion. We will create a fairly large distraction long enough for you to get in and plant the virus. A few minutes more and it will all be over. You need to get there quickly. Don't stop, don't give up. I got your back bro."

Connor couldn't believe he was agreeing and was surprised as he spoke the words "Ok. Will let you know when we get there,"

Connor disconnected from the call knowing it was the only option they had left.

————

Lucas sat in the Starbucks' in Brentwood. He took a long swig from his cappuccino and then logged into the experience pod. He was running hybrid with both the earpiece and his computer connection. This allowed him to multi-task and manage the multiple experience groups he was surfing. He was still feeling great, knowing that it was all about to go away. "Oh well" he said aloud "It was fun while it lasted."

He started a program that he composed when he first started in the experience world. The program allowed him to simultaneously connect to several dozen currently active experience pods. He affectionately called the program "1984" for its Orwellian implications. He was about to declare war on the system. The experience world, which was based on the concept of collaboration and sharing, was actually going to have a massive, no holds barred fight against itself. He started humming an old John Cougar tune.

His goal was simple. He was going to rally the experience world to launch an offensive against the network and cause it to pause and be confused. The familiar tingle across his scalp was much stronger today as he quickly connected to all of the experience groups that he identified as anarchists and libertarians.

In his mind's eye, he stood on a raised platform, as far as he could see members of the experience pods stood waiting. They were silent and still, anticipation and energy literally hung in the air, as they waited for him. His thought stream began to swirl out from him and weave through the crowd.

<Ladies and Gentlemen. I am Lucas. Thank you for joining me here today. I have interrupted your normally scheduled activities to enlist your assistance. We are faced with an incredible threat that undermines the core of our beliefs. We have been working in a world where we thought freedom and openness were the rule. We have been operating in a world where we could control and create a new world where the only limit is our imagination. Unfortunately, I have learned and confirmed that Tribe has sold us out. <Surprise moves like a sound wave across the group as the power of the group creates a visible shudder across the experience world the power of the connected group is immense> That's right - Tribe, our noble benefactor and provider of our world, has been secretly observing and in many cases influencing our thought streams. While we thought we were fighting the establishment, we were actually building it up. I can't tell you how many times this has happened, but I can assure you that it has happened consistently. We have become the cogs of the system that we have sworn to oppose. We have been played the fools<another massive wave of energy flows across the group><tremendous rush of emotions, anger, visions of action, visions of treachery> Everyone, we need to be purposeful in our response. We need to move quickly. We need to take back what is ours. We need to combine our strength; we need to break down the foundation that has deceived us.>

The crowd had swelled and the power of millions of people all connected together. Lucas felt waves of emotion flow over him, powerful, raw, and primitive. He felt his own power increase. He felt invincible. The group was responding and supporting him, driving him forward.

<Everyone here is critical. Each of you can control our destiny. Together we are the most powerful force in this universe. Now, I need you to work with me, to join me and to execute our plan of attack. We are in a war we didn't create, a fight we didn't pick, but we will be victorious. We will succeed and fight for everything that we stand for: our core beliefs of freedom from oppression and censorship, freedom to communicate, freedom to think and freedom to believe. We will create a tidal wave to take down the system, a tidal wave that will break down the foundation of Tribe. Our retaliation will be swift and concerted. It will break the authority of Tribe and will teach them not to challenge freedom and choice <swell of pride, ebullition, tremendous waves of power flowing and throbbing across the group> Now, about the thought we will deliver...>

Lucas sat back and watched the network traffic both spike and focus its thoughts and approach. He disconnected from the thought stream and using some old fashioned hacking entered the experience world naming service application. He hesitated only a moment before running his executable. The program asked him if "Enter start time for Apocalyptic?" He entered 4:06pm, exactly 30 minutes from now.

CHAPTER
44

Adam disconnected from his experience world console and felt like a tremendous weight was lifted from his being. He just finished implementing his plan in the financial services experience pod. He had planted the final thoughts across the entire experience world. He was sure his plan would work as planned.

Tess buzzed to tell him that the investor group had arrived and were gathering in the boardroom. Adam walked to the front of the room and turned to face the group of bankers and lawyers. "So, as you can see from our video overview, we have unprecedented growth, profitable operations, and some of the best looking people in the business." Everyone in the room chuckled and smiled to each other.

"Any overview of our company, however would be incomplete without an actual test drive of our experience world." Two attractive young women came from the back of the room and began distributing small plastic bags at the end of each row. "We are passing out preconfigured earpieces that will allow everyone to connect to the Tribe experience world. You will all be connecting to our financial services experience pod world. I have configured your earpieces to connect to the venture capital pod."

The group began inserting their earpieces, sounds in the room began to subside as people connected to the experience pod. Adam stood in the front of the room and once everyone was connected, he pulled out his own earpiece and jumped into the experience pod.

They all found themselves standing on the floor of the New York Stock Exchange. It was empty looking abandoned at the end of the trading day. The silence was disconcerting and caused many of the group to look confused and slightly nervous. Adam materialized at the front of the group, looking more handsome and striking than in the real world. The light in the space changed and warmed and immediately set everyone at ease.

Ladies and gentlemen, Adam here. Everything is acceptable I trust. You are now in the experience world. We have pre-configured this mind's eye space to a location that most of you should recognize.

He was greeted by a familiar flow of thoughts. He had hand-picked this pod and invited several well-known venture companies to the pod shortly before he connected to the investment group. He had also planted several thoughts earlier in the pod. These would be remembered when he started his presentation. He expected his goal would be achieved. He had also seeded a member of the finance team that would provide random positive comments about Tribe. His thoughts would be secondary and act more on the sub-conscious level.

This is amazing. I can't believe it – everything we heard is true – it's possible – amazing <vision of Cape Cod in the summer, boats and fishing and golf>I love Cape Cod – How many people have been to the Cape. Flurry of thoughts around Cape Cod. Memories flood in -<different times, events, kids swimming>I heard Steve Jobs is alive. <momentary confusion> He is going to make an announcement later today. Jobs is alive. I knew it. [Adam realized that someone else had infiltrated the group and was monopolizing the conversation. He attempted to take control] <snippets of Jobs

talking, presenting in front of the group> <emotions increasing, people are astounded><image of a slightly overweight man in black sweat suit appears> it's unmistakably Jobs. Amazing. I can't believe it. <Everyone getting excited about the possibility – begin to get caught up in the emotional wave>[Adam attempts to take control one more time. It's running out of control – he is shaken by someone and he breaks out from the experience world

Adam focused his eyes and looked over at John Riebold, his Chief Technology Officer, shaking his arm.

"Mr. MacArthur, we have a major problem. The network is starting to see unprecedented levels of use. Something is happening, something really big. If this continues, we are in danger of spiking the system. We need to respond."

Adam looked around the room and sees all of the participants lost in the experience pod. He hesitated, not sure of what to do, his options are limited.

He turned back to his CTO. "Don't do anything. I am confident our system will handle it. Do something to make sure we don't go down."

"But Adam, we are at risk."

"Didn't you fucking hear me?" Adam screamed. "Go back to your little cave and make sure the fucking system stays up. If it doesn't, you and your entire team will be fired today."

John quickly turned and scuttled to the door. Adam returned to the room as one of the bankers stood up abruptly and ripped the earpiece away.

"Something is wrong. People are out of control in there. You need to do something. It is getting scary." The man leaned down and shook the man next to him and reached to take out his earpiece. At almost the same moment, a woman sitting in the front row fell forward. Her head hit the desk with a loud thud. Several people began babbling and moaning, as others violently disconnected from the experience world. Adam turned and quickly moved out of the room.

He was greeted by panic in the halls. Several people sprinted through the hallways, heading for some other area of the office. Adam moved for the elevator intent on getting back to his office. As he moved he heard voices yelling across the open offices. "Dude, it's like we are under attack" and "Amazing how quickly the network traffic is surging" echoed off the walls. He stepped into the elevator and desperately pounded the close button door. The doors finally closed and returned the elevator to silence. He stared as the floor numbers quickly rolled up. But then he smiled, surprising himself, because he knew what was happening and he welcomed it. He wanted out. In that moment of pure clarity he realized what he had become, how we had been compromised and controlled. He had lost part of himself and now he realized that he welcomed the end of his nightmare.

CHAPTER
45

Dusk was falling over downtown Los Angeles. Connor and Alexis were dropped off unceremoniously in front of a non-descript building with no windows. As they neared the visible glass entry door, they could see the guard sitting confidently behind the main desk.

Connor turned to Alexis. "So it comes to this. We only need to get by one security guard and we are in the facility. Are you ready?"

As they opened the door, the guard looked up from his desk and studied Connor and Alexis. A flash of recognition passed across his face, but then was gone and he returned to his stoic stare. He mechanically moved his head to the left and looked at a small lobby seating area. Two people sat in the leather chairs awaiting their arrival.

The man was impeccably dressed in a suit and the woman was wearing a black jogging suit. Both stood and moved to greet Connor and Alexis. Connor's heart dropped as he recognized Rina and Tarun Patel. In a fraction of a second, it all made sense. The man behind all of this wasn't Adam MacArthur or someone in India; it was Tarun Patel. Connor looked quickly at the door planning to make a run for it.

The man reached out his hand as he crossed the small lobby. "Mr. Shaw and Ms. Mack, please don't attempt to leave. I have people outside who will cut you down where you walk. You will be much better off if you listen to me and follow directions." Tarun chuckled before continuing. "I have to admit, it is nice to finally get together. You have caused me considerable headaches and problems. I am Tarun Patel and I believe you already know my assistant Rina." Rina's face was a bloody mess and her left eye was swollen shut.

Connor and Alexis stood motionless and speechless.

"I am sure you have many questions. Please be so kind to join me to discuss this situation in a most civilized manner." Tarun motioned to a well-appointed conference room off the main lobby. Connor realized that this location was a setup. They had convinced Lucas that this was the proper location of the switching station and instead it was the den of the man controlling it all.

Connor's stomach dropped and he hesitated, "We're not going anywhere with you."

Tarun chuckled. "Mr. Shaw, my offer wasn't an invitation. Please join me or I will allow Rina to kill you right here."

Rina pulled out a handgun, which she was now pointing at Connor and Alexis. She smiled a broken smile, teasing them to test her. She motioned for them to start moving. They had no other choice then to enter the conference room.

———

At 4:06pm PST the program installer began working. It took three milliseconds to release the worlds most advanced and lethal computer virus ever created. Lucas recognized that redundancy is the key to success in programming. He and Connor would release the virus at the same time. It wouldn't hurt he thought if one didn't work.

The virus spread from the Tribe data center quickly and without notice. The virus, by its very design, exponentially replicated itself and spread across the telecommunications carrier wireless network. Unlike many previous viruses, it wasn't limited to a specific application or system deficiency. It was designed to be the first truly symbiotic program, taking on attributes of its host in order to replicate, and then quickly turning parasitic to destroy the host after it had infected the system.

The worm rode along with other programs, appearing as a complementary application or system extension, never damaging the carrier program, until it had been dispersed across the entire network. Once dispersed it was poised to destroy the network and chipset of all related and distributed communication hardware, including phones, tablets, and computers. The first aspect of the virus program worked flawlessly as it quickly infected the individual devices. It spread quickly across a wide geographical area, three states quickly became ten and then tripled to thirty as it kept growing.

The virus completely penetrated North America, infecting the network and infiltrating every connected wireless phone and device. The momentum of the virus increased as it jumped carriers and country borders. Canada and the United Kingdom were the first countries outside of North America to replicate the virus. With three major countries infected, the virus, moving like wildfire, spread quickly throughout the rest of the world.

Once the virus replicated itself across the global network, it executed its first command. It began to fry the chipset in every individual device. The program both overloaded the chipset processing and shut off any temperature control fail safes. This combination caused each chip to overheat. Devices simply stopped working and users were immediately disconnected from the network and the experience world

Within moments after the devices were disabled, the second phase started. It attacked the specific physical networks. The network failed in central California as the virus attacked and began erasing wireless network routing and directory applications. In quick succession three additional wireless networks went down across the state. The entire states of Oregon and Washington followed immediately thereafter. The dominoes of the wireless networks fell as the remainder of North America networks went down in a matter of minutes.

Within twenty two minutes of the release of the virus, the wireless carriers identified the cause of the network failures and determined it was a well-concealed virus. The broadband network and communications companies moved quickly to save their networks realizing they were facing a massive network failure. As designed and expected, the wireless carriers' system administrators implemented their disaster recovery processes and began to take networks off-line to run their standard network diagnostic and virus scan programs. They were attempting to quarantine the virus and destroy it before it could do any more harm. Unfortunately for the system administrators, the virus had already completely infected the networks and, more importantly, the virus was designed to anticipate their response. Adam's painstaking research knew each wireless carrier's disaster recovery program. The information, now publicly available through the beauty of new corporate disclosure laws, was relatively easy to access and download as well as design a response that avoided and exploited the recovery process.

Once the network diagnostics were started, the first component of the virus was identified and eliminated. The sacrificial lamb was given up to trick the system administrators into believing they had found and eliminated the virus. Since the primary threat was eliminated, the administrators followed their usual routine and restarted their standard network diagnostics to identify and repair any damage. Unknown to any of these technical managers was the second component of the virus. It lay hidden, waiting to attack the overall network management applications after the diagnostics were completed. This part of the program, disguised as a network utility, followed in the wake of the diagnostic software, neatly resetting the network configurations and overwriting data and programs. As the network management utilities ran, the virus efficiently began to eliminate the network infrastructure and backbone management programs. The virus attacked in its second phase and was discovered in a matter of minutes as the networks continued to fail. The wireless carrier administrators had no other option than to bring down each of the networks and restart them in manual control mode. This would allow them to bring application components on-line individually in an attempt to isolate the virus location.

The final and most elegant component of the virus, which became legend in the hacker community for years, was designed for this contingency. Once the networks were brought down and restarted, the virus attacked at the machine code level. Upon restart, the virus rewrote chipsets, memory, and caused complete failure of all applications, hardware, and networks. The administrators could do nothing to save the system other than completely cutting power. Unfortunately, the ability to cut power was the most protected and controlled aspect of their systems. There was no simple way to bring an entire data center down. As a result, the wireless carriers were forced to sit and watch in horror as a little program destroyed everything.

———

"Would you like a coffee or tea?" Tarun asked Connor and Alexis as they sat in the expansive conference room.

The surreal situation was not lost on either of them as Rina sat next to them holding the handgun. Her disfigured face was malevolent. She was ready to pounce and inflict considerable harm for her injuries.

"No," Connor replied.

Tarun removed his jacket and hung it in a concealed closet. He moved effortlessly and sat down across from them with a practiced air. Crossing his leg and tightening the crease in his pants, he sipped coffee before speaking.

"Please put in your earpieces. We are going to go for a little walk in the experience world" Tarun held up his earpiece and showed it to both of them to reinforce the point.

"No" is all Connor said, Rina moved with lightning quick reflexes and hit him with the gun across his right cheek. He fell to the floor as blood flowed from a gash in his face.

"Put in your earpieces, or I will allow her to beat you to death. You really have no choice. Get it?" Tarun said cheerfully, winking and smiling a devilish grin.

Connor pulled himself back onto the chair and for an instant, considered rushing Rina. Rina noticed the slight change in his demeanor, and almost as if she was reading his mind, raised her gun slightly and shook her head slowly.

"Are you alright?" Alexis whispered as she helped Connor back into the chair. She was genuinely concerned as she considered that they were not going to make it out of this situation alive.

"I'm fine. I think we need to do what they say. I'm sorry for everything." That was all that Connor could muster. He grabbed Alexis' hand and gave it a strong squeeze. "Let's do this together." They both put their earpieces in with their free hand and felt the familiar tingle across their scalp. Tarun sat down behind his desk, and put in his own earpiece.

Connor and Alexis were greeted with a flurry of images and emotions as they connected to the experience world. This was the most visceral and powerful experience they had ever met, and they were unable to switch between their minds eye and the actual physical world. They were locked into Tarun's experience pod. They felt the power and knew immediately that the center and source of the entire experience world was funneling through this room and Tarun. They finally found themselves in a rural, pastoral setting. It looked like a European countryside. Connor and Alexis were still holding hands and as Tarun and Rina dissolved in front of them.

Alexis directed her thoughts at Connor "Your face is back to normal." Connor reached up in the experience world and touched his cheek which did not have the large gash.

Tarun observed this exchange. "We can't have that, tsk, tsk." He waved his finger at Connor in a downward stroke and a large bloody gash appeared in his cheek. "That's better" Tarun's thoughts replied. "Come join me for walk. I would like to take you to some of my special places." Tarun motioned to begin walking.

Connor and Alexis turned and their hearts dropped. Directly behind them stood an iron gate leading to a cobblestone street with old brick buildings on one side and an open field on the other. There were three words on the top of the gate. *ARBEIT MACHT FREI.* Both Connor and Alexis knew they were in an Auschwitz experience world. As they walked toward the gate, people began to appear onto both sides of the path. All the figures were clothed in dark grey tunics and stood completely motionless. They stared at Connor and Alexis with visible hatred and their thought streams swirled around each with red, violent, and dangerous thoughts. The pressure began to build as the number of people appearing increased. Soon the path was a narrow space between the grey tunics as far as they could see.

Connor and Alexis' thoughts swirled with concern and fear, they could hardly contain their trepidation and terror.

Tarun's thoughts came fast and forcefully. "You do not truly understand my power. This is but a sample of what I can do. If I chose, I could have these people attack your consciousness and rip apart every shred of your psyche. You would literally go mad as they tear away your mind, piece by piece."

Connor saw that Alexis was close to collapsing and pushed his thoughts hard at her. "It's okay, please relax." Connor stopped and turned toward Tarun and forced his fears back to challenge him. "So why did you bring us here?"

Tarun stopped and smiled. The grey tunics blinked out of existence and the scene changed as well. They were now standing in an ancient laboratory. The old wooden floor was buckled and irregular and there was a constant rattling of the windows facing the Boston Bay. Strong winds buffeted the glass as if they were trying to shake the panes free from their wooden frames. The howling wind looked like the harbinger of an imminent storm. Connor turned and looked out the window at the Bay frothed as the cold winds drew the water into a white frenzy. The icy water spilled onto the piers and sidewalks coating everything in a cold wet blanket.

Tarun spread his arms and smiled again. "Welcome to one of my favorite places. This is Alexander Graham Bell's laboratory, the birthplace of modern technology. As you most surely know Alexander Graham Bell and Tom Watson invented the harmonic telegraph on March 10, 1876. A year later, Graham and two investors formed the Bell Telephone Company, and the first commercial applications of the harmonic telegraph were quickly developed. Their invention and company created the foundation for the global telephone and the telecommunications industry. Their discovery went on to become one of the most important inventions of all time, leading the world into a new era of communication and economic growth. The harmonic telegraph simply changed the entire world forever. I walk in the shadows of my forefathers, and like Bell and Watson, I am poised to change the world as well." Tarun pulled up an old wooden stool and sat, motioning for Alexis and Connor to sit down as well.

"But I jump to the end of the story. Let me give you some background and let me go back to the beginning and give you some

background. Today I am the most successful venture capitalist in the world. My personal investments are in the hundreds of billions. I sit on some of the most prestigious corporate and philanthropic boards in the world. I can call Presidents, Prime Ministers, CEOs directly and get through every time. I have more homes, cars, and great works of art than I can recall. My opinions move markets. I am quite literally at the top of the game."

"But I didn't start out here. No, my early years were filled with hardship. I struggled for survival as a young child. Many times my family couldn't put food on our table for days. I wore clothes, so threadbare, that I was always shivering. I didn't have any support from my family, as they were in the same predicament, barely surviving. The back of the laboratory dissolved as a grainy image of India appeared the feeling of loneliness, sadness and hardship swirled around the room. The scene froze on a hobbled Indian man. When my father died at a very early age, killed actually, in the fields over an argument for grain, I made a promise to myself that I would never allow the same to happen to me. I promised that I would get out of this god-forsaken country and get the United States. From that day on, I worked tirelessly for my chance to come to the United States to study. Fortunately for me, my intelligence was above average and I was given an opportunity by a local teacher." Tarun paused before returning to his story.

"You must realize that America represented the land of opportunity for a poor, uneducated farmer's son from India. The American movies which we used to sneak into showed a beautiful country, with beautiful people and blue skies with panoramas painted by God's hand. The scene changed again and images of the Rocky Mountains, fields of grain waving in the wind, feelings of *pride, comfort, and safety flowed over the room. The scene changed to people all dressed in well-tailored clothes, the hustle and bustle of the big cities in the 50s, men holding doors for well-tailored women. The message was clear. America allows anyone, regardless of social status to fulfill their dreams, to accomplish their heart's desire." Tarun said clearly connecting with his fond memories.*

His tone and the image changed quickly "So what happened when I came to the US for college? It wasn't at all like the movies or the books. It was all a lie. A cheap fabricated lie. I was disgusted. The beauty that I had seen in the movies didn't exist. Americans had such tremendous resources that it bordered on the obscene. The scene changed with images of homelessness, violence, fires, prisons, fat people sitting at a sporting event, a scene of people on a couch in a daze as the blue flickering light of television illuminated their faces. The housing, transportation, the food, all of it immediately available for anyone to pursue to their heart's desire. The well-choreographed city scenes of the movies were in reality a brutal, hard life, where people stepped on each other to get ahead unaware of how blessed they were. For a poor boy from India, it was a tremendous shock. I was terrified of this world into which I had been thrust. I didn't understand the rules. I didn't understand how things worked. Every day was a struggle, albeit in a different, admittedly ironic way from my upbringing." Tarun looked off in the distance momentarily lost in his thoughts with feelings of aggression, anger, violence swirling.

The scene went blank as Tarun's thoughts continued "I want you to realize that I didn't begin with any ill will to my American classmates or the American system, but over time it developed into a loathing of everything American. Your government, your economy, your people, your educational system it was all in shambles and nobody recognized it or did anything about it. The complacency was addictive. It hid behind a façade and the framework behind it was crumbling. The US was controlling the world with its conspicuous consumption. I realized that Americans are fat, both metaphorically and literally. You all sat on the top of the pyramid looking down for so long you forgot what got you there in the first place. Fat, lazy, and stupid. Fat, lazy, and stupid." The entire scene turned blood red and pulsated with power and anger. Tarun's thoughts continued forcefully directing his comments specifically at Connor and Alexis and they felt the pressure building around them.

"So, it was during this time, I came to an amazing realization. Your insatiable American appetite could be used for my benefit. I could exploit you. I could use this greed and desire to succeed. I would use what my intellect, my one true and pure strength to get back at the US, to punish this country for its hedonistic, devil-may-care attitude. A part of me wanted you all to see how corrupt and compromised you had all become. I wanted to treat you like you treated the world. I vowed to take advantage of you, to consume you to destroy you while enjoying it." Feelings of superiority and dominance swirled around the laboratory, the scene changed to images of server farms, communication switches, and computers, people working in clean rooms, images of technology came faster and faster.

"So my plan started with technology. I identified high growth areas in consumer and business technology. I made initially small, but strategic, investments in such areas as AS/400 development and hardware. This inevitably led to PC hardware and software.

At first, my intention was to gain economic superiority and use my capital to combat the moral and ethical decline of the US. While funding several groups that shared my philosophy, I was well on my way to achieving this strategy when I accidentally stumbled upon a scientist doing some interesting work in distributed computing for DARPA. His work utilized the current defense department network to distribute content using a new programming language he had written called html. I immediately recognized that this simple concept would someday drive centralized applications and communication. Call it luck, but this little discovery gave me a glimpse into the future. I changed my investment strategy to networking, data, analytics and internet technologies, on-demand applications, and eventually social media."

Connor interrupted pushing his thoughts against this tide of images and feelings "Why are you telling us this?"

Tarun continued, ignoring his question. "You must realize that my investments gave me access to the largest companies in the world. Images of power, kings, queens, presidents, celebrities surrounded the laboratory while feelings of success and pride, winning, achieving power swirled in and out. I regularly met with CEOs and Boards of Directors and, as you know, sat on many Boards myself. Through this connection, my companies began to create standards, to define the technology world, to establish the protocols, the rules of how the world uses technology and information. As my wealth and power increased, I began to influence the success and failure of companies. I began to influence politics. I could influence the wealth of states and countries. I could influence and control the livelihood of hundreds of thousands of people, and for the first time had the ability to change people's thinking. Don't let anyone tell you otherwise the most powerful elixir is making someone believe something. Once you have this power, nothing else compares."

"So, as I said, quite by coincidence, my investments all began to converge on the conclusion that I could achieve my goal of bringing down America and now the world from within, by using my investments, influence, and power to disrupt the economic order. You must realize that in the future the most powerful entities are not countries but companies. Business will continue its expansion to control all aspects of our lives. It's actually quite ironic that the final piece of the puzzle came, not from the US, but rather India. I sat on the board of TG, a technology company I had cultivated to compete with many of the US based hardware companies. The founder, Ravi, a poor brilliant lost soul, actually invented an unbelievable program that enabled people to share their thoughts. An unintended by-product was the ability to control electronic equipment. A real plus I must say in the end. It seems that Ravi was motivated much like me. He was determined to right a perceived wrong with Kashmir by creating a network where he could also control people's thoughts. Don't you see the symmetry and cosmic alignment here?" Images of a new world order with people all dressed in grey tunics, smiling, automatic in their emotional response. Tarun smiled and clasped his hands in front of him, pleased with himself and ego-involved in his accomplishment.

"No, not at all." was all Connor could respond. He was disgusted by this madman and how we viewed the world. Alexis sat wide-eyed terrified by the thoughts, feelings and the situation.

She felt like she was in a mental straight jacket and the scene from Clockwork Orange came to mind. She looked to Connor, hoping he knew what he was doing.

"Mr. Shaw, maybe you are not as smart as my operatives have led me to believe. Regardless, most genius has been misunderstood. But to be completely honest, it doesn't matter what you think, because with this invention and the experience world created by Tribe, I will tell you and everyone else what to think, to do, to say, and how to live. Don't you see the connection here? The convergence of these technologies, the culture, and human nature has created a platform where everyone is connected, where everyone is exposed, available, willing to interact. We live in a world where people want to share their most intimate secrets. Nothing is sacred. Nothing is secret. This little discovery, the experience world is the final piece of the puzzle that has been developing for the last 20 years. All of these pieces have come together to give us what we have today. Once we were willing to share with faceless friends incredibly intimate details, the next step was the experience world. In which our thoughts, combined experiences, our feelings all laid bare, open for anyone who wants to connect. Convergence is what makes it all work." Images of Tarun sitting above the world, God like, looking down on his creation. Tarun finished talking, turning his attention directly on Connor and Alexis.

"The reason you are sitting here now is that both of you served your purpose and are now a considerable threat to the experience world and more importantly to me. My greater consciousness allows me to control everything. I can dictate thoughts and people actually think it is their own. I can control people. You are not going to

limit or stop the power that I have created. I can dictate religion to people and tell them what to believe. If I don't like a particular religion I can change it or better yet create a new religion. It only takes a few well-placed thoughts in the most evangelical groups and you would be amazed at what can occur. I recently tested an approach to bring the Nazi's back into the mainstream. You know what happened? The poor, defenseless public actually began to believe that the Nazis weren't all that bad. Can you believe that? Forget about religion. In the future I control the moral and ethical standards of cultures, or control politics by telling the voting populace who is the best candidate. Finally, and probably most importantly, I can control the economy, what people buy, how they buy it, what companies win and lose. The experience world makes me the most powerful man in the world. I control the hearts and minds of every single person connected to the experience world. I tell them what to do, when to do it, how to do it. I am omnipotent. I am God."

Tarun's face became a mask of rage as he stood up and pointed at both of them, his voice becoming a scream. The scene around them turned into a dark red pulsating field of color. The feelings roiled with aggression, violence and anger. Red fingers and hands reached out from the walls of the laboratory at Connor and Alexis, trying to pull them into the hell that was seething behind Tarun. "And the two of you thought you could stop me, stop the experience world. You are both going to meet a very violent death. I am going to demonstrate my power, and kill you both in the experience world. I am going to allow Rina to get inside your minds and slowly disassemble them piece by piece. She is going to toy with both of you *and make sure you never get out of the experience world again. It is going to be very enjoyable to watch you suffer."*

Tarun stood up and walked to the window facing the bay "Fitting isn't it that the network you mean to destroy will actually destroy you? Rina, any time you are ready."

"Good bye." He said without turning from the window.

Immediately Tarun felt a wave of tremendous weight pushing back on him. He had difficulty breathing. His autonomic nervous system became confused. His heart was fluttering, his vision blurring> What is happening? This has never occurred before. Something is wrong, too much pressure on my thoughts, cannot keep focus I am going to destroy these two how can this be something wrong need to disconnect need to disconnect>

Rina moved toward Alexis first and reached her hands out to grasp both sides of her head. She began to squeeze, impossibly strong, and Alexis felt her enter her mind. It felt like a violation, a crude and blunt instrument that entered her thoughts and began pushing deeper and harder. She recoiled and tried to fight back but she was held firm. Connor tried to move but his body was frozen, as if an invisible hand grasped him. He could only turn his head to witness the violation of Alexis. He pushed with all his mental power against the invisible bonds only managing to move his right hand slightly. He never felt more helpless and terrified in his entire life.

Quickly the pressure and feeling in the room changed, as Tarun's body stiffened and he fell to the wooden floor. His hands and arms flailed and his back arched. He began to shake uncontrollably while his eyes bulged and his head banged the floor repeatedly. Sensing the change, Rina momentarily hesitated and released Alexis to turn toward Tarun. Tarun's seizure stopped immediately and he lay unconscious on the rough wooden floor. His tongue was hanging from his mouth as drool rolled from his lips.

The laboratory disappeared and Connor sensing his advantage moved quickly and yanked out both of their earpieces throwing them across the office.

Their mind's eye blinked closed and they found themselves back in Tarun's office. Rina disconnected from the experience pod and blinked slowly while she considered her options. She saw Tarun's limp body lying on the floor. She immediately realized that all life was extinguished from the once powerful man. As she took stock of her situation, she looked down and realized she still held the gun. Slowly, she raised the gun ready to pull the trigger to eliminate Connor and Alexis. She smiled and slowly as her finger moved on the trigger.

At the same moment, the conference room window behind her shattered and the front of her head exploded. Her gun fired wildly at the ceiling as her body fell to the floor next to Tarun.

Connor and Alexis fell to the floor and crawled for the door. The main door exploded inward and several SWAT team members rushed into the room. Two officers went to Tarun and Rina, and two hovered over Connor and Alexis.

"All clear, Sir," said one of the team members into his headset.

At that Hamlin entered the room with Ari Peck. "Everything is alright now. You're safe. Nothing more to worry about."

Ari Peck looked to Connor and Alexis "Are you okay?"

Connor nodded weakly "I suppose, but I'm not really sure what just happened."

"Let's move outside to the car and I can explain everything." Ari Peck motioned for Connor to follow Hamlin and Alexis.

Within two hours of the release of the virus, after the wireless carriers fought valiantly, the majority of the world's cell phones and personal devices were permanently disabled. Every wireless chipset was burned and locked. Entire wireless networks fell like dominoes and all forms of electronic communication began to become disabled.

Several financial markets halted trading as the normal rush of electronic transactions ceased. Investors began to flood the markets with sell-offs, unsure of the impact of the breakdown on the system and trading. The Internet backbone, with its impenetrable original design by the Department of Defense, came to a stand-still as it no longer could access wireless networks.

Tribe, the company that started it all, suffered disastrously. The entire Tribe network was overwhelmed by an unprovoked experience usage attack prior to the release of the virus. This attack was an effective diversion that kept the Tribe system administrators distracted as they watched network traffic spike to all time levels. Once the virus hit, the Tribe experience servers overloaded and shut down automatically. This caused the experience pods to disappear from the network. Each blinked out of existence, as the network connection and the experience phones were destroyed.

Adam sat at his desk as Tribe crumbled before his eyes. He felt relieved.

Four hours and eleven minutes after the virus was released, the entire global wireless communication network was destroyed.

Every single wireless phone, tablet, and computer permanently lost its wireless network connection.

All wireless communication on the planet ceased to exist.

———

Connor, Alexis, Hamlin and Ari Peck sat at in a rundown deli just off six[th] street. The television carried news reports from across the globe about the recent events. Reporters from various countries discussed how the massive network failure was changing the world. The India and Pakistan situation seemed to disappear as both countries focused on the network loss. China's military and ruling government took no action as multiple protests tore across the country.

"So how did you know it was Tarun?" asked Connor.

"The NSA actually put all the pieces together. They had intelligence reports that came in during the last several days that definitively pointed to one person behind all of it. Their intelligence identified several operatives working in various companies as well as government agencies that were tied to one technology group."

Ari continued "So then through some good, old fashioned police work, and unbelievably tax and corporate compliance documents, we identified that the common link in all of the companies was Tarun Patel. We were able to mobilize the local SWAT team and we were headed here to arrest him. Our surveillance reported that he had you both hostage so we put our sharpshooters in position and waited to see how it developed. We were ready to go, but once you entered the experience world, we held off to see what happened. " Hamlin turned to Ari.

"The interesting thing is that we still don't know what happened to Tarun in the experience world. It looks like he connected to the network and went into some type of coma. Also, as the news is showing, it looks like someone released a network virus that brought everything down. It is going to be some time before we put this all together."

"Lucas…" Alexis whispered.

"What was that?" asked Hamlin

"Nothing, forget it." said Alexis.

The group turned to the television as a reporter, with his close cropped gray hair and expensive suit stood in Times Square, New York. Thousands of people flooded the streets behind him.

"Like many moments of great change, this came quickly. One moment we were all operating in a world where we knew the rules, where we were comfortable and secure. The next moment, everything has changed. The world as we know it is no more. I have spoken with many people in the last several hours, and I have to say that everyone seemed to be coming out of a daze. They were shaking away the haze that has clouded our lives for so many years."

Connor turned to Alexis and smiled a knowing smile. Alexis returned the smile and reached across the table to grab his hand.

"Everything is going to be alright" Connor said leaning close.

Alexis nodded slowly, not believing what she was hearing.

CHAPTER
46

"I am going to head back to my apartment, and then see if I can find Lucas. We have a lot to talk about." Alexis moved forward to hug Connor and whispered in his ear "This is all because of you. You saved the world."

Alexis left Connor standing on the sidewalk as she got in the car with Hamlin and pulled away from the curb. Connor needed to walk. He finally found a Starbucks. As he stood in line, he looked around the room and noticed a perceptible change, people were talking to each other and interacting. What a refreshing change he thought.

———

Adam stood next to his convertible and stared at the dark offices of Tribe. He was holding numerous letters and documents that he had been receiving constantly over the last two days.

It seemed like everyone was bringing a suit against Tribe and the government was quickly building a case against them. He shrugged his shoulders slightly and walked over to the trash can just sitting off of the sidewalk. He threw away the papers, brushed off his hands and returned to his car. Without another look at the building, he pulled into traffic and drove away, leaving Tribe behind at the beach in Santa Monica.

EPILOGUE

"Kids time for dinner. Come on down." a woman's voice echoed through the oldest boy's room.

"Alright, we will be right down" the four yelled in unison. The oldest boy sat at his desk piled high with various electronic equipment. He was making the final connection to a conglomeration of boxes and wires. He smiled and picked up an earpiece and slipped it into his ear.

The other siblings reclining on the bed and chairs across the room sat up expectantly. "Are we ready to try it?"

"Put in your earpieces" said the oldest brother. The younger kids followed the instructions and sat waiting. A moment later they felt a tingling across their head and were greeted with a flurry of colors and feelings.

<relax. It's ok. I'm here. Oh, ok. This is cool. Dad will kill us if he finds out you set this up. What, no way, it's an experiment, besides we created our own network, we technically didn't break his rule. Uh, ok. Hey what are you doing?>

The three younger children's' right arms moved up and down and then their left started to do the same. <that's not funny. How can you control our arms. Dunno, buts its kind cool.>

The younger children ripped out their headsets and screamed in unison "Mom" before the older boy could stop them.

"Alright, alright, no more. Shhh. Don't say anything." The kids left their room and headed downstairs for dinner. The pile of electronic equipment hummed softly in the empty room.